Demon Huntress: Love Me To Hell And Back

Elizabeth Mason

www.darkstroke.com

Discover us online:
www.darkstroke.com

Find us on instagram:
www.instagram.com/darkstrokebooks

Include **#darkstroke** in a photo of yourself
holding this book on Instagram and
something nice will happen.

This book is for you, Justin.

Thank you for supporting me during this exceptionally long journey.

And always helping me with the quick clean.

Acknowledgements

First and foremost, I'm forever thankful to my family. My two handsome boys, Aiden and Brae, thank you for giving me an hour or two of silence so I could write. And Justin, my perfect husband, thank you for always telling me to focus on my writing. I love y'all to infinity and beyond.

A very special thank you to my friend, Loni LeCain. If I didn't say, "fuck it," I'd still be editing.

I especially want to thank Leigh Shulman for being my mentor and giving me the courage and knowledge to finish my book.

After years of writing, seeing my book come to existence is a surreal feeling, and I'd like to thank darkstroke for making that happen. A special thanks to Laurence for your editorial help, cover design, ongoing support, and for tolerating my picky personality. You have the patience of a saint.

Finally, and most importantly, I thank you, God, for all your blessings.

About the Author

Elizabeth is a Cali girl who should enjoy the California sun more than she does. She's content being indoors writing and creating spooky stories with strong leading women and bad boy leading men. With a degree in psychology, Elizabeth is drawn to the complexities of human behavior. The diversity of personalities, interactions, emotions, and relationships reflect in her writing.

When Elizabeth isn't busy typing away, she enjoys time with her husband, two boys, and her two Weimaraner pups. And thanks to her love for lattes, she enjoys reading paranormal romance late into the night. Her husband and her two boys inspired her to never give up, and thanks to them, she's proud to announce her debut novel: Love Me To Hell And Back. A haunting tale of self-reflection and forgiveness, even in the darkness of Hell.

Demon Huntress: Love Me To Hell And Back

Chapter One

MAEVE

We stood outside an old, abandoned cotton factory in an alley that smelled of mildew and rotting garbage. Someone had cut the chain and left the heavy door into the unit ajar. We squeezed between the narrow opening without a sound. Dust and rust filled the air, and I paused and listened. Open-air flowed through the cracks and broken windows, mice skittered in the walls, and...a muffled cry.

I pointed up to the floor above us, and Emerich nodded his chin at a set of rusty stairs. I followed closely behind as we crept up the steps. He withdrew his gun from his holster, and urged me to unsheathe one of my knives. On the second floor, right at the top of the stairs, was an open doorway. Emerich stopped, peered around the corner, and winced. I ground my molars. I knew damn well that what he had seen wasn't good.

Emerich pointed to the other side of the room, and I nodded once before I snuck across, holding my knife at my waistline. There were trash bins, old crates, and a pile of stained sheets. I crouched behind one of the old containers and peeked around the base.

There she was, the woman from Emerich's vision. Naked, bruised, and savagely beaten. Her arms and legs were bound by rope to a thick wooden post. Strands of saliva dripped from her trembling lips as the jinn stalked around her, dragging a long, c-curved knife with jagged edges across her battered belly. I swallowed the bile that burned the back of my throat. *I'm going to slaughter that fucker.* I lifted my knife, ready to kill, but Emerich shook his head, a silent warning to stay put. He was right. If I acted rashly, an innocent woman could die.

She begged and whimpered—her voice, hoarse and barely audible.

"Shhh. It won't be long now," said the jinn. There were candles set in a circle around the woman and other ritual items like a dead snake, crow's feet, and…was that human bones? Probably. Jinns were evil fucks. They might have been angels once upon a time, but that didn't mean they had an ounce of sympathy or remorse. This jinn had tortured this poor woman, but hopefully he didn't rape her too. A common occurrence. God, I loved my job. Hunting these fallen angels, otherwise known as jinn, gave me a reason to live.

Emerich stepped around the corner into a wide stance. He wore black cargo pants, black boots, and a black tee, making him hard to spot in this dark space, but thanks to the magic of my nevus, I clearly saw him. He held up his handgun with the barrel pointed at the jinn's head. "Drop the knife, asshole."

The jinn put one foot before the other and pivoted around. He smiled, seemingly pleased, as he bowed forward. "The name's Lucas."

He and Emerich sized each other up, but Lucas didn't stand a chance. Not against us. We were trained to hunt and kill.

Lucas grinned. He was damn gorgeous—all jinn were. His features were sharp and exotic. "Nice to finally meet you, prophet."

Whoa, pump the breaks. Lucas knew Emerich was a prophet, but how?

Emerich flashed me a sideways glance, and I sighed. Damn it, Ems. You just gave up my location.

Looking my way, Lucas's smile grew from ear to ear. "You brought a dinner guest."

Why did all jinn sound like hissing snakes? Oh, maybe because they were evil shits?

I stood tall and stepped behind the bin, holding my knife at my thigh. My fingers twitched around the handle as Lucas's eyes slid up my body from toes to head. He licked his lips, and a sudden wave of nausea settled in my gut.

Lucas's nostrils flared as he inhaled. "Mmm…I like a woman in leather. The smell reminds me of a raunchy fuck with an unadulterated bitch." His choice of words made me cringe, and I couldn't stop the wave of revulsion.

I glanced down the length of me. My clothes weren't leather. They were a unique material, created to reflect fire and keep my body cool, but that dip shit didn't need to know the details of my fucking clothes.

"Help!" the woman cried. She pulled on the rope tied around her wrists. It was a pointless attempt to free herself.

"You'll be okay." Emerich snapped his mouth shut as Lucas swung around and backhanded the woman across the face. The post cracked and split, and I winced. The bastard knocked her out, but at least she had a moment to rest.

Lucas swept his hands together as if they were dirty. "Fucking rude." Lucas stared at Emerich with a smile that reminded me more of a toad swallowing a worm. "Now… where were we?"

Emerich held his stance and his gun steady. "Cut the shit, Lucas. You're going back to Hell. You know it, I know it, so quit wasting our time." Emerich's fingers played with the trigger.

Lucas held up an index finger. "Correct. I am going to Hell, but not until I finish my job."

"What job?" I asked.

Lucas turned to me. He wore a wicked grin too wide and unnatural. "Levi sends his love."

Levi? Where had I heard that name before? Was Emerich confused too? It was hard to tell. He glared at Lucas with his fingers wrapped around the trigger, ready to shoot.

"Not yet, Ems," I whispered. We still needed answers, but it was too late.

A loud pop, my breathing stopped, and Lucas bent back as if he had no spine, dodging the bullet. Except for the ringing in my ears, all was silent. *Please, oh, God, tell me that bullet didn't hit the woman.* The shot broke through the brick wall behind her. *Oh, thank you, Lord.* I slapped a hand to my heart, relieved. *She wasn't hit.* I glared at Emerich. What was he thinking? He could have killed her. Emerich held firm, pointing the barrel of the gun at Lucas's head. Did he shoot purposely to frighten Lucas? Emerich was an excellent shot, but sometimes he played too close to the edge, putting innocent lives in danger.

Lucas glanced over his shoulder, smiling. "Holy shit," he laughed. "That was fucking close." Emerich had the gun aimed at Lucas, waiting for the right moment, and he wouldn't miss again. Lucas pointed and waved a finger at him, still smiling. "You, my friend, I like you." Emerich didn't budge or blink. "And I have something for you."

"I'm not your fucking friend," shouted Emerich at the same time I yelled,

"Who the fuck is Levi?" I swayed back and forth on my toes, eager to kill this bastard.

Lucas looked at me like an evil clown. "Your parents say hi."

I ground my molars as his words brought back painful memories. *That's it! You're dead, motherfucker.* I swung my arm up, holding my knife by my ear, ready to throw when… *pop*! Another shot was fired.

The bullet hit Lucas in the eye. He stumbled back a few feet but didn't fall. He reached into the socket where his eye had been and pulled out chunks of tissue and nerves. They hit the ground. *Plop.* Blood and tissue splattered on the floor by his feet.

Damn, jinn, gross shits, were hard to kill.

Lucas reached into his jacket and pulled out a flask. He took a swig, filling his mouth with whatever it was inside, winked at me with his one eye, and turned toward the woman.

Now, what was he doing?

Lucas spat what looked like a clear liquid, coving the front of the woman's body, and thank the good Lord, she stayed unconscious. Her chin still resting on her chest. Lucas reached into his jacket again, but this time he pulled out what looked like…a match? *Shit, it was.* He stroked the head of the matchstick and looked at me. "Someone told me that you like fire." He flicked the match at the woman, and fire spread across her body. That was all it took: the sight, the smell, the noise. My vision dimmed, and in a few short seconds, I was back at my childhood home.

Four wrists tied to the headboard. Four ankles tied at the base with one angry flame and zero room to move. The heat creeps across my face, sweat drips from my brow. The smell of burning flesh assaults my nostrils, and their primal screams pierce my eardrums. My heartbeat is thrashing in my ears. Save them, but my legs are weak.

"Mae bear!" Emerich, he was calling me. "Mae bear!" He used my nickname to break into my subconscious mind. It worked nearly every time. "Mae bear, come back."

My flashback faded.

The fire flickered into darkness. The screams faded into distant whispers. The abandoned factory. The woman on the post, screaming. Fire. Save her.

I snatched one of the old, crumpled cloths from the pile I had spotted earlier, a few feet away. The burning wood broke in half, and the charred rope snapped. I freed the woman, threw her to the ground, and smothered the flames with the cloth. The fire died, and my heart pumped faster as I slid the fabric back.

"No." I covered my mouth with the back of my hand. "No, no, no! No again."

Most of her skin was black with exposed patches of bloody tissue and muscle. *I couldn't save her.* I curled my hands into fists. The girl was dead because of me, no, not me —Lucas.

I sprang to my feet and spun around. Lucas had Emerich by the neck. Emerich's face was red, and he tried to pry loose Lucas's hand.

"Fucking asshole!" I screamed. I threw my knife. It sliced through the air the same time Lucas leaned forward and kissed Emerich on the lips.

My knife hit Lucas, puncturing his head right above his

temporal bone.

Bull's eye.

He dropped Emerich, stumbled back, and looked at me with my knife sticking out from the side of his head. "Fucking bitch." He tried to yank the knife out. "What the fuck is this shit?" He tugged and tugged on the blade, pulling his head down at the same time.

"That shit is a knife made of steel, melted and mended together with a special stone, capable of turning jinn to ash and sending assholes like you back to Hell."

I yanked my knife free. Black blood squirted out and dripped down Lucus's face. He used the back of his hand to wipe it off, and that was when he noticed his hand was burning away.

The ground trembled, right on cue, and I crouched, using my arm as a kickstand to keep my balance. A piece of space pulled inward, suction-like, morphing into what looked like a small black hole to Hell.

Lucas's body was nothing more than a black cloud of sulfur, sucked through the hole like spaghetti. I covered my ears and hummed, but nothing could mask the cries and moans that drifted out from the depths of Hell. I waited for Lucas to disappear and for the hole to close—the longest ten seconds of my life, every time.

Chapter Two

EZRA

I drove down Washington Boulevard, toward the city, in a daze. Damn, I was tired. Work's been non-stop, and I needed a break. The job last night was nothing new. I hunted the jinn, killed the jinn, and got paid, but locating the fucker took days. Thank the Gods, the traffic was down, but for how long? Chicago's traffic started early, and I had a few short minutes before sunrise. I combed my fingers through my hair and yawned. I couldn't wait to be home. Shit. How long has it been? Two, three weeks? I hadn't slept at all—only a few more miles.

My cell rang.

Are you fucking kidding me? I squeezed the steering wheel until my knuckles burned, which didn't take long, thanks to the fight I had with the jinn last night. I flexed my fingers to kill the tension before I reached for my cell. "Yeah?"

"Mister Virunas. How nice to hear from you," Dorian said in a pompous manner. I loathed the guy.

"It's Ezra, and you called me." I bit my lip to stop myself from cursing. I wanted to tell him to get fucked, but he was my boss, and I was a slave to his wishes.

"I assumed you finished the job." Straight to the point, the only thing I like about the pretentious prick.

"Have I always finished the job?" Dorian awaited the day I failed. Well, that fucker would be waiting a long time. I've never flopped a case assigned by The Order, yet every damn time, Dorian would call to verify my work. "I didn't torture the asshole." Like The Order wished. "But I got the job done."

"Perfect. I need you to begin a new case."

I held the phone up to my ear with my shoulder as I geared right to exit the highway. "Fuck, Dorian. I haven't slept in my own—"

"Levi broke the law. But this time, Mr. Virunas, I'm ordering you to kill him."

I laughed, purposely sounding cynical. "Are you serious? Kill him? That's a bit harsh. What has he done this time? It better be fucking serious."

"He stole the Sacred Seals."

I pulled to the side of the road, forming a cloud of dirt and dust, and turned the car off. I sat in silence, letting his words seep in. Did I hear him correctly? Levi wasn't that fucking stupid. Stubborn, yes, but not stupid.

"Mr. Virunas? Are you there?"

"I misunderstood. For a moment there, I thought you said that Levi took the seals."

"No, Mr. Virunas, you heard correctly."

Something in Dorian's tone had me crushing my molars. "Are you referring to The Sacred Seals?"

"Yes."

I pinched the bridge of my nose. "Are you sure?"

"Mr. Virunas—"

"It's Ezra, Dorian. For fuck sake, call me Ezra."

"Okay, *Ezra,* I understand this sounds—"

"Fucking absurd?"

"Ezra—"

"It was someone else. It had to be. Levi isn't that stupid. The seals are protected by the fucking Arch Assembly."

"Tell me, Ezra, do you know someone else with that sort of power? Unless…you took them?"

Damn, it was getting hot in here. I rolled the window down. "What do you think, Dorian? I don't need the seals, but Levi…" He craved power, and the seals, the keys to the apocalypse, would undoubtedly give him that. My guess, he planned to rule the world alongside the mighty Grigori. The kings and lords of Hell, fuck that, they meant shit to me and fuck the Arch Assembly too. "The damn Arch Assembly.

How can they protect humans if they couldn't even keep the seals safe?" I laughed. They called themselves archangels; those wannabe badasses were worthless shits.

I hit the steering wheel. "Shit!" Killing Levi was the last damn thing I wanted to do, but someone had to. That motherfucker would end the world. "Alright, Dorian. I'll do the job, but," I sat up straighter, "if I kill Levi, I no longer work for The Order."

I waited for the argument—a lame excuse to keep me. Dorian didn't want to let me go. I knew that, and my words were met with an awkward silence.

"You're the best we've got, Ezra. Do you not enjoy protecting humans from rogue jinn?" I couldn't blame him. I was the best damn hunter they had.

"I'm done with the round-the-clock jobs, Dorian. I need rest, and let's face it, you're asking me to kill Levi. That goes against our contract." I white-knuckled the steering wheel. Why the fuck did I need to explain myself? Gods, I hated being tied to The Order. "I'm sorry, but that's my only condition. Levi's death for my freedom. Take it or leave it."

There was a pause, followed by a lengthy sigh. "Okay, Ezra, as you wish. But this case won't be easy. You'll need the Book of Raziel to kill Levi."

"Are you fucking with me? Nobody knows where that book is."

"Winston is the keeper of the book, and he lives in Savannah, Georgia."

I threw my head back and laughed. "I know for sure you're fucking with me. That wizard has killed more jinn than the archangels combined."

"You have no other choice, Ezra! You need the book to kill Levi." Correction…I needed a spell from the book. One powerful enough to kill Levi. Dorian was right. "Do not waste my time, Mr. Virunas. Go to Savannah, locate the Demon Control Unit, where he works."

"You mean the DCU?" I laughed. What Dorian was asking of me was ludicrous. "Dorian, don't fuck with me. There's a reason why the Arch Assembly put Winston in charge of the

DCU."

"That's why you'll find a lead. Don't waste your time with Winston. He is too powerful and will kill you on the spot." *Obviously.* "Instead, find someone close to him. Someone he trusts. An informant to locate the book." There was a pause, followed by another lengthy sigh. "Another thing, Ezra, and you must keep this a secret, but the rumor is a prophet works for Winston."

"Well, no shit. I have to keep that secret." A single prophet was born once every few years, and it has been what, over a hundred years since I've learned of one surviving? When word got out that a prophet had been born, rogue jinn usually hunted and killed them. Luckily, Winston protected this one.

"He's young, tall, and lean. He's also a jinn hunter, and his work partner is a young female."

"Hold on, Dorian. We need to think this shit through. You're asking me to get a banned book. What if this is what Levi wants?" The asshole was a master of trickery and manipulation.

"We don't have time to think this shit through. Get the book before Levi does." He ended the call. No goodbye and no thank you—fucker. Damn, but Dorian was right. Levi needed the book to open the seals. *If I don't get that book and kill him...hello apocalypse.*

I tossed my cell to the passenger seat and started the engine. My mind was spinning, trying to make sense of everything—an impossible task. *Everything I've done for Levi, and this is how he repays me.* The only reason I worked for The Order was to save him.

Now, I'm ordered to kill him.

Chapter Three

MAEVE

Finally the hole to Hell disappeared. Yeah, I wished we were leaving with more info, but I'm pleased Lucas was back where he belonged—in Hell. I stood, dusting the dirt from my hands. Where's Emerich? I looked around.

"What the...shit!"

He was lying on the ground, and his arms and legs were sprawled in all directions. "Ems!" I rushed over and slid to my knees beside him. "Emerich, you okay?" I shook his shoulders and patted his chest. "Ems?"

He scrunched his face and groaned. "Fuck"—he grabbed both sides of his head— "it hurts."

I scanned his body for apparent injuries. "What hurts?" I didn't see any broken bones or blood. "Is it only your head? Is it difficult to breathe? Fuck, Ems. You need to talk to me."

He rocked his head back and forth, clenching his teeth. "Fuuuck me."

I've seen him with broken bones, deep cuts, and even a bullet wound. He had handled the injuries like a champ each time. Not now. This was a first. "Okay, try to relax." I thought back, trying to figure out what happened. *Lucas had been shot in the eye, the woman had been set on fire, a flashback. Focus, Maeve, what happened next? The woman had died, Lucas had kissed Emerich, and I had killed Lucas, sent him back to Hell.* I snapped my fingers. "Lucas kissed you."

"Shit, Maeve. Don't fucking remind me," he said, hissing through his teeth.

I sat back on my heels. "I'm sorry, Ems. I just...I don't know what happened."

Your post dramatic stress disorder, that's what happened, fucking PTSD. It's my fault.

Emerich's face was still scrunched in pain, and he was still squeezing his temples as if that would alleviate the pain. "You probably hit your head when you fell or something."

"Landed on my ass."

Fuck. Now, I was squeezing my temples. "Well, whatever happened, we'll have to figure that out later." I stood and leaned over Emerich, grabbing him under the armpits. This wasn't going to be easy; Emerich was a tall guy, but I had the strength. Thank you, Nevus. "Let's get you to the doctors at the DCU, have your head examined." I helped him up. "Lord, you're heavy. Should've skipped that pizza for lunch," I joked. Yeah, the joke wasn't funny. In fact, it was stupid, but the situation needed a bit of humor to keep me sane—somewhat.

I hung his arm over my shoulders and wrapped my arm around his waist, and before we left, I glanced over my shoulder. Damn. Bless her soul, that poor woman, I had to remember to call the cleanup crew when we got to the car. This was the worst part of my job, seeing the innocent hurt or dead because of some evil jinn.

I helped Emerich down the rickety old stairs one shaky step at a time. "Here we are." I blew a strand of hair from my face and steadied him before I let him go. "Finally, we made it. I thought those damn stairs were going to break." I squeezed through the heavy door, followed by Emerich. Once we were in the alley, I wrapped my arm around his, but he pulled away. "What? What's the matter?" Vomit shot out of his mouth, a thick stream of brown mush. "Shit!" I said, covering my nose with the palm of my hand to block the sour odor in the air.

Emerich folded over and rested his forearms on his thighs. Should I stay back? Give him space? He spat a few times before he stood. He crossed his arms over his chest and sucked up a string of saliva that hung from his bottom lip. "It's cold." Cold? It was July in Savannah. I aimed my ear toward him, he wasn't easy to hear, and his chattering teeth didn't help.

14

I hopped over the long stream of puke. "Sorry, Ems. I didn't hear you." I rubbed tiny circles on his back and waited for him to talk. He didn't. "Okay...um.... Come on, let's get outta here." I softly nudged him, but he didn't budge. "Em? Are you okay?" What a stupid question. He obviously wasn't okay, but at least I tried to comfort him.

He shook his head and stepped away from me. "Em?" I pointed my thumb over my shoulder toward our parked car. "We should go. You need to get your head checked." I tapped the crown of my head.

Silence again.

I scratched my temple, completely confused. Em's eye watered, and he seemed unsettled and a bit bewildered. What was up with him? I had no fucking clue. I ran my fingers through my hair, glancing around as if I could find answers written on the brick walls. What was he doing? I kept my distance in case he got sick again, yet close enough to keep him safe.

He stood on his toes and looked skyward with his chest jutted out and his arms limp at his sides. He opened his mouth wide. Was he going to scream? Nope, not a sound. This evening was getting damn weird. Oh, hell, I should have known. His eyes blazed with a familiar white light—a premonition. "Crap, Em. Perfect timing." I grabbed his hand and led him to the shadows along the wall.

Poor guy. It was hard for him as a prophet. He had zero warning before a vision. I reached into his pocket for his sunglasses. He usually had a pair on him to hide his eyes in case of a sudden premonition, but of course he forgot them. I glanced down the alley. They were probably in the car, but by the time I got back, his vision would have gone. They lasted, what, a minute, maybe less? I waited, rubbing tiny circles on his hand with my thumb.

Emerich's face was stiff. He looked more terrified than usual. What was he seeing? Whatever it was, it was awful. I reached up and rubbed the folds that formed between his brows.

A rush of adrenaline tingled through my body at the sound

of glass breaking. I spun around to find a man standing behind me, shaking in apparent fear. His face was pallid, and he reeked of booze and sweat. There was a broken beer bottle at his feet, and I sighed, relieved. Drunks were simpler to persuade. "Sir," I started. "This isn't what it seems. You've had a lot to drink." I held up my hands, palms facing him, as I attempted to calm the man.

He lifted a shaky finger and pointed at Emerich. "Devil," he said with tremors in his voice. *Great. We got another one.* I had little choice. I acted quickly, and with zero thought. I knocked the guy out with a sharp right to the jaw. There was nothing to worry about. He'd wake up sick and confused, probably forgetting everything he had just saw. Em and I dealt with this kinda stuff all the time, and usually, a quick jab to the chin did the trick. They never remembered a thing.

I dragged the man across the ground and sat him against the wall when...*thump.* I turned around. Emerich had hit the concrete hard and was twitching and foaming at the mouth. "What the hell?" White lights during a vision, typical, but having a seizure wasn't.

I dropped to my knees next to Emerich. I took off my vest and pushed it under his head. I didn't need him getting more injuries—particularly to his head. I rolled him onto his side just in case he got sick and bit down on my lower lip, running it between my front teeth as I waited for the seizure to subside. This was the worse night ever. I couldn't keep up with the madness. Well, at least his eyes were no longer glowing, but his face and hands—they were twisted in pain.

Emerich's skin stretched tightly around his skull, and his coloring went pale grey. His cheekbones were more pronounced, and his eye sockets were hollow. Something wasn't right. His brown bear eyes, wide smile, and deep dimples gave him that all-American-boy-next-door kinda look. Now he was like a damn corpse—literally. I reached into my back pocket for my cell and dialed.

"Maeve?" Sal answered before it even had a chance to ring.

I opened my mouth, ready to speak, when...I couldn't

believe my eyes. Welts—everywhere—formed on Emerich's face, arms, and hands. They rapidly became sores, marking his flesh in a red oozing mess. One after the other, they popped and bled.

I covered my mouth with the back of my hand. I wanted to scream for help, but that would draw attention to us. "Maeve?" Sal's muffled voice cut through my bewilderment, and with an unsteady hand, I grabbed my phone and brought it to my ear.

"Sal, something's wrong—"

Emerich grabbed my wrist and yanked me to him, causing me to drop the phone yet again. "It's happening." I could clearly hear the fear in his voice.

"What? What's happening?" I was trying to free my wrist, I hated being touched, especially being grabbed, but his grip was firm.

"They're coming."

"Who's coming?" I freed my wrist from his grip and rubbed it with my other hand.

He closed his eyes, holding a hand over his chest as he gritted his teeth. "Help me."

"Okay, I will! I'll try, but you need to talk to me. What do you need me to do?" He dragged his nails down his left cheek before crossing his arms over his chest, hugging his shoulders. "Emerich, don't do that." I winced when I saw the bloody lines he had left on his face. I'd never seen him like this, desperate and suffering. My heart hurt for him.

"Help me."

"Okay, I will." I nodded continuously, as if my words were insufficient.

He shook his head forcefully. "No!" he shouted before he grabbed my shirt and yanked me closer to his face. "Promise me you'll stop him. You're the only one. Promise? Only you." He squeezed his eyes shut and shuddered. I pulled my shirt free from his grip and wiped the spit he sputtered on my face with the back of my arm. "Promise, Maeve?" His voice, so full of pain and worry. I didn't press for more information. He was hurting, and I could always ask later. So I made the promise. Even though I had no idea exactly what I was promising, I still made it. For him, I'd do anything.

Emerich mouthed, *thank you*, and closed his eyes.

I reached for my cell, shaking like a scared dog. "Sal," I said.

A loud clatter sounded behind me. I glanced over my shoulder in time to see the man I knocked out had woken up. He was running away, frantically looking over his shoulder. I spotted the source of the noise, a toppled trashcan. He must have run into it when he wasn't looking, announcing his getaway.

I stood and slapped my knee. "Shit!" Would the man talk? Would he tell someone about Emerich and his glowing eyes? He was drunk. Nobody would believe him. Fuck, I should run after him. No! I can't leave Ems. Right? Oh, damn it. The man was already gone.

"Maeve," said a voice from behind me.

I spun around. My knuckles slid across a man's jaw with a *thwap*! "Sal?"

"What the fuck, Maeve?" He was rubbing his chin.

"Sorry, I wasn't expecting you so quickly."

He moved his jaw right and left before looking down at Emerich's unconscious body. "What happened?"

"Well, I don't know for sure. We just finished a hunt when he started complaining about his head hurting. Then, he had a vision, and after, this happened." I gestured to Emerich's body.

Sal squatted beside Emerich, his brows lowered, hovering over his concerned eyes. He studied Emerich's injuries before he clapped his bear-sized hands together with a *slap*. *And here came the best part.* Sal rubbed his hands together, faster and fiercer, before he placed them on Emerich's chest. In no time, Emerich's skin turned a healthy hue, his body grew thick with weight, and his sores disappeared one-by-one. I've seen many mysterious things, but Sal's incredible powers always amazed me.

Sal stared at Emerich, pressing his lips into a fine line as if he were trying to solve a puzzle. Seconds later and he

18

reached into his jean's pocket for his cell and dialed. "I need a medical pickup, code red." He gave the person our location and hung up without a *thank you or goodbye*. I searched his dark eyes for answers. He seemed confused or worried; I wasn't sure which. He wasn't the easiest man to read.

"What's going on, Sal?" I asked.

He shook his head while staring at Emerich like a coroner would a dead body. "I can't cure him."

"What?" I held out my hands, palms up. "But he looks fine. The sores are gone." For the first time tonight, he was relaxed. Oh how I wished I could see his brown bear eyes, wide smile, and deep dimples. His aura could soften even the hardest-boiled, insensitive person, including me. But he was sick, and I was sad, angry, confused, guilty. *This was my fault.*

Sal pinched his bottom lip, still shaking his head, and sighed. "He caught something, a virus. One I've never felt before." He looked at me, fear in his eyes. "You said this happened after a vision?"

I nodded.

He stood, rubbing his eyebrows and muttering to himself. My chest felt tight as the stress kept building, and building, combined with the vibes Sal was emitting, was far from positive. "Thank God we have an emergency medical crew in Savannah," I said. "One positive thing to come from this stupid night." Our headquarters for the DCU was in the middle of the Okefenokee Swamp. It made for an excellent hiding spot but was so damn far from Savannah, where all the demon-action was.

"Still, the medical staff needs to transport him to the DCU, where our specialists are located. That's two hours from here."

I leaned my shoulders against the brick wall and looked up into the night sky. "Yeah, but at least the emergency medical vehicle has all of the necessary equipment to stabilize him if needed."

Sal and I didn't have to wait long for the medical crew. They worked quickly, checking Emerich's vitals before placing an oxygen mask over his mouth. We followed them as they lifted Emerich onto the gurney and rolled him into a van read *Quarantine Facility.*

I rushed across the street to my car. Sal had parked his Harley behind me, and while he was putting on his helmet, I scanned the area one last time.

What the hell? What was that? Something moved and disappeared into the shadows along the street.

"What are you looking at?" Sal followed my gaze.

I squinted as if that would help me see better. "I thought I saw eyes like animal eyes." That sounded stupid, but after every shitty thing that had happened tonight, was it really all that stupid? Not so much.

He nodded his chin at my right hand. "Is your Nevus burning?" I turned my hand around, and on the back of my wrist was my Nevus—a tattoo-like mark. I ran my fingers over the ancient print that formed two small circles, one inside the other. My Nevus gave me added strength and heightened senses; that was how I spotted the eyes so far away. I shook my head, still scanning the area, when Sal pointed to a spot that had flattened cardboard boxes over broken wood pallets. "Probably a cat."

"Yeah...probably." The eyes were the color of gold, or more like amber, too animal-like to be human. Except, something inside told me it wasn't a cat. I should've investigated. The assassin in me was thirsty for redemption. Still, when the van took off down the road with Emerich inside, nothing else mattered. Besides, Sal was right. If it were a demon or a jinn, my Nevus would have burned, alerting me of their presence.

Chapter Four

MAEVE

The quarantine van barely came to a stop when the medical crew opened the doors, pulled the stretcher from the back, and rolled Emerich into the DCU's hospital wing. I parked the car in front of the hospital and ran after them, but two beefy guards had stepped in front of me by the time I reached the quarantine zone.

"Stop there," said one of the guards, and I skidded to a stop. "Sorry, Maeve, you're not allowed beyond this point."

My jaw dropped. "Says who?"

"The boss," said the other guard.

"Come on! You know my name." Both guards tilted their heads, probably wondering why they should care.

I waved my hand between the guards and me. "You know my name. We're friends." I had never seen these guards before, but it was worth the shot. They folded their arms across their broad chests and shook their hoods.

"Fuck," I spat. *What now?* I pressed my fingers to my temples.

"All we can do is wait." I turned and saw Sal pointing to the waiting area.

I shook my head. "Nope. I hate hospitals." They were too cold and smelt like bleach…and death. I didn't wait to hear what he had to say. On my heel, I turned and went out the entrance. I sat on the brick steps outside the building, and seconds later I heard the entrance doors slide open. Sal strolled out and sat beside me.

"Why are you here when you should be with Emerich?" I asked.

A scratching sound told me that Sal was rubbing his short black beard on his chin. "The DCU has the best doctors in the world who specialize in a variety of disciplines, including the supernatural." So I guessed he was putting his trust in the doctors. God, I hoped he was right. If something happened to Emerich...well, it was my fault.

We sat in silence, staring into the dark, swampy backdrop. The DCU was like Area 51 but without the dessert, and we didn't hunt aliens; we hunted demons (animal-like beasts born in Hell) and jinn. We also had an airfield, housing, a hospital, labs, and training centers with school rooms.

The Okefenokee Swamp was the perfect hiding spot. We were surrounded by alligator-infested water, as black as a cast-iron kettle, and tall pine and cypress trees, making the location hard to spot and dangerous to trespass.

I sniffled and wiped my runny nose with the back of my hand. My eyes were watery. I wasn't crying, but I wanted to. I was tired. I was hungry, but I wasn't in the mood to eat. I brought my nose to my armpit and sniffed. Yup, I smelt like shit and needed a shower too.

How was Emerich? Was he better now? What were they doing in there? Probably running tests. My mind bounced from one random thought to the next, probably trying to cope with the craziness.

Sal wrapped his arms around me and squeezed. It was then that I wanted to let go of my cool façade and cry on his shoulder like I did when I was a child. Sal was six feet, four inches of pure muscle, intimidating to many, but not to me. He was, and always will be, my pushover protector.

The door to the hospital opened, and Winston stormed out. "Salazar, is she clear?" Winston asked Sal, and God bless his soul, he was always straight to the point.

I jumped up and gave my attention to Winston. He wore newly shined boots and a trench coat that nearly swept the floor. "What do you mean, *clear*?" I asked. "Clear of what?"

Winston had an unlit cigarette between his fingers. "With the same virus?" He pointed toward the hospital with the fingers holding the cigarette.

Sal stood and straightened his worn jeans and white tee before he calmly answered Winston, "She's fine."

Obviously. I didn't have a fucking seizure and bloody welts. "How's Emerich," I asked.

Winston was headmaster of the DCU, and a powerful wizard. If anyone had answers, he would be the one. He stared at me and sighed. His eyes were dark and tired, and the wrinkles around them seemed more profound. "We're doing everything we can to nurse him back to health, but..." He pulled a lighter from his pocket and lit the cigarette. "The cause of his sickness is supernatural. That's why Salazar couldn't heal him. He's in quarantine."

Supernatural Virus? I sucked in a sharp breath as I remembered learning about those in Demonology class. They usually meant certain death. "But he seemed better after Sal healed him. Everything went away."

Sal shook his head and looked at me with his deep blue eyes. "I was only able to cure him externally...not internally." The muscles in his jaw tic. Sal didn't fail at much, and I could tell that this had bothered him. "Those viruses can only be created and passed by select jinn, powerful ones."

"Tremendously powerful ones," Winston clarified. He held the cigarette between his lips, and it bounced up and down as he spoke. I swore, one day, his greying beard that draped just past his chin would catch fire. He grabbed the cigarette and pointed at me. "What happened?"

I rubbed my eyes and ran my hand down my face. I was tired, my mind was foggy, but I could do this. *This was your fault!* I shook my head. I had better shake my guilt and tell them what had happened. "Emerich had a vision sometime yesterday morning about a jinn sacrificing a woman, so we left here and drove to Savannah. The jinn killed the woman, him and Emerich fought, and I killed the jinn. After that, Emerich complained about his head hurting. At first, I thought nothing of it." I tensed as I thought back. "I guess I'd get a headache too if a jinn kissed me." I shuddered at the thought.

"Kiss?" Sal and Winston both asked.

I nodded as I looked between the two of them. "Yeah, he kissed Emerich seconds before I killed him." *You could have prevented this entire thing. Tell them. No. Not yet? Should I?*

"Fuck," said Sal. He frowned, creating deep wrinkles between his brows. He was in deep thought about something. "That sounds like a Devil's Kiss." Winston nodded as if he thought the same thing. Sal looked at me. "Did this jinn have a name?"

"Lucas," I answered.

"Was he alone?" Sal asked.

"Lucas?" Sal and Winston nodded. "He had a victim. A girl—"

"Another jinn?" Sal interrupted.

I shook my head. "No. No other jinn."

Winston flicked the ash from his cigarette. "Impossible," he snapped. "That curse hasn't been used for millennia."

Sal folded his arms over his chest. His bulging biceps were as big and as round as my head. If only he could beat the shit out of this virus. "I'm certain it's the Devil's Kiss."

I lifted my hands, palms up. "What the hell is this Devil's Kiss?" I asked, my eyes bounced back-and-forth between the two.

Sal placed a hand on my shoulder, probably to calm me down. "It's ancient magic created by the Grigori. It's a spell used to pass a supernatural virus from one host to another."

Winston eyed me. "And you killed Lucas?" I nodded, and he shook his head. "Impossible. If the jinn was powerful enough to summon a Devil's Kiss, he would have been too powerful to kill."

Sal looked at Winston. "What are you saying?"

"Yeah, thanks for the vote of confidence. You don't believe me strong enough to kill a powerful jinn?"

Winston snuffed the cigarette using the sole of his shoe. "What I'm saying," said Winston, looking at Sal, "is that someone else is behind this."

"Who?" I asked.

Winston brought his attention back to me. "I'm not sure

who, but I have my suspicions." He and Sal exchanged a quick glance. *Suspicions? With whom?* "What happened after?"

I scratched my temple, thinking back, which was hard when your mind was full of questions. "I helped Emerich out of the factory, and he had another vision. But it wasn't like other visions. His eyes glowed three times brighter, and afterward, he had a seizure, and his skin blistered and bled and—"

"He had another vision?" Winston interrupted my rambling. "Did he tell you what he saw?"

"No. He asked me to help. Begged me to stop him."

"Him? As in himself?" Winston asked.

Both men eyed me like a Jury would a criminal. I shook my head. "I don't think so. He was too sick and passed out before I could ask him questions."

"Do you think his vision showed the perpetrator?" Sal asked Winston.

Winston ran his fingers down his short beard. "I don't know. But let's hope so...for Emerich's sake."

"Is he going to be okay?" I asked Winston. "There must be a cure."

Winston thought for a moment, his brows hard over his eyes before he shook his head. "I need to speak to the Arch Assembly."

"What? No," I yelled. "There must be something you can do. Some sort of magic voodoo." I wiggled my fingers up and down.

Winston started to argue when Sal spoke up. "The Devil's Kiss acts like a virus. Once inside the human body, the curse hijacks the cell's replication machinery and starts making copies of itself, making it difficult to penetrate and destroy."

I threw my hands into the air. "This is bullshit." My hands fell to the sides with a slap.

"Enough," yelled Winston. "The curse is in Emerich, in his cells, taking them one-by-one. If we act carelessly, we may kill him while attempting to break the curse."

I looked to the heavens, pleading for answers. "We can't."

My voice was a sad whisper. "We can't let him die."
Winston's features softened at the sight of my tears. "There
must be something I can do."

"You're too emotionally involved." He took a step closer
with his chin held high. "I'm ordering you to take a break."

My mouth popped open. Was I being punished? "For how
long?" I thought a day, maybe two.

Winston opened the door to the hospital. "For the
remainder of this month."

Where's Sal? Was he not going to help me? He turned his
head away.

I laughed at the absurdity of the situation. "That's fucking
three and a half weeks."

"You heard me, Maeve. Stay away from this and away
from Emerich," Winston commanded before disappearing
into the hospital wing.

Sal touched my shoulder, and I jerked away. His arm fell
to his side with a *slap*. "He's right, Maeve. Being
emotionally involved can make you…unstable."

He was referring to my PTSD, but I was too weak from
anger and sadness to argue. I held my stomach as if I were
about to get sick. "I can't handle losing someone else." I used
the back of my hand to wipe away a tear.

"Even when you get hurt, you never let it defeat you," he
whispered. He'd been telling me that since I was six, the day
he rescued me, brought me to the DCU, and gave me a home
when I didn't have one. It was his way of helping me cope
with my past, the past that still haunted me, one flashback at
a time.

"But it is defeating me, Sal. My past, my hurt, my PTSD,
all of it, defeating me…and endangering others."

"What are you talking about, Maeve?"

"Emerich is sick because…I had another flashback. I
should have been there for him, but I let myself get
distracted." Fire was my trigger, and when Lucas lit that
girl… Oh, God. For years, I used my PTSD as a weapon. The
mind-crippling disorder gave me strength and reason to hunt
and kill jinn, and with time, I came to appreciate the sickness.

It was a gift, that was what I had told myself, but now, I wasn't so sure.

My chin quivered, and I felt a wave of regret settle into my gut. "I could have prevented this whole damn thing. Emerich might die because of ME!" I screamed as I formed tight fists. I wanted to hit something—anything—but there was only me. I lifted my fist and pounded down on my chest, one good punch to the heart. I relished the pain.

Sal grabbed my wrist. "Stop it," he snapped.

I jerked my wrist free from his grip and stepped away. Tears gathered and slowly ran down my warm cheeks. Sal's shoulders lifted and fell with his deep sigh. Was he feeling helpless? Angry? Was he going to help me? Help Emerich? "Maeve, I—" Didn't sound like it.

I held up a hand. "Tonight, in the alley, Emerich asked me to help him, and I promised him I would." Emerich was more than a work partner; he was my best friend. My mind was made. "Do you know what it's like to watch someone you love die, knowing you could have saved them? I can't let that happen. I can't let someone else die. Not again."

Chapter Five

EZRA

Seven days had passed since The Order assigned me this fucking job: my final assignment, and here I was sitting in a stuffy bar, listening to old men bluster over who had the better and most believable fish story. It was a sure way to hear tales of the town. The men told ridiculous stories, but I knew, in some cases, they might be true. Their outrageous stories could be leads that would get me closer to the DCU, thus helping me find the damned place.

I threw back a shot of whiskey and enjoyed the burn it caused before I slid the shot glass down the bar. The swift bartender caught it and looked at me. I held up a finger; one more shot. Finding the Book of Raziel might have been more effortless than locating that damned government unit. I hammered the bar with my fist, and the bartender eyed me. *What the fuck was I doing here?* There had to be a better place than this stuffy old bar, an area with a younger crowd.

I stood and tossed a few twenties on the bar when an old man stumbled in. He slipped on a soggy cardboard beer coaster—another drunk bustard. I reached out to catch the guy, but instead of thanking me, he pulled my arm and brought his mouth to my ear. I turned my head away from his bitter breath.

"I saw the Devil," he said. "I saw him. He had glowing eyes."

I looked the guy in the eyes. The other men at the bar laughed. Not me.

He swayed, but his eyes remained steady on mine. "What do you mean...glowing eyes?" I asked.

His breath reeked of beer and cigarettes. I had a fleeting moment of doubt, but then he said, "His eyes were like headlights, bright and white."

I grabbed the man's shirt. He closed his eyes and turned his head. The fool thought I was going to punch him. "Where?" I asked. The guy had a fresh bruise on his chin, and if he didn't talk, he'd have another between his eyes.

He pointed a shaky finger. "The alley just down the street," he said.

I let go of the guy's shirt and patted him on the shoulder. "Thanks," I said and ran out the door.

"He will take your soul!" The old man yelled after me. I swatted the air. *Nobody wants my dark soul.*

The man with glowing eyes had to be a prophet. It's been known for years, prophets' eyes glowed white during a premonition. I ran a short distance from the bar, not even a block away, and slowed my pace to a stop, and peeked around the corner of the alley. It was dark. Not a single streetlamp flickered in the night. I crept closer for a better look, minding my step so as not to be heard. I hid behind a large dumpster.

A man and a young woman stood nearby as a medical crew hauled another, younger-looking man into a quarantine van.

The young-looking man I assumed was the prophet. He was just as described to me by The Order: tall, thin, and young. The other man didn't fit the bill. He was tall too but also muscular and maybe in his late thirties.

My thoughts froze. It wasn't common for a prophet to be quarantined after a vision. I looked around for answers. Nothing out of the ordinary. No evidence to give a reason for quarantine.

The crew worked quickly and had the prophet loaded and ready to leave in seconds. I had to move fast if I planned to follow them.

I turned to leave when my mark pulsated. I rubbed its location at the back of my neck and made a quick inspection in the surrounding area, and that's when I noticed.

The young woman was staring at me. *Was she the*

prophet's partner? Dorian mentioned the prophet having a female partner.

I stepped behind the dumpster, hoping she didn't see me, and pushed my back flush against the wall. Fuck me, that girl had a sharp eye. How did she see me? I was half a mile away from where she stood and was well hidden in the dark. There wasn't one working streetlamp at this end of the alley.

I peered around the dumpster, hoping the coast was clear. *Phew.* I was able to breathe again. The female had gone. My shoulders relaxed, but then the sound of car engines followed by a roar of a motorcycle told me they were leaving. "Fuck." I sprinted to my vehicle.

Thanks to my incredible speed, I was sat in my car with the engine on in seconds. I pulled onto the road when I spotted the van, followed by a Harley and an old Chevrolet Camaro. I followed the vehicles through old Savannah to an open highway lined with swampy trees and dense shrubs. The drive was so damn long. I'm surprised they hadn't spotted me. Still, I followed closely behind with my lights off without being seen or heard thanks to my superb eyesight and electric engine.

Forty long minutes later, I saw brake lights. The van was the first to slow. Why the hell were they stopping? There was nothing around, not a building or fucking convenient store. I slowed my pace to maintain a safe distance. The van turned right, off the road and into the brush, followed by the Harley and Camaro.

I parked behind some thick vegetation and walked the rest of the way in a hurry. The path the vehicles turned onto was more like a thin trail, hardly enough space for a car, let alone a van.

Of course, the DCU would be in the middle of a fucking swamp. I should have guessed. I kept an eye on my surroundings, and just to my luck, I stepped in something mushy. "Fuck," I muttered. "This better be the fucking DCU." I kicked off as much of the sticky mud as I could—hoping it was mud—and moved forward. I traveled a few more yards when I heard the roar of the motorcycle. I picked up my pace, and even in the thick muck, I caught up to them. They were waiting for an entrance gate to open. This was it, the final truth. Had I found the DCU?

Keeping to the thick brush, which seemed to line the compound, I stayed unnoticed. I followed the vehicles to a building labeled DCU Hospital Wing.

Finally! I found it! I felt as if I could fly. I was that fucking ecstatic. If only I had wings, I'd do flips in the air, but not all of us were that fortunate, and my muddy boots would agree.

The quarantine crew rolled the prophet inside, and the young woman and large man followed. It was too dark to see beyond the hospital building. There were no streetlights or lamps except for the light above the hospital door. I glanced over my shoulder and saw nothing, complete darkness, but I was far from being alone. I heard an occasional splash of swamp water or frog croak. This wasn't ideal, but I had no choice but to hide in the brush next to fucking alligator-infested water.

I waited a short few minutes when the door to the hospital opened.

The woman I spotted in the alley stepped out of the building. Her leather clothes fit her like another skin, showcasing her feminine curves.

She sat on the first step leading to the entrance, gazing forward toward the swamp that enclosed the compound. I was immediately taken by her. She was a contradiction. How could she fight? She wasn't a typical build for a demon hunter. Too petite.

A moment later, the brawny man from the alley came out and sat beside her. He amplified a bright light in the space around him, unnoticeable to the untrained eye; his glow seemed holy in nature; pure white like angels.

I watched as the man carefully interacted with the woman. He took her hand and squeezed. She smiled before taking a deep breath, and I detected a paternal-like relationship between the two. That pleased me. Wait, for fuck-sake, what the hell was wrong with me? I don't give two shits about their relationship.

Ahhh, finally, the man I'd been waiting for. Winston, the wizard, and keeper of the Book of Raziel stepped out of the hospital. He was tall, old, and confident. I felt the thickness in the air. Waves of static energy ran through me, prickling my skin and lifting the hairs on the back of my neck. I had met many creatures with great power, but his strength was comparable to the nuclear fusion that gives stars their energy.

Winston stopped to talk with the woman and man from the alley. I could hear pieces of their conversation as they spoke about the prophet. He had a vision and became sick with....

I'll be damned...A Devil's Kiss?

Who could carry out such a curse?

Oh, shit. My mind drifted to one person, and I had a sickening feeling in the pit of my stomach. Only a few beings were strong enough to pass a Devil's Kiss, and Levi was one of them. Could it have been him? It had to had been. It all made perfect sense. Levi had a plan, and the prophet would expose that plan to the DCU, to Winston, so Levi cursed him with the Devil's Kiss to keep him quiet.

That blasted sneaky bastard.

I observed the three of them. Winston spoke to the man with respect, and with the woman, judging by his open body language, he was firm yet watchful. He lifted his chin while talking to her yet watched her with gentle eyes, aware of her grief.

Interesting.

Winston raised his voice. He told the woman to go home, and fuck did that piss her off. She was desperate to save this prophet, said something about 'making a promise'.

Hmmm...

Perhaps I could use her desperate disposition to my advantage?

Dorian suggested I use the prophet as an informant to get the info I needed, but he was cursed and dying, the fate of the Devil's Kiss. But what about the woman?

Chapter Six

MAEVE

I slumped onto the couch with an oomph followed by a tired sigh. Sleep. Oh, that sounded good. A nice nap. No. I couldn't sleep. Memories of Emerich filled my mind. Last year, Emerich and I had bought a house in Savannah. It wasn't anything special, but we had been raised at the DCU, confined, and protected within the compound's gates, so to us, it was perfect.

I smiled at the memory. After we had signed the papers, Emerich went shopping. He was so eager to make our house feel like a home, and a week later, we had furniture and decor, both old and new. I was lying on our granny couch when I ran my hand over the rough cloth. The poor thing was falling apart, but hey, at least we could somewhat comfortably watch movies on our new flat screen tv. I blew out, making my lips rumble and sputter. "Yeah, like we have time to watch movies," I said with a laugh. I glanced back, expecting to hear Emerich argue that fact, but for the first time in a long time, I was alone.

I had a sickening feeling in my gut. It was quiet. Too quiet. The kind of quiet that ran chills down my neck. Living with Emerich was like living on the streets of Savannah: full of life. He had danced and sang to his music that could be heard from across the street. I had hated it.

Until now.

I curled into a fetal position and closed my eyes. Emerich was dying, and it was my fault. My best friend, my roommate, my work partner—dying. He had warned me not to go on this last hunt, and what had I done? I had ignored him and his warnings. I squeezed my eyes shut as the memory came to drown me.

"We were trained to listen to our intuition, Maeve, and this vision makes me feel uneasy," says Emerich.

"Why?" I'm asking. "And might I remind you, we work for the DCU—a secret government sector—and our job is to control and eliminate any-and-all supernatural wrong-doings." Emerich was rolling his eyes as if he's heard this a million times. I'm sure he has, but I don't care. "No, Emerich, you need to listen. Your visions show us future unlawful jinn activities, right? Well, why is that? I mean, why not have visions of your future instead? Because you're a prophet, and prophets are born to help rid this world of evil shits, otherwise known as jinn. Since I could remember, your visions are the basis of nearly all our cases."

He gives me a look, silently calling me a bitch. "You're one stubborn..." I lift a brow, daring him to finish that sentence. His hands fly to the sky and fall with a slap on his thighs. "Geesh, Maeve, you just don't get it. I don't think we can handle this one."

I roll my eyes and sputter. "That's hogwash! I get it, Emerich, I do. We were trained to listen to our intuition, but above all else, we're trained—"

"Yeah, I know, we're trained to kill jinn." He grabs my arm, forcing me to look up at him. "This vision was dark, Maeve, and unsettling. I've never felt anything like it. I have a bad feeling."

I pull my arm free from his hold and flex my fingers. I hate being grabbed. "I hear you, Emerich, but we don't have time to contemplate your feelings." I look directly into his eyes. "It's our job to protect the people, Ems. You saw a dying girl in your vision, and you, of all people, know I can't allow that to happen."

His shoulders slump upon hearing my plea. "Let me get my gun," he grumbles.

I punch the air. "That's my boy. I'll pull the car around. Meet me out front."

I sniffled and ran the back of my hand across my runny nose. I could no longer hold back the tears that streamed down my face.

I cried. And I cried. And I cried some more. I cried until I drifted off to sleep.

I'm walking down a dark alley. Alone. A hand taps my shoulder, I turn around. It's me. I am face-to-face with my evil doppelgänger. *She wears a fixed smile on her face and a devious glint in her eyes. Weird.*

"I can fix this," I say, but my doppelgänger *shakes her head. I open my mouth to argue, but nothing comes out. I grab my throat, and my* doppelgänger *fades away.*

I was standing in a room. Too dark to see, but the smell of fire tells me I was in my childhood home. A hand taps my shoulder again. I turn and see a tall figure cloaked in ash and smoke standing behind me.

"Wake up," he says.

I tilt my head like a confused pup. He opens his mouth, and out comes a loud ring.

Ring! Ring!

I sprang up into a seated position, gasping for air.

Ring! Ring!

I turned around, twisting at the waist, expected to see the smokey figure, but I was alone.

Fuck me. It was only a dream. I placed a hand over my speeding heart.

Ring! Ring!

"Shit! My phone!" I jumped up, stubbed my toe on the coffee table, and hissed. "Oh, mother of…that hurt! Stupid Table." While bouncing on one foot, I grabbed my cell and hit answer. "Hello," I hollered.

"It's me," said Sal, "Are you okay? You sound—"

I was balancing on one foot. "Yes, yes," I said, rubbing my hurt toe. "How's Emerich?"

Sal sighed, and unfortunately, it was a sad sigh. "It's not looking good, Maeve. His breathing patterns keep changing drastically, and his blood pressure dropped. We were able to wake him, though it wasn't easy. He was extremely agitated.

I've never seen him like that. Thankfully, Winston was able to calm him enough to tell us about his vision."

Wait. Did Sal say vision? "Did he see who cursed him?"

Sal sighed again, instantly deflating my hope. "No. He saw the Grigori on horseback."

I jerked my head back. "Wait…what? I don't get it." The Grigori: the first fallen angels banned to Hell; the most dangerous and evil of devils, including Satan himself. "But why did he see them on horseback?"

"Think back to your theological studies of apocalyptic events."

I thought back to my theological classes, and it hit me. "No fucking way," I said as understanding dawned on me. The Grigori were locked away somewhere deep in the darkest depths of Hell. Yet, according to the archangels and their prophecy, the Grigori will one day return to Earth on horseback, seeking to take over the world.

"Don't worry, Maeve. I'm sure we would have heard from the Arch Assembly. No, doubt, they would tell us to prepare. It's our job to keep the people safe. If the Grigori returned to Earth, there would be a war between them and us."

"Wait, so you haven't heard from them yet?"

Knowing Sal, he was probably pinching the bridge of his nose, stressed to the max. "No," he whispered.

My mounting frustration caused my thoughts to blank, and with nothing else to say, I hung up.

The Arch Assembly were a bunch of narcissistic know-it-alls. Emerich would die before they decided to help. I threaded my fingers through my hair and spun around as if looking for answers when I spotted a photo of Emerich and me.

It was taken last year. Emerich and I had just finished our training, and with sweat and blood, we had finally become jinn hunters. It was our goal, our dream, our common bond. For an entire year, from sunup to sundown, we endured hours of training in skills like sabotage, infiltration, and combat using various abilities and weaponry. The worst part was conditioning under the heat of the Georgia sun or in the swampy humidity. The classrooms were no better: musty, old, and confined. The training was grueling work, and every night before we passed out from exhaustion, I would ask, "What if I fail?" and he would say, "I will not let you."

Emerich was my strength, and in this photo, on this night, we became work partners. It was a snapshot of us taking our oath. We held our hands over our hearts, wearing grins that reached ear-to-ear, as we made a joint pledge. The pledge was to always obey the DCU's partnership contract. We both pledged to protect and respect each other as partners both on and off the job.

I remember that evening so clearly. Em, Sal, and I celebrated until late in the night. It was so fun and perfect. As the night was coming to an end, I asked Emerich, "What if I fail?"

After he took a swig of his beer, he said, "I will not let you."

I smiled, my cheeks sore from grinning all night. "Nor will I let you." He was my strength, and I was his.

Winston and Sal said I shouldn't get involved.

Pfft.

I showered and dressed.

In the alley, Emerich asked me to help him, and I promised I would. I took the photo from the frame and slipped it into my back pants pocket as a reminder. That night, I pledged to protect my partner, and that's what I'd do.

I stepped outside and locked the door behind me.

I needed answers. A cure. Information. I usually used the DCU's archives, but Winston had suspended me. My only option was to find a jinn and hope it could tell me what it knows about the Devil's Kiss.

Chapter Seven

MAEVE

There was a line of people waiting outside to be let into one of Savannah's most popular nightclubs, The Banshee. The club was dark and bright at the same time. Flashing lights danced around the room, highlighting the shine of the black tiled floor. The smell of sex and alcohol filled the air, making it the perfect gathering spot for jinn.

I motioned for the bartender. "Grey Goose and cranberry," I yelled over the music. Once he delivered my drink, I sat on a stool and scanned the crowd. Night clubs weren't my thing. I hated being touched, and just seeing all the sweaty bodies tangled together gave me anxiety.

A young woman pushed by to stand at the bar. She wore a tight leather skirt and knee-high boots, and to bring the sexy up a notch, she pressed her arms together, showing her cleavage to every hungry man at the bar. If she wasn't easy, she sent the wrong message or tried to get a free drink. I scoffed. "Not going to work," I muttered, smiling into the rim of my glass.

She looked down her skinny nose at me. "Excuse me," she said, or more like squeaked as she had a mousey voice.

I pointed back at the bartender with my thumb. "He's not into women."

Confusion was written all over her face. "Whatever," she spat before she strolled to the other side of the bar with an I'll-sleep-with-anybody-I-want swag.

"Whatever," I mocked. At least she was gone.

I moved the ice around in my glass with the tiny black straw before I took another sip. My gaze drifted to the back of the club. I wished I could sit somewhere less crowded, but this seat offered the best view, and I was on the hunt for a jinn.

In the meantime, I waited and observed. I had to admit, the bass pulsed through me, making my blood hum with excitement. The energy passing between the dancers revived my senses, and that's when I felt it—a presence watching me. I was expecting to see the young woman staring daggers at me, but she left out the side door.

There, peering down from the second-floor balcony, the same eyes I spotted in the alley. *Amber Eyes.*

I threw back a mouthful of liquor and dashed toward the stairs, making my way through the maze of people as quickly as possible. Dancing bodies rubbed up against me, but I didn't mind; it was the fastest way across the room. I went up the stairs, two steps at a time, and was at the balcony in under a minute, but Amber Eyes was gone.

"Fuck," I cursed under my breath. I grabbed a handful of hair and spun around, looking for those eyes. "Where did you go?"

I searched every corner of the second floor, studied each person's faces, hoping to find those eyes. I even checked the men's room. *How did he get away unnoticed?* He was like a damn ghost, there one second and gone the next. I headed downstairs, determined to find this person when my Nevus burned.

A jinn was nearby.

I paused as a thought crossed my mind. *Wait one damn minute... was Amber Eyes a jinn?*

I shook my head. My Nevus would have burned when I spotted him in the alley last night. Then, what was he? His eyes were too unusual to be human. *Maybe an angel?* I wasn't sure, but either way, a jinn was near, and it wasn't Amber Eyes.

My sense of smell took over. My nostrils flared as I inhaled. *Bingo.* I smelled sulfur. Jinn and demons have a faint sulfur scent, primarily undetected by humans. I followed the trail down to the first level. My mark burned fiercer. I inhaled again. The smell was more pungent to my right.

I headed to the rear of the club to the back door that led to the alley. A faint cry for help echoed outside. I looked behind me. Nobody was there, so I retrieved my blades and slipped outside. The alley was dimly lit and smelled like old booze and urine. I swallowed the foul flavor that tainted my taste buds as I took in the scene.

The jinn pressed a girl against the brick wall. Her shirt was ripped open, exposing her breasts, and her skirt was bunched up around her tiny waist. Go figure, it was the woman from the bar. She found herself some trouble. He squeezed her neck to stop her cries while his other hand was buried between her legs—s*ick bastard.*

I stepped forward, ready to throw a knife, when a gunshot fired, a loud pop followed by a quick thump.

I turned to see the shooter.

I sucked in a quick breath. *Go figure. It was Amber Eyes.*

"You!" I shouted. "Who are you?"

Amber Eyes nodded toward the girl. She was screaming hysterically, and if I didn't calm her, I'd have to explain a dead body to a crowd of curious clubbers.

Amber Eyes winked at me before disappearing around the corner.

I stomped my foot. Damn it! He got away. Again. I wanted to run after him, but I had a job to do. I tried to calm the girl, but a lot happened at once. The ground trembled, and the jinn turned to ash. Then as expected, a hole to Hell appeared, sucking the pile of ashy jinn through the small opening until there was nothing left but the bullet that had killed him. I stepped away from the girl, bent down, and grabbed the shell, wiping away the blood. It seemed like a regular bullet, yet it worked like my knives, sending the jinn to Hell.

"Interesting," I said. I flipped the bullet around in my hand a few times before I slid it into my pocket. Who was this Amber Eyes? Was he a hunter like me? If so, who did he work for? More questions were tossed on top of the ever-growing pile of other questions I needed answered.

The girl stared vacantly at the spot where the hole to Hell

had just disappeared. She was stiff and not breathing, and...

"Shit," I spat. The girl passed out. Thanks to my quick reflexes, I caught her just before her nose hit the pavement. I sat her against the wall, and her head slumped forward like the drunk guy I had punched out last night. I reached into my pocket for my cell. I couldn't erase a person's memory, so I called the DCU's cleanup crew. They used one of Winston's potions to erase memories.

Twenty minutes later, and the team finally arrived. I was anxious to continue my hunt for a jinn, so I didn't stick around. I had visited one other club and a rave, hoping to find a jinn, but the night was abnormally quiet. I glanced at my watch, almost midnight. The Den, an underground gambling joint for jinn, opened in ten minutes. Silas, the owner, was stunning but also a sleazy, arrogant asshole. I would have killed him years ago, but his club was valuable for information, and he'd never crossed the line, giving us a reason to kill the bastard. I'd bet my knives that he'd heard something among the jinn. They liked to talk, especially after a few drinks.

The security guard recognized me and let me in without a word. I took the elevator down to the basement. The dive was small and dingy, and there were no windows to ventilate the smell of sweaty armpits and cigarettes.

My Nevus prickled like a bad sunburn as I walked through the room, scanning the faces of all the gamblers. I chose a table near the bar where I could quickly survey the room and spot Silas.

"Front money?" asked the dealer, and I nodded. "Bet?"

"Dollar bet," I said, looking at the only other player seated at the table. Common in places like this, he wore a hood and dark glasses that kept me from seeing his face. I hated that. As a jinn hunter, it was part of my job to memorize faces and read facial expressions. On top of that, I couldn't tell if he was human or jinn, as the Den had a good mixture of both. It was hard to tell who was and who wasn't human.

"Call," said the dealer. I slid two chips into the ante and blind, and the dealer dealt the cards.

"Is Silas here?" I asked the dealer.

"Pair," the dealer called, adding chips to my ante.

"Is Silas here tonight?" I asked again, placing a large pile in the trips, which seemed to perk the other player, and he matched my bet.

"Two pairs," called the dealer. Ugh. He wasn't going to answer me.

"You play well," said the other player. His voice was deep and resonated in a calm sexy manner.

I shrugged and answered, "Had lots of practice." It was true. Em, and I had played all the time while growing up.

"Odd hobby for a young lady," the other player said.

I smiled. "I wasn't into high school dances and shopping."

The other player laughed a deep rumble that went straight to my core. "I see that," he said. If his face matched his tone of voice, he was damn sexy. If only I could pull back his hood and get a look.

"Three of a kind," announced the dealer.

The other player sat back, looking at his dealt hand. "You win again," he said with evident surprise in his voice.

I glanced toward the bar and around the room. The dealer dealt the next hand, and I slid all my chips in. "Case bet," I called, hoping to make a scene and draw out Silas.

The guy stared at my chips, shaking his head, and matched my bet. "That's an interesting tattoo. Where did you get it?"

My hands rested on the table. I glanced at my Nevus. "Tattoo parlor," I said. I mean, what could I say? *Oh, this old thing? It's a Marking Spell that my wizard boss bestowed upon me when I was only a child to help protect me from all the evil spirits.*

The dealer flipped the cards. "A straight."

"And the design?" the other player asked.

"A friend of mine found it in a book—"

Someone touched my shoulders. "Are you taking this poor man's money?" A*h, just the guy I was looking for.* Silas sat down beside me, with his two stout bodyguards standing behind him. "Nice to see you," he said. "What brings you here tonight? And don't tell me it's for money."

"I need info," I said. Why beat around the bush. I needed info, and I needed it now.

He looked around me. "Where's your partner?"

"He's a little under the weather."

He nodded, stood up, and pulled on the hem of his expensive-looking jacket. "Well," he said. "Let's talk in my office?"

I stood after him. "Lead the way, asshole," I said. The other player laughed.

Silas pretended not to hear. "This way," he said and placed a hand on the small of my back. I rolled my fingers into two tight fists, struggling not to jerk away from his touch. I didn't want to piss off the man I needed information from.

Think of Emerich. Think of Emerich.

I glanced over my shoulder at the other player. I hoped to get a peek of him, but he had left. Silas removed his hand from my back and stepped in front of me. We maneuvered around the narrow spaces between the tables. He smelled of expensive cologne with a hint of sulfur. He was a foot taller than me and dressed in designer clothes like those Hollywood gangsters you'd see in movies.

I followed him down a long hallway that reminded me of a hotel with doors all the way down on both sides. Soft moans and breathless grunting could be heard from behind them. I guess sex was a standard bet.

We reached the end of the hall, and Silas opened the door. "After you," he said, and placed a hand at the small of my back again, guiding me in.

"Well," I said, looking around, "This wasn't what I was expecting."

What was I expecting? Maybe a cold room with a single desk littered with stacks of money or bags of drugs. Instead, everything was big and lavish: dark wood, tiled floor, and velvet textiles. I admired the expensive paintings on the walls.

"These yours?" I asked, resting my eyes on a painting that stood out from the rest. It was a young girl staring at a vast terrain of fire, and I wondered if the girl was in Hell. In a

43

twisted kind of way, she reminded me of myself, scared and alone. The painting consumed my thoughts so thoroughly that I failed to notice how close Silas was to me.

Damn it, Maeve. Lately I'd allowed my mind to wander. In this line of work, a distraction could get me killed. I need to be more vigilant.

He ran two fingers down my arm, and my lip curled. "Don't forget I'm trained to kill your kind," I said in a deep, menacing tone.

He lifted his hands in the air, palms facing out. "Touché. What do you want to know?"

I didn't have time to waste, so I got straight to the point. "I need to break a curse called the Devil's Kiss?"

His face turned ashen. A slight change to his appearance, but I caught it. "Only the Grigori can pass such a curse."

I noted a slight tremor in his voice when he said Grigori, and I rolled my eyes. "Well, I can guarantee the jinn who cursed my partner was not a Grigori," I said. "I need a cure." Silas kept looking at the door. "Are you expecting someone?"

His face transformed, showing his true self. His canine teeth grew into long, pointy fangs, and his eyes darkened into two black voids. They were called vampires in literature and film, but that was just a fancy name for blood-craving jinn. The Grigori had cursed them, had doomed them to live among humans and drink their blood to survive. Yet, I had heard somewhere that that was only a myth, and vampires were created when a jinn impregnated a woman. Either way, they fucking sucked, and the thought of having sex with a jinn gave me willies.

"If your partner is cursed with the Devil's Kiss, then you're dealing with someone powerful." He pointed to the door. "You need to leave. I refuse to meddle with the Grigori."

I rolled my eyes. "Quit being a dramatic puss and tell me what you know!"

The paintings fell from the walls. The couch slid across the room and slammed against the door, trapping me inside. "I told you to leave. You had your chance." Papers from the printer flew up and scattered. Then, in a blur of motion, he grabbed my wrist, twisted it behind me, and shoved it up between my shoulder blades. He wrapped his other arm around my neck, pressing the front of his body against my back. His breath, hot and moist, crept across my neck, and I hissed when his fangs punctured my skin. He stuck his tongue out and lapped the blood that formed.

If he was expecting fear, he was going to be disappointed. I slid a knife out of its harness and shouted, "Not tonight, asshole." I headbutted him with the back of my head, connecting with his chin. He let me go, and I shoved my knife into the side of his neck.

He staggered back, and his appearance changed back to beautiful. He grabbed the knife's handle and pulled. It didn't budge.

"Only I can remove it," I said, smiling as pieces of his flesh flaked off and fluttered to the floor. He was slowly burning away. "Your time is running out. I can let you stay or send you back to Hell." It was a lie that seemed to work. Once I stabbed a jinn, they were doomed to Hell.

He stood taller and rolled his shoulders back, but no matter what he did, he looked stupid with that handle sticking out of his neck. "Yes! There's a way to break the curse."

"Tell me!"

"It's a hex found in a—"

Just then, someone burst through the door, and the couch slid back as if it was nothing more than a tiny dollhouse miniature. A gun fired. The bullet blew through Silas's head, splattering flesh and blood on the books that lined the shelves behind him.

"His ticket to Hell was long overdue," said the gunman.

My muscles tensed as I realized the gunman was the other player at the poker table. "Are you fucking kidding me?" I yelled. "I needed him alive. I need information, asshole." Fuck, I was so close. What was I going to do now?

The gunman slid his glasses down his nose and winked at me.

Amber Eyes!

45

I pointed at him. "You," I said, nearly growling the word. I was that pissed.

"Meet me at Colonial Park Cemetery after midnight. I have the cure you're looking for." He pushed his glasses back up before darting from the room and disappearing down the hall.

"Oh, hell no," I hissed, "You're not getting away this time." Silas was about to tell me where to find a cure. *His ass was mine*. I grabbed my knife from Silas's neck and ran after Amber Eyes. Curious and naked onlookers stuck their nosey little heads out the door. "Go back to your room," I yelled. "Nothing to see here." I jumped over two dead bodies—Silas's bodyguards. Amber Eyes must have killed them too.

The entire cardroom fell quiet. Some were standing, and others still sitting, but every gambling jinn had their eyes on me. I didn't care because I was searching for Amber Eyes.

"Did you see a guy with a gun?" I asked a man to my right. He shook his head, so I asked the guy on my left. "You?" He also shook his head. "Fucking idiots."

I gave the crowd one last look, eyeing each man, but nobody seemed out of sorts or suspicious. I glanced at my watch; thirty minutes until midnight.

It was time to finally meet this mysterious Amber Eyes, and he had better have answers, or I swore to God I'd fucking kill him.

Chapter Eight

EZRA

I've visited many graves in my lifetime. Usually I run into an angry ghost or two, some nosy kids, or a random gravedigger looking to sell bones on the black market. Still, this grave was quiet—the perfect spot to talk in secret.

Maeve leaned against a brick wall with hanging tombs. Her hair was like the feathers of a raven, black and shiny, and it hung in waves to her slender waist. Her eyes, deep and dark, had an intense, penetrating stare. They emphasized the soft spray of freckles across her cheeks and nose. She was an unusual beauty, gothic yet innocent, a paradoxical mystery, inside and out.

She looked pointedly at her watch and then at me with a lifted brow. "About time," she muttered.

I stepped under the light of the nearby lamppost and placed my hands over my heart. "Forgive me?"

She pushed herself from the brick wall. Her eyes grazed my body from head to toe and back until our eyes met again. "You ran from me twice. Why talk now? Why not sooner? Do you enjoy playing these immature games?"

I coughed into my fist to disguise my laugh, but I wasn't so sure I hid my smile well enough. Maeve cocked a brow and puckered her lips, seemingly annoyed with me. I cleared my throat before answering. "This humidity gets to me." She tilted her head to the other side and folded her arms across her chest. To me, it was apparent that she was silently demanding an answer, so I gave her the truth. "I was watching you."

She moved her hands until they hovered over the holsters

that held her knives. "Why were you fucking watching me?"

I raised my hands, palms facing her. "Easy, love. I don't mean you harm."

She took a step closer, and I inhaled her scent. I got a hint of apple and cigarette smoke, probably from being at the Den. That place was a fucking dump.

"Answer the question," she demanded.

"I couldn't very well talk to you at a club or gambling joint—too many ears."

"You're dodging my question."

This time, I took a step closer, and surprisingly, she didn't move away. Instead, she widened her stance, lifted her chin, and kept a steady hand over her knives. She was a woman who demanded respect. I liked that. "I need something from you."

"Really?" she asked. "And what could that be?"

"A book."

She lifted a brow. "A book? Well, there are these places called libraries."

I took another step closer. "It's a special book."

"Pfft...whatever you say, Amber Eyes."

Did she just call me *Amber Eyes*? "I prefer Ezra. But you can call me what you wish, sweetheart."

"Okay, *Ezra*," she said. "What were you doing in the alley last night?"

I shrugged my shoulders and smiled. "I was walking home from the bar."

She eyed me suspiciously. "Why were you at the Den? Are you jinn?"

"I have a feeling you already know that answer, but I assure you, I'm not a jinn."

"An angel?"

I threw my head back and laughed. "Fuck, no!"

"You said you have a cure? I'm assuming you were listening to my conversation with Silas?"

"Yes, I know how to help the prophet."

She unsheathed a knife and spun around me until the blade pressed against my Adam's apple. *Damn, she was fast.*

"How do you know about Emerich?" Her tone, abruptly deeper with a trace of edge. God, she was a turn-on.

"I know many things, love." I grabbed her wrist and twisted it back until she dropped her weapon. Then, I crushed her into a bear-hug, brought my lips to her ear, and whispered, "I can help him, but that is if you're willing to cooperate."

"Let go of me, asshole," she said through clenched teeth. Her chest rose and fell along with her heavy breathing.

"I wouldn't squirm," I said, licking my lips. "It turns me on." She froze, and I laughed, letting her go.

She reached down and grabbed her knife, pulled out the other, and pointing them both at me. "Do that again and I'll kill you. Now, tell me how you think I can help my partner."

I picked some lint from my sleeve, bored with her silly threats and those ridiculous knives. "Put the knives away, love. You're not going to harm me." She spun them around in her hands, and I thought she was going to put them away. I was wrong. She held them steady and pointed at me. Of course, she was a stubborn woman.

"How can you help my partner?" she asked again.

"Not until you get me the book."

"What book?"

I pointed at her wrist. "The same book that gave you that Nevus."

She narrowed her eyes at me. "How do you know about my Nevus?"

I shrugged. "Like I said, *love*, I know a lot of things."

Narrowing her eyes, she said, "My name's Maeve."

"Considering your career choice, what I do not understand is why you would want a Patriarchal Blood Nevus. It's a Marking Spell meant for the elite in the underworld." I lifted a brow. "That explains how you're strong enough to do your line of work."

She snorted. "So, let me get this right. You think this," she tapped her wrist, "is meant for jinn?"

"For the elite jinn, mostly the Grigori."

She held up her wrist with her Nevus facing me. "I would

never, *ever* scar my body with a mark meant for Grigori."
She practically spat the last word, and I cringed. "And what
do my Nevus and this book have to do with Emerich?"

"Bring me the book, and I'll tell you."

She threw her hands up. "What fucking book?"

"The Book of Raziel, sweetheart."

"Never heard of it."

"Winston is the keeper of the book."

She squinted as if looking inward before clearing her
throat. "And why do you need this book?"

"I need to stop a war from happening. I'm sure you've
heard, a war between the damned and the divine?"

She paused, deep in thought, biting the inside of her
cheeks, her expression downcast. "War? As in the
apocalypse?"

"Yes."

She lifted a brow, bestowing upon me a contemptuous
attitude. "And...how can this book prevent this war?"

"It's an ancient book of spells and knowledge of medicine,
magic, and weaponry."

She folded her arms over her chest and eyed me. "And if I
get this book, how can I trust you won't take it and run?"

I leaned forward and stared directly into her dark eyes.
"You have no other choice."

She laughed dismissively. "There are always choices. And
I work with powerful people."

She was right about that. She worked with influential
people, Winston being one of them. I stepped back and lifted
my hands, palms up. "Well, forgive me. I'm wasting your
time."

I pivoted around on my heel and went to leave, but she
stopped me just as I had predicted. She was desperate to find
a cure for her partner, and nobody had an answer except for
me.

"The prophet was cursed by a powerful spell called the
Devil's Kiss," I said, "It's a nasty spell that causes
excruciating pain before death. The prophet doesn't have
much time, Maeve. Sometimes life is about taking risks."

Her eyes were fixed on mine, but they were distant as if she were deep in thought, hopefully contemplating my words. Seconds later, she stood tall, pushed her shoulders back, and lifted her chin. "Fine! Meet me here tomorrow, just after sunset."

Chapter Nine

MAEVE

I had a plan, and I was sure of that plan. After speaking to Ezra, I drove straight to the DCU the second I left the grave, determined to search through Winston's house to find that book. When I was nine, Sal had mentioned a room with top-secret stuff located somewhere in Winston's home. Now that I was here, parked at the back of his house, I felt sick to my stomach, feeling nervous or guilty; I wasn't sure which. Did I really want to break into his house and look for something I knew was top secret and most likely forbidden?

Winston's old pick-up truck was parked outside the office building, just as I had anticipated. Knowing him, he most likely wouldn't be home for another hour or more. Everything was going perfectly. It couldn't have started better, yet, here I sat, contemplating my plan. My conscience was beating at my brain, telling me to do the right thing. *What was the right thing to do?*

Either I confront Winston with everything I'd learned and hope he'd help me or break into his house and look for the Book of Raziel myself. If Winston were willing to use the book to help Emerich, he would have already, and if I confront him, he'd probably send me home. I refused to leave empty-handed. I had no choice, Winston would be home soon, so I had better go.

I jogged around to the front of his cabin-like home and peered through a window. I immediately spotted a flashing red light, a security alarm. I tried the door. It was locked. *Geesh...what a spaz. Who else would break-in?* His house was in the DCU; the entire compound was gated and guarded. Was there someone who worked for him that he didn't trust? Or maybe he was protecting something significant. *Like the Book of Raziel?*

Thanks to my training, I deactivated the alarm and unlocked the door without breaking a thing or making a sound. I was inside in under a minute.

The last time I was here, I was nine, and if memory served me right, Sal mentioned something about a room with top-secret files and objects.

I pivoted around, forming a visual map of the layout. I rechecked the time. Dang, I'd been here longer than had needed. I better get my ass in gear. After all, I drove straight here after speaking to Ezra, determined to find the book quickly, and leave.

I searched every room from top to bottom. I looked under furniture and rugs and behind hanging picture frames. I even felt around drawers and other cracks and crevices for some sort of switch to open a hidden door or wall.

A sickening feeling settled in my gut as I slowly realized that there was nothing here. I pressed the center of my forehead with my fingers. "Think, Maeve. Think."

The sound of an engine, a car door opening then closing, footsteps on the gravel. *Someone's coming.*

"Shit!" I looked right and then left before darting to the back of the room. I opened what ended up being a closet door and hid behind a row of hanging coats. Damn, I knew Winston like trench coats, but an entire closet dedicated to them? He had taken the detective look to a whole new level.

Footsteps.

I rolled my lips in, held my breath, and pushed my body flush against the wall. "Ouch. What the..." Something poked me from behind—I felt the wall. There was a small metal lever, hardly noticeable.

I opened my eyes wide. *Could it be?*

A soft click of a door closing. Shit, I had better hurry. I pulled the lever with zero hesitation, and a hatch, the size of a small door, popped open. *It could be.* I stepped inside and felt around for a light switch, which I found to my right.

The light lit up the area, and I shuffled back. "Holy shit," I whispered with my hand over my heart. Thank God I located the light. One step more and I would have nosedived down a steep, spiral stairway.

I looked over my shoulder, knowing it was now or never. Someone was bound to hear me if I stuck around. I took the stairs as fast as I could without falling, and when I reached the bottom, I found a narrow hallway, dimly lit straight ahead. I glanced back up the stairs, second-guessing my plan again. What if I was caught? Winston would suspend me for a year, maybe two. Oh, hell. I made it this far. It was too late to turn back now. I crept ahead, taking deep breaths as the air was stifling.

At the end of the hall was a sizeable open space. It was nothing special. In fact, the room was rather bare. Wow, all of that for this? A secret door, booby-trap-like stairs, and a long creepy hall for what, an empty space?

I wanted to slap my forehead, feeling disappointed, but I refused to give up so soon. There had to be something here, so I scanned the area. There were two bookshelves with a handful of books, a single desk with nothing on it, and a glass box perched on a thick wooden stand right smack in the center of the room.

I rolled my eyes. *Really? Could it be more obvious?*

Whatever it was inside that box was essential. I glanced over my shoulder, grinning and feeling smug. *This was too easy.* Break-in. Find the book. Take the book. Done. I mentally patted myself on the back as I crept closer to the box.

I looked inside the glass, and a sudden onset of nausea hit my gut like a brick. "Fuck…" There was no book, only a glass vial with a label. "Damn it!" And to top it off, the print on the label was faint and written in a language I didn't know, maybe Emean writing. Either way, it seemed ancient. I was about to leave, look about the room when I spotted it—a word.

Raziel.

I pumped my fist into the air. "Booyah!" It wasn't the

book. "But it was something," I whispered to myself. It was a flicker of hope, and I was taking it. I felt around, searching for a button, a switch, or a knob. Anything, but there was nothing—a common theme lately. I pulled the glass, but it didn't budge. I needed something to break it, but there was nothing heavy enough.

"What are you doing?"

I jumped and gulped down a breath to hold back a scream. "Fuck, Sal?" I held my heart as it felt like it was about to explode. People don't sneak up on me. Thanks to my Nevus, I heard them coming before they even entered the room, except for Sal. He was the only one.

His eyes ping-ponged between me and the box. "What are you doing here?"

Uhm.... "What are *you* doing here?" Oh, a good one, Maeve. I wanted to roll my eyes hard. Come on, I needed to be brighter than that lame-ass comeback. If I didn't find an excuse and a damned good one, my ass was in deep shit.

"Does Winston know you're here?" Sal asked, eyeing me.

"Well...no."

He pinched the bridge of his nose and squeezed his eyes shut. Yep, I was in deep shit. "Fuck, Maeve. You—"

"I found a way to help Emerich," I spat out. This time, I didn't *mentally* slap my forehead. I physically did and hard.

Sal crossed his arms over his broad chest. "How?"

Oh, well, what better choice did I have but to be honest. It was that or what? Come up with a blatant lie? He'd see right through me. "The Book of Raziel," I blurted without much more thought.

His mouth fell open in shock. "Who? How? Who told you about that book?" If I didn't know him well, I would have been intimidated. He was an ox with a hundred percent muscle, but it wasn't his size that was threatening. It was the feeling I got while around him. He seemed to know everything about me as if he could see into my soul. Sometimes, I felt uneasy just thinking around him as if he could reach into my very mind. It was damn intimidating.

"Does it matter?"

He leaned in, getting closer. "You shouldn't know about that book."

I didn't step back. I refused to cower. "Why?" Why shouldn't I have known about this book? What was the big deal?

"The Arch Assembly banned the book from ever being used again."

I couldn't help but lift a quizzical brow. "Why?" This book was obviously powerful, but was it powerful enough to save Emerich and prevent the apocalypse? I could only hope.

"It's a book full of dark magic and forbidden knowledge." *I guess Ezra had been honest about the book.*

A sudden surge of frustration ran through my veins. This conversation was going in circles. "Okay, but Emerich's life is on the line, so I'll take my chances with the Arch Assembly." I wasn't scared of those self-loving-flying-wanna-be-badasses. "Can you at least tell me where it is?"

He shook his head. "No."

"Wow. Just like that? Look, Sal, I know Winston used that book to give me my Nevus, and I know he's the keeper and —"

Oh, no. The vein on Sal's right temple pulsed along with the pop of his jaw muscles as he clenched his molars. He was either getting upset, or he already was. "Who's giving you this information?"

I threw my hands up, getting angry myself. "Tell me."

He pinched the bridge of his nose again. It was his signature move when he was irritated. I've learned to read Sal's emotions through the years. Not that it was hard as he plainly wore them on his sleeve, one just had to be observant like me.

"Winston can't use the book to save Emerich. He sealed it years ago."

"So, the book *could* save him?" The anger in my voice fizzled away as Sal confirmed my hope, making it a reality. *I can save Emerich.* "How did he seal it?"

Sal pressed his lips into a straight line. "It doesn't matter."

Did I hear him correctly? "It doesn't matter? Emerich

matters, Sal!" Now I was the one pinching the bridge of my nose. The whole damn situation was fucked, and before I continued, I inhaled a calming breath. "Look...according to Emerich's vision, there's a war coming, and from what I've heard, the book can stop it." He didn't respond, so I kept talking. "One death is better than the lives of an entire human population."

He shook his head. "It isn't time for war. Like I said, we would have heard from the Arch Assembly."

I shook my head. "No, Sal. Emerich's visions are never wrong."

"It's a forbidden book."

"And it's Emerich." Finally I saw his features soften. *About fucking time!*

"I want to help him. I do. But I can't, Maeve. The book is sealed."

"How?"

He shook his head. "Doesn't matter." I bit the inside of my cheeks until I tasted blood. I wanted to hit something— anything. *Why does Sal keep saying that?* "Emerich matters, Sal!" I screamed, hitting my fist on the glass box. "Tell me!"

"With blood! He can't use the book because it's sealed shut with fucking blood!"

I investigated the box. It sure did look like blood in that vial. Did Sal know what was in it? I brought my attention back to Sal before he noticed his mistake. "Winston can't, or he won't?"

He snapped his mouth shut and looked away. Sal used to be a jinn hunter, Winston's partner, in fact, until Emerich and I came along. After that, he gave up the hunt to teach and train us, but we all knew that he was more like a father than a mentor.

"I once asked you why ...why you gave up hunting? You remember what you said?" I didn't wait for an answer. "You said, 'I need you and Emerich to know how to protect yourselves.' Why? I asked. You said, 'Because you and Emerich matter to me.'" I stood on my toes. Why? I wasn't sure. Maybe it was to appear taller or to drive my point home. Either way, it didn't matter because what I had said next was enough to break even a bear of a man like Sal. "Because you love us."

He swayed and stumbled back as if I had stabbed him. "I'm...."

I folded my arms across my chest and turned my head away from him. His sad eyes hurt to see, but I had to keep Emerich at the forefront of my mind. Remind me that his life was more important than who I hurt. "He trusted you, Sal." My voice broke.

He didn't say anything, so I dared a glance at him. He brought his eyes to meet mine, and I saw a glossy sheen of tears covering them. My heart hurt for him, but at the same time, I selfishly felt pride as I was plainly winning this argument. I had to win. Emerich's life depended on it.

"I'm sorry, Mae. I—"

Still, he wasn't going to talk. I was winning this argument. Was it an argument or more like a desperate plea? In any respect, I shook my head, wanting desperately to scream—just scream. My mounting frustration was building. "We need to help him."

"No!"

This time it was me that stumbled back as if I was shot in the heart. "No?"

He lifted his chin and peered down at me. "No," he sternly stated.

He was looking down at me like I was a child, and something in me snapped. I formed a fist, open my mouth, and let him have it. "Yes!" I screamed that one word, not giving two shits who heard me or who I hurt. I was pissed.

Sal wasn't fazed by my antics. "Go home, Maeve. Get some rest. We can talk about this in the morning."

I wanted to scream, cry, and fight. I wanted *Sal* to fight. I wanted him to fight to save Emerich. I wanted him to do something—anything. But I got nothing.

I was too angry. Too ashamed to look at him, so without another word, another fight, or another glance his way, I left.

***

After that argument with Sal, I felt drained, but I couldn't leave the DCU until I saw Emerich. I needed to feel grounded in my reason to save him. As it seemed, I might have to break the rules and go up against Sal and even Winston.

Earlier today, Dr. Lee said he'd have better insight into Emerich's health later in the night, so I went to the hospital. The doors slid open, and the assistant at the front desk asked if I needed help. I walked past her without a word and went straight to the quarantine area. Dr. Lee was waiting for me. "Well?" I asked.

"Come inside." He ushered me into the hall of the quarantine area. It was late, so it was just the two of us. "We got his blood work back."

"And…"

"His cells are dying." He didn't beat around the bush, and I respected that.

"How long does he have?"

His features softened. "A week, maybe a little more."

A sudden, painful lump formed in my throat, and my eyes grew moist. I tried to speak but choked on a sob. I clutched my body as if to hold it together, but I was falling apart. Dr. Lee wanted to comfort me, but I swatted him away.

I pointed at Lee and shook my head. "Don't you dare stop me, or so help me, God, I'll…." I didn't know what to say. I couldn't threaten the doctor's life. After all, he was trying to save Emerich, but I had to be sure he wouldn't stop me. I was getting tired of people telling me no or to go home. Lee lifted his hands and lowered his head, submitting to my threat. I took off down the hall toward the quarantine room.

It wasn't hard to spot. Emerich was in a room that had a wall of glass, probably for easy observation. He lay on the bed with dozens of wires connected to him. He was pale and thin, as if he'd been sick for weeks. I heard the rhythmic beep of the heart monitor. I touched the glass with my fingers and reflected on the situation.

Where did I fit in all of this?

It seemed no matter which direction I turned, I ended up hurting someone. But the hurt was not like death, and that was Emerich's fate. Winston told me not to get involved. Sal said I was too emotionally tied to Emerich that I should hold back.

"I can't," I said. *I can't hold back.* If I kept questioning the what-ifs, Emerich might die. He only had a week, a fucking week. What was I waiting for?

I pushed myself from the glass.

If they weren't going to help, I was.

Even if it meant risking my fucking life.

I walked down the hall, driven by determination. I turned the corner and spotted an ax next to a fire extinguisher. *Perfect.* I could use the ax to break the glass and get the vial. I opened the fire extinguisher box, grabbed the ax, and headed toward the exit.

Dr. Lee spotted the ax in my hands as I walked by. "Maeve? What are you doing?"

"I'm sorry, Lee, but somebody needs to help Emerich."

The assistant muttered a whole slew of profanities, and I winked at her as I strolled by and straight out the exit.

I jumped into my ride, tossed the ax onto the passenger seat, and drove straight to Winston's. I smirked and giggled. If only Emerich saw me now, he'd be proud. No worries, I told myself. He'll hear about this soon enough when I saved him.

I parked in front of Winston's, grabbed the ax, and threw it over my shoulder. I didn't have time to waste, so I kicked Winston's door open. Neither did I have the time to worry about the things that got in my way, and once inside, I went straight to his coat closet. Then, I hit the lever and went down to the basement. Nothing could stop me now. I stepped up to the box, lifted the ax high above my head, and swung down. The glass cracked but didn't break, so I tried again. And again. And again. Until the glass shattered into a million glittering pieces.

I threw the ax to the ground and grabbed the vial, slipping

it into my pocket. Wow, I thought I would feel guilty, taking something obviously important, but I felt...right. This was the right thing to do; to save Emerich no matter what. My shoes crunched the bits of broken glass as I darted toward the exit. I was eager to talk to Ezra and show him what I had found. I jogged down the hall, up the stairs, through the closet, and out the front door.

I thought I had done it, undiscovered and unseen. Yeah, I was wrong.

Winston was sat in a chair on his front porch, waiting for me. I looked up to the heavens and cursed. He was sitting in his rocking chair, rocking back and forth while smoking a cigarette.

"He will kill you," he said. His voice was hoarse.

I glanced around, looking for someone. "Who?" I asked.

"Shamsiel. He'll kill anybody who attempts to steal the Book of Raziel. He has a sword with blue flames, and stories say, one hit can kill an army of men." What? Shamsiel was an angel—that's all I knew.

Wait, how did Winston know I wanted the book? Sal must have told him.

I raised an eyebrow. "Why aren't you stopping me?"

"Do you want me to?"

Was that a trick question?

I glanced around again, but this time as if I would find someone else with the answer. "No," I said, feeling uneasy. I wasn't sure what was happening? What did he want me to say? Did he want to scare me, stop me from getting the book? Where was the book?

He pointed at me with the hand holding the cigarette. "You will fail," he simply stated. "You still hold onto your past, and that...is your weakness."

Okay, that was harsh and uncalled for. "Thanks for the vote of confidence," I said. "But you're wrong." *My past gave me a reason. It gave me the strength to do what I do.* Hunt and kill jinn. I didn't tell him that. I didn't feel I needed to because it only mattered to me.

He stood, and I mentally patted myself on the shoulder for

not faltering back a step or two. The man could be intimidating. "For Emerich's sake and yours, I hope I am wrong."

"I can help Emerich. I just need the book."

He flicked the cigarette into a nearby bush. "Good luck." He headed indoors.

"You need to help Emerich! You have the blood to unseal the book! He's dying!" I screamed like my life depended on my words. Though Emerich's life did.

His hand on the door handle, Winston didn't look at me as he spoke. "If I could, I would, but things must unfold as they are written." Then, without another word, he went inside and shut the door, leaving me with more questions than answers and more doubt than hope.

What the hell did that mean?

Chapter Ten

EZRA

I poured myself a shot of bourbon from the mini bar, savoring the burn as it slowly slid down my throat. I hadn't slept in weeks, and last night wasn't any different. The Bohemian Hotel was an excellent property with river-view rooms, but I grew tired of the constant traveling. The smell of old carpet and cleaners, the sound of water gurgling in the pipes within the walls and toilets flushing, was all enough to drive any man insane.

I sat in the hotel's scratchy lounge chair by the large window. The evening sun was slowly fading behind the river's horizon, and the crowd of people that occupied the streets was slowly retreating indoors, except for a few night owls. I spotted a young woman strolling by, blissful of the possible dangers that surrounded her. She reminded me of Maeve. Maeve wasn't naïve, especially to the dangers in the world. Winston made sure of that. Still, she was petite, just like the woman strolling along.

My thumb ring clanked against the base as I tapped the glass with my thumb. Maeve, that woman was a mystery. Why had Winston given her a Nevus? Sure, it gave her physical strength, which explained her role as an assassin for the DCU, but why would he risk his life using the Book of Raziel. And why not use it to save the prophet and kill Levi? How much does he know about Levi? *I'm sure he's read through the Book of Raziel. He must understand what Levi can do.*

There were several rumors about why the Arch Assembly couldn't guard the book: it cursed their dreams; it caught fire, burning half their territory; or my favorite, the book released an awful smell of rotting flesh and sulfur.

The truth was, like everything sinful, the temptation to use the book's powers was unbearable. Even the Arch Assembly's angels weren't strong enough to resist its influence, so they made Winston—a human—keeper of the book and gave him eternal life. It was the perfect solution until Winston was also tempted. I believe he dabbled in spells and magic, and that's how he became powerful - really fucking powerful.

He used to hunt and kill jinn, and word on the street was he'd kill jinn with a single thought or a flick of a wrist. Ha, I've met numerous archangels with fewer powers.

My cell vibrated, and I snatched it up from the small end table.

I didn't check to see who it was. I didn't need to. There was only one person who ever called me. "Dorian," I said, pinching my temples. His high-pitched voice scraped at my middle ear, so I turned down the volume.

"Don't sound so glum, Ezra. How's the case?"

"Why would the wizard give a human a Nevus?" I asked, without thinking first of the consequences. There was no telling what The Order would do to a human with a powerful marking spell. My guess was nothing, being that she was human and not a jinn. There was little they could do when it came to meddling in human affairs.

There was a beat of silence. "I beg your pardon?"

"Why would Winston use such great power on a human? She must be someone important to the wizard." There was something different about her. I felt it when I touched her— the energy that flowed through her. It was faint yet untainted and robust.

"She? Who's She?"

"She works at the DCU." *Whoa. Time to pump the breaks, Ezra.* I wasn't sure I wanted him to know too much about this mysterious woman of mine.

"Give me her name and age."

Damn. I shouldn't have blurted out that question. I raked

my fingers through my hair as my frustrations mounted. Fuck, I needed sleep; the lack of had to account for my rash idiocy. "She isn't important now. The case is going..." What could I say? It was too soon to know how the case was going. *Is it going well? I don't fucking know.* I had just found the DCU yesterday, for fuck's sake. *Is it going to shit?* Was a better question. It was just too damn soon to know. "I'll call you when I have more details." I hung up before he said another word.

Dorian was just as shocked as I was about the girl's Nevus, making her even more intriguing. I was willing to bet the wizard didn't consider the possibility of the Grigori's release. *Not during the girl's lifetime.* If he had felt such an option, he would have known the consequences.

Dorian was just as clueless as I was when it came to the big bad wizard. I hung up and checked my watch. Finally, time to meet Maeve. The eagerness and excitement to see her gave me a burst of energy. I went to stand when a sickening feeling settled in my gut. Was I eager to get my hands on the book, or was I excited to see Maeve? It was the book. It had to be about the book. I don't fall for women—not anymore. Plus, the book was the key to my freedom from The Order.

At least, that's what I told myself as I headed out the door.

***

I found Maeve at the same place we met last night by the same tombstone. She was dressed from head to toe in black leather that hugged her body, accentuating her curves, and her hair hung in long, black, shiny waves again.

She lifted a brow. What was she thinking? "I didn't come here to be drooled on."

I couldn't help but smile. I liked a woman with spice. "Don't flatter yourself, love. You're not my type." I usually sought out redheads, but I'd make an exception for one night.

"Whatever," she said, lifting her chin. "I'm here to make a deal."

I stopped a foot away from her, close enough to be

intimidating. I needed the upper hand as I was sure she would bargain her way to the cure without giving up the book. "Straight to business. I like that... Let's talk."

"We work together, and once we finish our job, we'll return the book."

I leaned in with a stiff smile. "How can I trust you?" I trusted nobody, especially women.

She let out an arrogant laugh and tossed her raven-black hair over one shoulder. "How can I trust *you*?"

"Touché," I said, moving my eyes up her body. She was fit with lean muscle, I gave her that, but she was just too damn petite. "You're not strong enough to work alongside me."

She withdrew her knives and spun them in her hands. "Is that a challenge?" she confronted.

I covered my mouth with my fist to hide my smile. "Sorry, sweetheart, but I work alone." I turned around on my heel, tucking my hands into my pants pockets, and walked away. It was a test, of course, to see how desperate she was.

"Good luck finding the book," she countered.

Damn it! I should've known.

She could manipulate and control a situation like a boss. I peeked over my shoulder. She wore a devilish grin. A damn, sexy grin, I had to admit.

I turned back around and peered down at her. "Do you have the book?"

She shook her head, keeping her chin high and steady. "First...the deal," she said, holding out her hand. *Mental note: add determination to her personality,* I thought.

Narrowing my eyes, I tested her again. "How important is this to you, love?"

She held intense eye contact with me. "I will go to Hell and back to save Emerich!" she stated without hesitation or fear.

"I doubt you'll have to go to Hell," I said, but she might have to come face-to-face with Levi, and that was just as bad.

I shook my head and closed my eyes. What I was about to do was probably going to end up being a colossal mistake. Fuck it. With a resigned sigh, I took her delicate hand and shook it.

The corners of her mouth turned up. She had the confident smile of a woman used to getting her way. "I'm glad we're on the same page." She sauntered past me with a slightly lethal yet mostly seductive sway. When she realized I wasn't following her, she glanced over her shoulder. "Are you coming?" Her tone was deep and smooth—sexy as fuck, and she had a hint of fire in her eyes. I fought the shiver of arousal. I was in deep shit. This woman was going to be a distraction, something I couldn't afford.

Down boy, I mentally said to my manhood growing below. We have a job to do…first.

I shifted my fly and followed her out of the cemetery and across the street. "This is my house," she said, jogging up the steps. She didn't live far—how convenient. She opened the door and allowed me in, tossing her belongings aside before showing me to the kitchen.

"Would you like a drink?" she offered.

"Bourbon?"

"Sorry, I'm a gin girl."

I lifted a brow and smirked. "Is that so? I thought you hunt and kill jinn."

She rolled her eyes. "Ha-ha. Funny, guy. Sorry, buddy, but that was a lame joke."

I shook my head and slid my hands into my pockets before leaning against the kitchen counter. "Not all jinn are bad, you know."

She popped open a soda and scoffed at me. "Are you serious?" she asked, "They're vile, sadistic monsters." Her voice became ice cold and sharp as a scalpel. "Anyway, gin is all I have as in g-i-n, gin."

I pushed myself off the counter. "No, thank you," I said, looking around. "So, tell me…do you have the book?" I asked, following her to a small kitchenette table where we sat. She smelled of vanilla and Cherry Coke.

"No, but" she grabbed something from her pocket, "I found this." She lifted her hand, showing me a small glass vial. "Salazar, my mentor, told me that the book is sealed with blood. I think this might be that blood." She turned the vial. "Can you read this?" She indicated a label with Emean writing.

I reached out to grab it from her to get a better look, but she yanked her hand back. I slowly moved my eyes to meet hers. "Say please," she said, her voice as soft as butter.

I sat back, casually crossing one leg over the other and crossing my arms over my chest. "Are you flirting with me?"

The corners of her mouth turned down. "You wish," she muttered, handing me the vial before leaning back uneasily.

I smiled, liking her sudden attitude change while taking the vial. It read: *Sol porta invenire tutum sanguine in Libro Raziel sit in sacro terram custodiebantur a Shamsiel, princeps quartus realm.*

I rubbed my chin. "Find the Gate of the Sun, protected by blood; the Book of Raziel rests in the sacred land, guarded by Shamsiel, ruler of the fourth realm." I shook my head. *Is this for real?* "I can't believe it."

Maeve leaned forward. "What?"

My smile grew wide. "You found it."

She lifted her brow, something she often did. It gave her personality more oomph in arrogance and pride. Typically, I would have been turned off, but the zesty attitude suited her well. "Found what?"

"The book's fucking location. It's written right here." I turned the vial so the words faced her.

She wrapped her hands around mine and slowly withdrew the vial from my hold. "Be careful with that. We might need it to break the seal." She slid it into her vest pocket and patted it as if to reassure its protection.

"It's not possible," I muttered. I heard Maeve say something, but my mind was consumed. I stood up and paced the small space. "We need to visit an old friend."

"Who?"

It wasn't possible. Fuck, Winston found the most excellent hiding spot. I had to keep this secret. Not even The Order can know this. I couldn't risk this info falling into the wrong hands, and I can't trust The Order. They were chatty fuckers.

I laughed to myself. For centuries, jinn and angels had

searched for the book. It was ironic that Maeve, a human girl, found its location in less than twenty-four hours.

Maeve snapped her fingers. "Hello? Earth to Ezra."

I stopped pacing and faced her. "We need to find the Garden."

She made her signature move and lifted a brow. "Garden?"

"Indeed, love. Not just any garden—*the garden*. The Earth's origin, the cradle of divination, the fertile land, holy valley, the land of the living, Dilmun, best known as…the Garden of Eden."

She sat back and chuckled. "Garden of Eden? That place was destroyed a long time ago. The great flood – remember?"

I darted to the front door. "Prepared to be shocked, love," I called over my shoulder.

"Wait. Where are you going?" She came from the kitchen.

"Charleston," I answered, walking across the street, back to the grave where I parked.

"Charleston, South Carolina?"

"Yes, and you're going too, so get ready and pack light." I turned to face her, walking backward. "Be ready in ten." She stared at me with uncertainty in her eyes, but then she turned on her heel and went inside. I pulled my cell from my pocket and dialed Philip's number.

It rang once before he answered, "Ezra, my dear friend, how are you?" His voice soothed my soul.

I clicked the unlock button on my car key to unlock the doors. "I'm alive," I answered as I slid into the driver's seat.

He let out a boisterous laugh, an addicting sound, and I laughed along with him. "Yes, son. That is always a good thing."

"For me it is." He knew how dangerous my job was. We both laughed again, a short moment before our laughter died off into silence.

"Well, what can I do for you?"

I drew in a deep breath, expanding my lungs, before allowing the words to spill from my mouth. "Levi broke the law, and I've been ordered to kill him."

Philip kept silent; I could feel his uncertainty. "And how

do you plan to do that?" he asked.

I rubbed my temples, unsure how he was going to take to my request. "I think I found a way, but I need your help."

There was a lengthy pause, then, with a long, low sigh, he said, "I will try my best."

"Do you mind if I visit?" I looked in the review mirror, hoping to see Maeve.

"Of course not."

Thank the Gods he didn't press for more information. I preferred not to discuss work over the phone, never knew who might be listening, so I said thanks and good-bye just as Maeve opened the door and threw a bag in the back seat. A fresh scent of vanilla and strawberries invaded my senses. Damn, what the fuck was wrong with me? *Since when I give a shit about lotions or perfumes.*

"Apparently, trusting you means going across state lines?" She asked, pulling the seat belt over and clicking it in place. Her hair fell to the side like expensive silk, and I had a sudden urge to run my fingers through the strands to see if they were as soft as they appeared. *Why the fuck was I admiring her hair?*

I pushed the ignition button, my car didn't need a key, and the engine roared. "Across state lines and possibly across realms."

Her hazel eyes lit up. They were long and exotic in shape and lined with black lashes. They reminded me of an ancient Egyptian queen—obsolete beauty and mystery. *Fuck!* Now I was admiring her eyes? *What the fuck is wrong with me?* I shook my head as if to shake thoughts of Maeve from my mind and stepped on the gas.

She tossed her cell in the cupholder. "So, why Charleston?"

I kept my eyes on the road as I answered, "A friend of mine named Philip lives there. He has one of the finest collections of rarities in the world, including the largest library of ancient text."

"What kind of ancient text? I mean, if the Garden is still around, we'll need stone tablets from the dawn of Creation, which, if we're lucky, only one or two may exist. So, if you believe your friend has what we're looking for, he must be one powerful guy with loads of cash. And, with that kind of money, why would he choose to live in Charleston of all places?"

"Philip is one of the few, an initiate of the High Priesthood of Mysteries, selected to protect the Keys of Divine Knowledge. There's a whole different level of knowledge that you need to learn, and Philip comes from a long line of religious leaders. He has a collection of artifacts that have been passed down, such as ancient maps, early texts, and other biblical relics. So, to answer your last question, Charleston is known as the Holy City."

She scratched her temple and looked inward. What was she thinking? "Priesthood of Mysteries...yeah, Winston's a member, but he refuses to talk about it. It's too sacred for the masses," she said, using air quotes to show her disdain. "What are the Keys of Divine Knowledge?"

"Sacred knowledge protected from jinn." *The location of the Sacred Seals was sacred knowledge, yet Levi knew where to find them. Maybe there was a rat in the Priesthood of Mysteries? Or perhaps Levi had known where to find them all along. He'd been around long enough.*

"Anyway," Maeve interrupted my internal ranting, "tell me why your friend is open to discussing knowledge gifted only to the exclusive?"

I tapped my fingers on the steering wheel. We were at a red light, and I was anxious to get to Philips. "He owes me a favor," I answered.

When the light turned green, I stepped on the gas. "Why?" she asked.

"Uh, that's more of his story to tell." She nodded, not pushing the subject. "Plus, he trusts me. We've been friends for years." I placed an elbow on the center console and shot her a pointed look. "However, he doesn't know you, so he may not trust you."

She snorted, which was not lady-like but still adorable. "Yeah, he wouldn't be the only one," she said.

I raised a brow. "Who else doesn't trust you?"

She gazed out the front window. "I just learned that Winston and Sal don't trust me with certain info either. They're cautious around me as if I'm a fucking loose cannon." She shrugged as if accepting it as fact.

What she said caught my attention. What did she mean by *loose cannon*? Was she referring to a quick temper? Though we had only just met, I could see that in her.

She shrugged her shoulders. "Maybe I am…. So, tell me, how does a demon hunter afford toys like this?" She held her hands out, motioning to my Ferrari.

I smiled and was about to answer when a shadow appeared and covered the car completely. I didn't believe it was a cloud. It popped up too suddenly.

"What are you looking at?" Maeve asked as she followed my eyes with hers, looking over her shoulder. But the shadow had vanished just as quickly as it appeared.

I looked in the rearview mirror, moving it around, hoping to spot it. "You didn't notice?"

"Notice what?" She was now looking through the passenger side mirror.

"The shadow?" I pointed up with my thumb.

She leaned forward, looking through the windshield. Her neck muscles strained as she tried to look up. When she didn't see anything, she sat back and looked at me.

"Never mind," I said, looking in the review mirror at nothing but a stretch of road. "To answer your previous question, I've been working for a long time." I forced my body to relax one muscle at a time, hoping the shadow was only my imagination. After all, I hadn't slept in over a fucking month.

"Yeah, well, you would have to hunt for an eternity to save enough money for this kind of luxury."

You have no idea. I laughed, inwardly mocking my own thoughts. "I have stocks, side businesses, investments, real estate, and years of savings."

"So, in other words, you're from old money."

I smiled at her. "Something like that," I said with a wink.

Her cheeks flushed a soft pink. "Umm...." She tucked a strand of hair behind her ear. *Was she coy?* I might like this side of her too. A sprinkle of sweetness to her spice makes the perfect meal. "So...why did you become a hunter?"

I shook my head to rid the thoughts that crept into my mind before they traveled down to my cock. "I hunt to pay off debt."

"What sort of debt?"

I raised my lips on one side into a slight smirk. "Do you normally ask this many questions?" She frowned and lifted that brow of hers, which encouraged me to laugh. "Okay. To save a friend," I answered. *A friend, yeah fucking right. Now, I'm ordered to kill him.*

"What happened to your friend?"

"I'm not in the mood to discuss that particular time in my life. What about you?" I asked, diverting the conversation away from me.

"What about me?" she asked, sitting straighter and looking tense. "I don't have much to tell."

Like her, I lifted a brow. "I doubt that, but okay, how did you start working for the DCU?" I was legitimately curious. Something about her felt pure and robust, like an inner power she had yet to discover and set free.

She broke eye contact to stare out the window. "That's a long story."

I gestured to the long stretch of road ahead. "We have a long drive ahead, sweetheart."

She dropped her shoulders and slumped in her seat. "Okay, fine, if you must know, I was brought to the DCU at a young age and raised there."

Interesting. "Why?"

"My parents died," she said as a matter of fact. Wow, I wasn't expecting that answer.

A swirl of feelings: sadness, regret, anger, or remorse were in her eyes. I wasn't sure, but whatever it was she was battling within herself, it defined her and not in a positive way. The negative feelings she harbored suppressed that power I had felt deep within her. Still, her innocent energy warmed me, and her negative energy pricked my skin like sharp particles in the air around me. If I were to guess, she kept her pain and heartache close to her heart. *I can relate because I did the same thing.*

"Mind me asking, what happened to your parents?"

Her features were expressionless. "Maeve?"

She pulled on her seatbelt as if it hurt and rolled up her sleeves. "It's hot in here," she said, lowering her window.

I turned the air on and shifted the vents toward her. "Are you okay?" She was visibly sweating and shaking. "Maeve?" I ran my thumb down her cheek, making her jump away from my touch.

She placed a hand over her heart. "Shit, Ezra. I... I'm sorry. It's just...I suffer from..." She waved a hand dismissively. "What were we talking about?"

What just happened? If I were to guess, she suffered from PTSD. I wasn't a damn doctor, but I've been around long enough to spot the symptoms. *Should I ask? Did I even care? No! Maybe? Get ahold of yourself, Ezra. Grow some fucking balls. Since when you give a fuck about a woman.*

I gripped the steering wheel, though I needed to get a damn grip on myself. "It doesn't matter what we were talking about." I kept my tone even and aloof. The more I learned, the more personal the relationship evolved. I kept everybody, especially women, at arm's length and for a good reason. My job kept me busy, and women are heartbreakers. I allowed a woman to break my heart once, but it wouldn't happen again.

"So, tell me about the prophet. Is it Emerich?"

She narrowed her eyes and glared at me. It was apparent, she was protective of her partner. Did she have feelings for him? "What do you want to know? And, yes, his name is Emerich."

I shrugged my shoulders, attempting to look callous and relaxed. I didn't want to spark doubt, especially while working with her. "Was he raised at the DCU?"

Maeve relaxed and sat back, nodding her head. "Yeah. Emerich and I were both raised in the DCU. He arrived a few months before I did. They found him as a baby, stuffed in a

74

gym bag behind a donut shop."

"How did you get to the DCU?"

"Sal...he found me. Took me to the DCU and cared for me."

"What was it like growing up there?"

She chuckled. "It was boring, to say the least. I didn't experience what normal girls got to experience. No school dances, sleepovers, or parties. We didn't hang Christmas lights, hunt for Easter eggs, or stuff our bellies with Thanksgiving turkey."

"Was it that bad?"

"Sometimes... it was like a military or boarding school, but instead of preparing us for service, we were trained to fight and hunt jinn." She giggled again, thinking about her past. "We even stayed in dorms and had workouts and discipline drills. But... I got to have Emerich in my life...and Sal."

She genuinely loved them. I saw it in her eyes. I knew then that she'd do anything for them. How much did she love them? Was it platonic? Was that a fucking pang of jealousy that I had felt?

The hairs on the back of my neck prickled. The shadow was back. It came and left, leaving us in the sunshine again. I leaned forward, trying to look up. I saw nothing. Though I wasn't sure what I was looking for, I was sure someone or something was following us. I felt a tingling at the back of my neck.

"Do you enjoy hunting?" Maeve asked, sidetracking me.

"Uhm...do you?" I asked while looking in the review mirror—nothing out of the ordinary.

"Don't deflect the question!"

I couldn't help but laugh. Maeve was sort of adorable when she was bossy.

"Okay, okay. I delight in protecting the innocent, but despite that, I tire of the hunt. It's a dark and lonely life, and I have no choice in the matter. I am loyal to my debt, and, like you, I was trained to fight and kill at a young age. I was twenty-eight when I joined The Order."

"The Order? I've never heard of anything but the DCU."

"The Order is a group of men selected to ensure jinn follow the laws set by the Grigori, but if you ask me, The Order is nothing but an irritating pain in the ass."

She rubbed her temples. "Wow...I thought I knew everything when it came to jinn, but after meeting you, it appears I still have a lot to learn. I never would have thought the Grigori had laws."

"Why not? Of course, Jinns need laws, especially those on Earth. You see, jinn can influence evil onto people, but they can't physically harm them. That would be against one of the laws set by the Grigori. I'm curious, isn't it the same at the DCU?"

She shook her head, telling me no. "We don't have laws set for jinn. We hunt and kill them all. They're evil, Ezra, regardless of established laws; they'll always do bad because they're evil."

The members of The Order are jinn. *Should I tell her?* "You're correct. You do have a lot to learn. Not all jinn are bad."

"You said that earlier, at my house, and that makes me wonder if I can trust you. Can I trust some who believe that not all jinn are evil? And what about The Order? They're making you get this book to stop the war, right? Well, what if they're behind this apocalyptic mess?"

I shouldn't tell her. She'd think I'm a jinn. I didn't want to deal with that...not now. "I'll kill them, but I assure you, they are not behind this apocalyptic mess."

"Can I trust you?"

I lifted my chin. "You have no choice but to trust me."

She shrugged. "I'm sure I can find this book without your help."

"And I'm sure the prophet's life is running out of time, but if you want to search for Eden on your own, then I'll pull over and let you out. But just remember, I am the only one in this car who can read Emean text...unless someone at the DCU is willing to help you?"

She bit her lip. "Touché, but how do you know the book is

written in Emean text?"

"Call it a lucky guess."

"Fine. But how can I be sure that you're not behind this apocalyptic mess and using me to get the book?"

I parked the car and took off my seatbelt.

"What are you doing?" she asked.

"I admit that's a fair question, but let's clear the air now before we go further. I can tell you that I'm not part of this fucking apocalyptic mess, but I don't have proof. Therefore, you have two options: I can drive you home, or you can take a risk with me, sweetheart, and never bring this shit up again."

She leaned forward, her eyes level with mine. Unlike most people, she didn't fear me. She challenged me. "While we're clearing the air, tell me, why were you in the alley that night Emerich got sick?"

I bit the inside of my cheeks, staring at her mouth. The beast in me growled, itching to taste her. For years, I've controlled that side of me, but in just a few short hours, Maeve awakened its lustful urges.

I squeezed my eyes shut, mentally talking myself out of my foolish desires. "I was ordered to kill the asshole attempting to start the war, and the only way to do that is with the Book of Raziel. I ran into a man scared shitless who said he saw the prophet, so I followed him to the alley." I leaned forward until I tasted the sweetness of her breath on my tongue—so pure and sweet. "I wish to prevent this war, and the only way to do it is with that book. So, tell me, love, are we in this together or not?"

Her tongue darted out, and I watched as she ran it along her bottom lip, making it moist and plump. "Who's trying to start the war?"

I sat back and ran my hands through my hair. "His name Leviathan, but he goes by Levi."

She narrowed her eyes and tapped her bottom lip. "I've heard that name before. Where? Oh, fuck! I remember. The other night, in the factory, a jinn, Lucas, mentioned the name Levi." She looked down and pressed her lips firmly together.

"It was him who cursed Emerick," she said to herself before looking back at me. "And you need the book to kill him?"

"He is powerful, and the only way to kill him is with a spell in that book." I rubbed the back of my neck, bending it from side to side, feeling the tension. That was a great reminder to keep Maeve at arm's length. If Levi thought she meant something to me, he'd use my feelings for her against me. He was smart, so keeping my mind focused was a must.

"I thought the Grigori were somehow behind the war. Although I'm not sure how they can do much of anything from their prisons."

"They're not shackled in jail cells. They are imprisoned in the last four realms of Hell, and they live like kings, free to roam those realms and do as they please. However, Levi plans to release them."

Her eyes grew wide. "What? How?"

I opened my mouth to answer when something on the side of the road caught my attention. I leaned forward, bending my neck to get a better view.

There stood a young woman with ashy skin and onyx eyes, wearing a white dress. She was oddly out of place, and before I could make sense of her presence, something hit the car hard.

Maeve's head went through the front window just as my forehead connected with the steering wheel. Red-hot pain shot through my body, and before the car came to a stop, I saw them.

A pair of glowing eyes gazing at Maeve with hunger.

Chapter Eleven

MAEVE

Open.
  Close.
  Open.
  Close.
  My eyelids were heavy.
  Open. Close.
  A muffled yell. *Ezra?*
  Open.
  I lifted myself up on my forearms, and immediately, I spotted Ezra's car on fire. Flames lashed inside like angry whips, and just like that, the orange flickering gave me a rush of anxiety, filling my insides. My heart rate surged. I closed my eyes, breathing slow, purposeful breaths, trying to escape what I knew was coming.
  It didn't work.
  Visions of fire engulfing two bodies run on a loop in my mind's eye.
  Screams followed by whispers of laughter in my ears.
  I do nothing.
  The room smells of sulfur and fire. The laughter in my ears grows louder, insulting my weakness.
  I do nothing.
  Red and orange flames consume them, melting them into nothing but ash, bone, and teeth.
  When it was over, the scene started again from the beginning.
  I squeezed my eyes shut, clenching and unclenching my fists, trying to escape the flashbacks.
  I'm going crazy— out of my fucking mind.

Flashes of a man cloaked in ash stood over me. I could only see his smile; it was too wide to be normal. I mumbled nonsense when a loud shriek pierced my eardrums, bringing on panic, followed by an intense feeling of sadness. I cried as the sadness grew into grief, and not just any grief, soul-sucking-sinister-all-consuming grief. There was only one demon that could produce such a scream, a Yomotsu-Shikome demon.

A year ago, Emerich and I were hunting a jinn when we came across a Yomotsu-Shikome demon. We killed its master, and it screamed the same deathly shriek, which was known to suck the happiness from a person's soul, leaving the victim weak with despair. It took Emerich and me an entire week to shake the depressed feelings.

I turned my head. Where was Ezra? A sudden heaviness settled in my chest and stomach, as I expected the worst. There he was, across the road, fighting... I was right. It was a Shikome demon. She was an old demonic hag with fierce claws, long and shaped like a hook. She moved so swiftly that it was hard to keep an eye on her movements. Was she walking on air? It sure did seem like it.

But, Ezra... he was also fast. And strong. He used a form of defense I'd never seen before. It was beautiful but lethal. His kicks and punches had both weight and force, and his jumps and spins seemed light and natural. He almost appeared to be flying.

I used my hands to help me stand. I swayed a little but quickly caught my balance. Ezra spotted me, a distraction that could cost him his life.

The Shikome demon jumped into the air, aimed right at Ezra, and grabbed his shoulders. She yanked him back until he fell, hitting the ground hard. Then, she landed on top of him, straddling his head with her legs. She lifted her arms above her head, revealing a long-curved knife that appeared out of nowhere.

"I don't think so, bitch." I reached for one of my knives, strapped to the harness at my hips, and flung it at her.

The demon didn't have time to act or even think about her

next move. My knife flew toward her with careful accuracy, hitting her between the eyes. I grinned from ear to ear, a menacing grin, as her body turned to ash. Demons didn't turn to smoke and get sucked back to Hell like jinn. They turned to ash, instantly wiping them from existence. "Night-night, evil bitch."

Ezra stood up, dusted the grime from his clothes, ran his fingers through his hair, and looked at me. I saw a mixture of emotions in his eyes: astonishment, reluctance, but above all, gratitude.

"Are you hurt?" he asked, scanning me for injuries.

"I'm fine." I pointed at my nevus. "I got this." I moved my eyes over his body, checking him for injuries. He had none. "Are you sure you're not a jinn?"

He folded his arms over his puffed-out chest and lifted a brow. "What do you think?"

I shrugged my shoulders and stuck out my bottom lip. Maybe a human/demon hybrid? *Did those exist?* I stared at him, running through the possibilities. "Then how the hell did you learn to fight like that with zero cuts or scratches or weapons or—"

"Easy, love. One question at a time." I inhaled, ready to ask again when he held his finger to my lips. I expected him to pull away, but his eyes were focused on my mouth.

"Thank you," he whispered, tracing the outline of my bottom lip with his thumb.

I should have run from him, but all I wanted was to be near him. "For...?" I was at a loss for words as my gaze was drawn to his lips, yearning to taste them. His cleft chin, straight cheekbones, and strong jawline classically defined his ample lips.

I opened my mouth as he stepped closer, bringing his mouth over mine and teasing me with his raw sensuality. Shame and desire mingled hot in my throat. He drew near, close enough to kiss if I dared. I wet my lips with my tongue, tempting him. Then, a cocky smile played across his face as he whispered, "Thanks for saving my life."

"Mmhmm..." I murmured just before he stepped away.

Uhhh...what just happened?

I cleared my throat and hoped the warm flush I felt didn't creep across my cheeks. "Oh, yeah," I said, dismissively waving a hand at him. "It's my job."

Ezra watched me for a moment with a curious stare. "Right, well"— he cleared his throat— "if you don't mind, I need to make a call." He pulled his cell from his pocket and dialed, turning his back to me as he spoke.

I reached up touched my lips with my fingertips. *Did I want to kiss him?* I squeezed my eyes shut. *No! I didn't! I can't. Should I? No, I shouldn't.* I almost died and failed to save Emerich. I couldn't afford distractions. *Yet...what did he taste like? Shit! No! Focus!*

Damn, all the damage. Ezra's beautiful car - ruined. I inhaled and looked up.

What the...

The air was distorted, thick, and hazy like I stood in a spooky snow globe. I swept a hand back and forth before me. The movement created a flow of waves and swirls that warped the sky.

"Those fuckers," said Ezra. I turned around, and he was flexing his fingers, opening, and closing them into fists. The muscles in his neck bulged out tightly.

"What's wrong?"

He curled his lip. "I just got off the phone with The Order. Those fuckers sent another hunter to keep an eye on me."

To keep an eye on him. Why? No matter how mad Winston or Sal got at me, they would never send someone to kill me. "Why?"

He laughed with an edge that left me uneasy. "Because they're paranoid pricks, that's why. But that fucker tried to kill me. He's always been an arrogant prick, and he hated me. I'm his competition, and he figured he'd kill me, finish the job, and prove his worth to The Order. The prick sent a Shikome demon to do his dirty work. He couldn't even face me like a man; fight me with his own two hands. That fucking coward."

"How do we stop him?"

"The Order said they'll handle it." He scoffed at the thought.

"Okay, is this other hunter a jinn? I mean, only they can control a Shikome demon."

Ezra narrowed his eyes and slowly shook his head. "Don't be so naive. Many wicked individuals crave power, and with the right knowledge, anyone can summon an evil creature. However, a Shikome demon is stronger in the Astral Plane, so he—"

I held up a hand to stop him from talking. "Did you just say Astral Plane?" Astral beings, better known as ghosts or spirits of the deceased, live in the Astral Plane. They're spirits that haven't correctly passed over to the next life. Some souls stay behind because they're scared of the unknown. Some remained because they're unaware they had died, living out their non-physical lives in a loop of dull unconscious existence.

I had a sickening feeling in my stomach. *Oh, God. What if I'm stuck here?*

"Yes, it's home to Shikome demons," said Ezra.

"Wait...no!" I shook my head vigorously before I pressed my temples with my fingers. "Wait a damn minute. We're in the Astral Plane? How?"

He pointed to the other side of the road.

Oh, good Lord, don't let that.... My stomach felt like it just dropped. Across the way, covered in dirt and rock, was a body. "Is that...." I covered my mouth with the back of my shaky hand. "Is...is that me? I'm...I'm dead!"

"Not completely. You see, the Astral Plane is a parallel universe to ours with similar physical laws. Technically, anybody can travel to and from Astral through metaphysical projection by separating their consciousness from their physical body. However, it takes years to master such mindfulness. Most people visit this place when they're *near* death."

My mouth hung open as I listened to Ezra ramble on about stuff I didn't care about. "What are you, a college professor? Please, Ezra, just tell me how to get the fuck out of here."

"Oh, Maeve, are you scared of the Reaper?"

Shit! I forgot about him. I reached for my blades just in case. This realm was home to the Grim Reaper, where he searches for Astral beings destined for Hell.

"Relax, love. He doesn't care about us."

"Ezra!" I snapped.

Ezra held up his hands, attempting to calm me. "Okay, okay. Do you meditate?"

"Um, no. We don't meditate at the DCU."

"Okay. Just relax. I'll explain everything. It's easy."

"Pfft," I scoffed at him. *"Yeah, I'll try to relax."*

"Focus, Maeve. Your spirit, or consciousness, is connected to your body by an invisible force. Have you ever heard of quantum entanglement?" *Was he serious?* I glared at him, lifted my hands, palms up, and shrugged my shoulders. Did he really expect me to know that answer? I wasn't a damn physicist. "Never mind, babe. Just let that invisible force guide you back to your body. It's easy."

I gawked at him. "Are you kidding? Tell me you're fucking joking." He shook his head. "What invisible force? How do I focus on something I can't see?"

He smiled, that cocky bastard smiled, and shook his head. *Geesh, someone, please shoot me. I'm going mad.*

"The invisible force is your energy, and you don't need to see it to feel it. Just close your eyes and focus."

"This better work, Ezra," I muttered as I closed my eyes and focused. Time ticked by, and still…wait…oh, wow. Ezra was right. At least in this realm, the atmosphere was thicker, specifically around my body. I felt a subtle vibration.

"I think I feel it," I said, almost giddy.

It took a few seconds, but it happened. The energy grew more robust, and then it happened. A force was pulling me inward. I couldn't fight it, and seconds later, a heavy sensation came over me, like a downward pull of gravity.

I was back in my body. I couldn't have been happier. Then….

Oh, God.

My damaged lungs snapped back into place. My spinal

cord uncurled in a sudden whip of motion, and little by little, muscle by muscle, my body healed. *Oh, fucking hell....* My injuries usually hurt when my nevus mended them, but that was nothing compared to this. A burning everywhere like fire ran through my veins.

The pain was so.... "Oh, God, please," I cried.

I tasted blood. I felt fire.

"Maeve! Stay...me...you...okay...Maeve." Ezra's voice was muffled. My ears were ringing. Then, everything went black.

I felt nothing.

Chapter Twelve

EZRA

Maeve had been asleep for some time, longer than I wanted. Amon, the other hunter, had almost killed her. The wreck mangled her body, and when her nevus healed her, the pain was too much. It overwhelmed her.

I gripped the arms of the chair, digging my nails into the fabric. When I finished this job and was free from The Order, I was going to hunt Amon. The fucker was at the top of my hit list. It wouldn't be easy, but I never went for easy. He used to be a strong commander of over forty legions of the finest knights in Hell, protectors of the Grigori, but one mistake, and he was demoted to a hunter for The Order. Ever since he'd been trying to prove himself.

Maeve moved her head ever so slightly side-to-side. "Uhhh...Where am I?" she asked, pressing her temples with her fingers.

I stood and went over to her side. "Philip's. We arrived an hour ago."

She opened an eye and peeked at me. "An hour? Shit, what time is it?" Her cheeks were flushed, giving her a childlike appearance.

"It's early morning. How are you feeling?" I asked, brushing a strand of hair away from her face.

She whimpered and pulled the blanket up just under her nose. "My head hurts. What happened?" She placed a hand over her eyes. "Good, Lord! My head hurts."

The beast within me wanted to take over, to seduce her, and it fights to take what it wants, but... *I'm stronger*. It's a part of me, of both of us, but I'm not like Levi. I've learned how to control the beast. I ran my hands through my hair, dragging my fingers through the tangles. Then, I reached through, "Always so many questions."

She pulled the blanket down to uncover her mouth as she spoke. "Apparently I have a lot to learn." She pulled the blanket up again, covering her mouth and making her eyes appear bigger...and adorable.

"You passed out. That bastard, Amon, sent a Gallu demon to hit our car. The impact nearly killed you."

"Amon?"

"The other hunter."

"That's right." She nodded. "A Gallu demon? That's what hit the car?"

Her chest, rising and falling to the pace of her calm breathing. Her nipples were hard, straining against the thin material. I wanted to free them, taste them, make her mine. The beast within me growled, and I shook my head to clear my running thoughts. *What the fuck's wrong with me.* I cleared my throat and brought my eyes back to hers. "Yes. Those demons are powerful." I cleared my throat again. "Are you cold?" She nodded, so I went to turn the heat on.

"I saw one once. A jinn had one tied to a leash." She was talking about a Gallu demon, and she shivered at the thought. "It looked like an evil dog with red eyes and long, razor-sharp teeth." She eyed me. "And you killed it?"

I looked around at anything other than her. "I did," I said; my voice was hoarse and thick with lust. Damn, I needed sex to calm my dick. It jumped at her every word and her every look.

"And I saved you?" She muttered the words to herself as if suspicious of her own memory.

I lifted my chin, slid my hands into my pants pockets, and stared down at her. I didn't need saving. Yet...after she killed that demon, I dared look at her in a way I had not before — with admiration. She was tough, genuine, and fucking beautiful. With pouty lips and eyes full of mystery, she was strikingly exotic. And those freckles that lightly sprayed her cheeks and nose gave her an innocent appearance with touches of raw beauty. She was…. a fucking distraction.

I cleared my throat and left the room without another word. I rushed to the bathroom and shut the door behind me a bit too aggressively. In front of the mirror, I gripped the edge of the sink. I was tired, and it showed. My face was marred with lines and dark circles. That was why I was thinking like a fool; I was exhausted.

It's because I like her.

I flinched. "No, I don't," I muttered to myself, shaking my head. Fuck that. *I'm not going there.* My sudden attraction to Maeve was becoming too much for me to handle, especially now. If I successfully finished this job, my debt to The Order would be paid—finally. I could walk away from them for good. Then, I could sleep with Maeve, make her mine for a night, and get her out of my system. Damn, the thought of fucking her got my dick hard. No, Ezra. Not now. Not until I finished the job.

I opened the medicine cabinet, grabbed what I needed, and left the restroom. "Here, take these." I tossed the bottle of Tylenol onto the bed before I went to leave.

I had sat here for too long, watching over her like a fucking fool.

I care about her.

I ran my fingers through my hair and tugged. Fuck, these thoughts, where in Hell were they coming from?

"Hold up," said Maeve. I paused at the door and turned my head until I spotted her eyeing me suspiciously. "Where are my blades?"

I lifted a quizzical brow. Did she think I took them? I scoffed. I didn't need a weapon to kill, especially with two measly little knives. "What? You think I took them?"

She pressed her lips into a thin line and lifted her brows. "Did you?"

Un-fucking-believable. I clenched my jaw shut to stop my anger from flying out of my mouth in the form of harsh words. Instead, I pointed to the bench at the end of the bed. "There." She sat up to look. I had placed them on top of her other belongings.

She looked away from me and muttered, "Thanks."

"Hopefully, I've earned a bit of your trust?"

She smiled. A genuine smile and my cock jumped. I wanted to kiss her. *Fuck that!* I needed to get away from her.

I shook my head, ridding all lustful thoughts of her from my mind, and I went to leave.

"Where are you going?"

I paused again and gripped the door handle, squeezing it until my knuckles hurt. "I need to speak to Philip." If someone were to see me at this very moment, they would have thought I was seething mad, maybe even a bit hysterical.

She kicked off the blanket and jumped up. "I'm coming too."

"No!" I shouted, making her look at me as if I had lost my ever-fucking mind. Ha, I was close. I pinched the bridge of my nose, reigning in control. "Please, get some rest."

"Your mad," she simply stated.

I chuckled and turned around; my back facing her. "You don't know me, love," I said over my shoulder.

"You're right, I don't know you well, but I can read men like you. Sal always pinched his nose when he was angry or frustrated."

I looked over my shoulder and glared at her. How dare she speak of another man in front of me. I opened my mouth to reprimand her but thought better of it. Instead, I told her, once again, to get some rest.

She folded the blanket back up, making the bed look clean and kept. Did this Sal guy drill her like a Sargent? Why straighten the bed so perfectly? I'd bet one of my Ferraris that the DCU was run like a military base.

Why do I give a fuck?

"Besides, I've had enough rest," she said.

I went to pinch my nose again but stopped. I didn't want to remind her of another man, so I rubbed the back of my neck instead. "Look, I need to speak to Philip in private."

She lifted a quizzical brow. Her signature expression. "Why?"

I turned around once again to fully face her. "If we approach Philip, the two of us, he might feel bombarded. Let me ease him into the situation before I introduce you."

Her brows drew together. "Yeah, whatever. Do what you need to do, but hurry because I'm only giving you fifteen minutes." She went to the restroom and slammed the door behind her.

The woman was infuriating.

You're letting her get under your skin.

Fuck that. I refused to allow that to happen.

***

Philip was in the library. Any passionate bookworm would piss their pants seeing this room. Floor to ceiling, the room was filled with books, rows, and rows of thick, aged volumes encased in leather bindings.

Philip sat in a worn, brown leather lounge chair, reading when he spotted me. "Ah, Ezra. You found me. How's Maeve?"

"She's doing well, thanks." I sat down in the empty seat beside him. He appeared open and warm, yet I worried his demeanor would change when I asked him where to find the Garden of Eden. He was protective of the Keys of Knowledge, and I needed to know the most sacred of secrets. I trusted the gravity of the impending apocalypse would be enough, and indeed, he would help me get out of my debt from The Order.

Plus, he owed me a favor, so why beat around the bush. I came right out with it, not holding back. "Tell me how to get to Eden."

His eyes flashed with interest. He sat up straighter and leaned in closer. "Why?"

"I believe the book is in Eden."

I could see the gears turning in his mind. "How do you know this?"

"A vial."

"A vial?" He was curious.

"Yes. A label on the vial, to be exact."

He was stroking his trimmed beard with his fingers. He was certainly intrigued. "And where did you get this...vial?" Or maybe doubtful.

"Maeve." I kept my answers short and uncomplicated.

"And how did she get it?"

I tugged my sleeves, taking my time to answer. After all, one wrong word, and I could lose the one man with the answers. Oh, hell, I wasn't going to get out of this conversation without the truth. So, let it be, the words flew from my mouth. "She works for Winston at the DCU."

He swallowed a mouthful of brandy and tapped the glass with his finger, making a clunking noise with his ring, deliberately taking his time, thinking. "So, you're telling me that Winston gave her this vial?"

I shrugged. "I didn't ask."

He removed his glasses and pinched the bridge of his nose. Damn, maybe Maeve was right about men pinching their noses when frustrated? "I don't know, Ezra. It's not wise to cause trouble with Winston."

"Levi stole the Divine Seals, Philip, and I was ordered to kill him." If words could slap a man stupid, then those words could surely knock a man out.

Philip set the glass down on the small table beside him, leaned forward, closer to me, and folded his hands over his lap. "What you're asking, it's...it's damn dangerous. You'd have better luck finding Levi."

"Impossible," I snapped.

"No, Ezra. Getting your hands on that book is impossible."

"I understand your concern, I do, but—"

"I know what you want."

I eyed him with a lifted brow and narrowed eyes. "And what's that?" I was a bit suspicious of his words.

"This is not the way to get her back."

I had a bad feeling settle in the pit of my gut. This conversation could go wrong, but that fate was in his hands. "Choose your words wisely." It was a warning. A warning he didn't take.

"You want Sky." He was too bold.

He might as well have punched me in the gut. His words forced the air from my lungs, yet I leaned forward with an eerie calmness, looking him dead in the eyes. The fool showed no fear. In fact, he dared to meet my gaze with an equal glare of his own. The muscles in my jaw tensed, but he did not falter.

Sky had been my wife before she deceived me and broke my heart.

"Don't speak about her again," I said between clenched teeth. I groaned, taking a deep breath to calm my anger—to calm the beast. I didn't want to upset Philip. He had what I needed. Plus, I liked the guy, appreciated him, and I believe he felt the same. "Look, Philip, if I kill Levi, I get my freedom."

He offered a deep sigh, followed by an understanding nod. He did care, but I still went in for the kill. "You owe me." His eyes locked with mine, set there for a moment. I wasn't sure what he was thinking.

"Okay," he said with a slight nod, "Okay. Eden is in Hell."

I jerked my head back. Hell?" How did I not know this?

"Yes." He poured himself another glass of bourbon. "But I don't know how to get to Eden from Hell. You will have to find that on your own."

He opened his coat and stuck his hand inside. "Take this," he said, handing me a key, "It'll help you get into a room where I keep my sacred artifacts and belongings. In there, I have various maps of Hell. You'll need to go through those."

I knew the room he spoke of. He showed it to me a few years ago. "I could use a shot now, thank you," I said, taking the key. *Of all the places, why in Hell? Am I mentally strong enough to go?* He poured a glass and handed it to me. I threw it back and hissed as it burned my throat. "How do we get into Hell?"

"I'll contact a friend of mine, Bones. He knows how to get souls in and out of Hell."

Things were moving too quickly for me to process, and images of what could happen flashed through my mind. I saw torture, fire, and...*I'm not going to think of him.* "I can't go.

There must be another way?"

Hell's not a physical realm, so only souls can enter. I knew that better than anyone. Physical items stayed behind.

This is fucking nuts.

Plus, souls get lost in Hell, trapping them there forever. *And my soul was just as vulnerable, if not more so.*

Philip patted my knee. "We both know there is no other way." His voice was softer now.

I raked my fingers through my hair, tugging on the ends as if the pain would relieve the sudden stress. "Fuck, Philip. Removing souls from the body for too long is dangerous."

"What's dangerous?" A voice echoed from across the library.

Both Philip and I jerked our heads toward the door where Maeve stood, looking from me to Philip and back to me again. Neither of us said a word.

How much did she hear?

Philip was the first to speak. "Join us."

She approached us, looking around the library, and her eyes grew big and bright as she took in all the books. Her hair was still wet from her shower, making it darker and longer, and her cheeks were rosy. I pulled a chair out for her as Philip introduced himself. Her lips were full of color, matching her reddish cheeks. *Why the fuck am I noticing her wet hair and lips?* I have other shit to worry about, like going to fucking Hell.

When we were all seated, Maeve asked, "What were you two talking about?"

"Philip knows where Eden is." *Why beat around the bush?*

"Oh, good." She looked at Philip. "Where?"

"Wait a minute, Ezra," said Philip. "I'm not sure I want to share this with others."

Philip wasn't sure he should trust Maeve. That was what he meant. "She works for the DCU," I reminded him.

"That's what I'm scared of," he muttered. "If Winston found out—"

"I'm trying to save a friend," Maeve interrupted. "I need help, and Winston won't help me."

"She can be trusted, Philip." I added."She needs to know. She's…my partner." Fuck, hopefully, that would be enough to convince him to trust her.

He removed his glasses and rubbed his eyes. "Fine." He put on his glasses and looked at Maeve. "You work for the DCU, so I'm assuming you can keep a secret. What we discuss never leaves this room." Maeve nodded. "Eden…is in Hell."

The rosy color in Maeve's face faded. I didn't want her to lose that fight of hers, so I asked, "Tell me, love, what do you fear most?"

She wore a confused expression, but then she looked inward, thinking. Finally, she answered, "Losing Emerich."

I knew she was going to say that, and I applauded her devotion to those she loved. She was indeed full of light, and her words and courage touched me, but was that enough to save her from Hell?

I leaned forward and stared directly into her eyes, but Philip spoke first. "If that's what you fear most, losing Emerich, then your heart is pure enough. Hold onto that purity, that desire to save your friend, and you might overcome the horrible obstacles thrown at you in Hell."

I shook my head, knowing the truth about Maeve. She wasn't that strong. Not yet. When she spoke of her parents, I felt something in her, something negative. Something about that night still haunted her spirit, weakening the energy around her. I felt it. It pricked my skin like tiny bee stings. "It's a start," I said. "But your spirit is weak."

"Timeout," she said, doing the universal sign for timeout used primarily in sports. "Eden is in Hell, right? What exactly are you guys talking about? What obstacles?"

Philip leaned over and placed a hand on her knee. "Nobody's making you go."

I removed Philip's hand from Maeve and replaced it with mine. "Looks like we're going to Hell after all, love," I said, trying to sound calm, though I was also losing my fucking mind. Maeve jerked her knee away from me. "If y'all are talking about going to Hell, that's not happening. I don't go to Hell; I send jinn to Hell. They'll find me and destroy me."

Chapter Thirteen

MAEVE

A hole opens after I kill a jinn. The wailing and crying from the tortured souls. Hell's the place I've sent many jinn, and I had no desire to face them again.

A buzz in my ears. My vision was blurred and dull. Oh, Lord, I was going to pass out? Ezra watched me, scratching his temple, probably wondering if I was going to be sick, and that would be a maybe. I needed to leave to get the hell outta here. "I need a moment," I whispered, getting up.

I walked out of the stuffy library and stopped at the grand staircase by the main entrance. Now, my vision jerked, and I heard a loud ringing in my ears.

Sit before you pass out.

I sat on the bottom step and hung my head between my knees, taking in deep breaths. I had a million questions running through my mind. How would I get into Hell? How would I survive? Maybe Sal was right. Getting the book was impossible.

I was sulking in my fear when the sound of footsteps approached. I expected to see Ezra, but it was Philip. He sat down beside me. There was so much about him that reminded me of Winston with a trimmed grey beard and rectangular glasses. Still, unlike Winston, Philip had sympathetic eyes and a calm demeanor.

Philip stayed quiet for a short moment before saying, "I know we've only just met, and I'm not trying to persuade you one way over the other. In fact, I advise you not to go."

I heard his words and considered them, but then an image of Emerich popped into my mind. He was in the alley, begging me for help. He was thin, pale, and covered in sores. That night, I made a promise that I would help him. Could I walk away or let him die without trying? Could I go on living knowing I could have saved him? I closed my eyes to process my fate. I thought about my parents. I could have prevented their deaths...*but I just did nothing.* "I have to. I made a promise, and I have to keep it, even if it means going through Hell and back—literally."

He didn't speak until I caught his eyes. They were kind, and I could tell, at that moment, why Ezra liked Philip. He was friendly and genuine. His soft, gentle voice soothed me. "Are you certain?" he asked.

I nodded without hesitation. "I'm positive."

He sighed. "Well, in that case. I have a friend, a witch doctor, and he can get you guys into Hell. I've seen him do it before."

"He's sent people to Hell before. Did they come back?"

He patted my back and stood up. "No."

I stopped breathing for a moment as I watched Philip leave the room without another word. "What the fuck..." I muttered to myself, "that was reassuring."

"Are you willing to take a risk, love?" Ezra was leaning against the door to the library. Just like Sal, Ezra was able to sneak around unheard and unseen.

I stretched my legs out in front of me and sighed. "I take risks all the time. It's part of the job." Ezra had one leg crossed over the other and his hands in his pockets, looking sexy with his hair touching his shoulders in golden waves. His hair closely matched his eye color, both like burnt honey, and his face was flawlessly sculpted: defined lips, a strong jaw, and a straight nose. Oddly enough, he looked like the Hollywood actors who played Jesus in the movies. Ha, he'll be a welcoming sight in Hell.

"So I guess we're going to Hell," I said, rubbing my achy legs. I hadn't rested well since Emerich got sick.

Ezra didn't answer. Instead, he stared at me with those amber eyes before reaching into his pocket and pulling out a hair tie. He tied his hair at the nape of his neck, leaving a few loose strands bordering his sharp jaw. Ezra might look like the Hollywood Jesus, but there was something about him… he had this sexy animalistic vibe.

It was damn addictive.

I wanted to forget about work, forget about duty, forget about Hell, and just…run my hands down his chest. It was probably hard and smooth.

I could use a fun pastime, even for a minute. After all, a healthy distraction here-and-there was good for the brain as it gave me a moment's rest to regroup. And Ezra was fun to look at, and if I was going to Hell, I might as well have a little fun. I'd never had a crush before. My lifestyle and job didn't give me time for relationships, and I admit, I was crushing hard. He was darkly mysterious, luring me in, which was ironic, given my job as a jinn hunter. Jinn were dark creatures but alluring too. In the same way that people are attracted to sin. Ezra was my guilty pleasure.

"We need to find where Eden is in Hell," Ezra said. His words brought me back to reality.

"How?" I asked.

He pushed himself off the doorframe and strolled over to me. He held out his hand to help me up. "Come on."

"Where are we going?"

"Philip keeps documents, maps, artifacts, books, and such in a room under his house."

Okay, this should be interesting, I thought.

I followed Ezra through a maze of hallways and rooms, through a secret door hidden behind a large mirror, and down a spiral staircase. At the bottom was a long, narrow walkway lined with metal walls. Motion-activated lights flickered on as we walked toward a large door at the far end. It reminded me of a bank vault with a five-spoke wheel like the helm of a ship.

Ezra let go of my hand and reached into his pocket, pulling out a key.

Did he hold my hand the entire time? And I didn't pull away or break a sweat? Hmmm…that's not common for me. I hated being touched. I must still be in shock. Telling someone that she's going to Hell would do that to a person.

Ezra stood beside the vault-like door and slid the key into a keyhole on the wall rather than the door itself. A small square section of the wall opened, and a security camera slid out. Ezra stepped forward, activating several beams of red light that scanned the details of his face.

I whistled in appreciation, impressed with the state-of-the-art technology. The DCU wasn't so advanced. The five-spoke wheel on the door turned several times on its own, and I heard the locks disengaging before it opened.

"Alright, let's go in," said Ezra.

I don't know what I imagined, but I didn't expect it to look so...medieval. Not with all the high-tech, we had just used to get inside. There were wooden tables with worn wooden chairs, old brick walls, a wood-burning stove, and no windows. Bookshelves were stuffed with books, ancient-looking artifacts were encased in glass boxes, and.... "Is that a—"

"Medical bed? Yes."

The bed was equipped with metal stirrups and leather restraints, something I'd seen in an old psychiatric hospital. Behind the bed was a bench littered with flasks, test tubes, metal clamps, and a burner.

"What does he use this for?" It was spooky.

Ezra shrugged his shoulders. "I'm not sure I want to know."

Was he joking? Was Philip as innocent as he seemed?

Ezra stood by the small iron stove and reached for a log. "Wait!" I yelled, catching my breath, immediately feeling stupid. *Way to keep it cool, Maeve.* He paused, holding the wooden log halfway into the stove. "Let's not light a fire. I don't like them much."

He was eerily still as he eyed me. *What was he thinking? Was he going to ask why?* Fire always triggered flashbacks, but I wasn't ready to tell him that. I didn't want him pointing out my weaknesses like Sal and Winston did.

He pressed his lips tight into a grimace and tossed the log back onto the pile. "You'll tell me why when you're ready," he said, standing up, dusting his hands on his pants.

Tell him what? Did he see my sudden stress? Of course, he

did. It was obvious. "Let's find Eden first," he suggested, and I looked heavenward, thankful he didn't push for answers.

"Did you know, the local historic churches used their steeples as landmarks to guide ships into the Charleston Harbor?" he asked. "Immigrants followed the earlier settlers, looking for religious freedom. This place was an underground basement of an ancient church that obviously no longer exists. It was where they kept their sacred books and such. Come." He nodded his chin in a follow-me way. We went to a wall lined with drawers, where he pulled out several boxes labeled *The History and Topography of Scheol.* In the Hebrew Bible, Scheol was another word for Hell. "We need to find where Eden is in Hell, so this is a good place to start."

He stacked the boxes on a table beside the stove. Then, he handed me a pair of white gloves and a magnifying glass. "This is going to be a fucking blast," his remark was tempered by humor.

I shrugged. "I don't mind reading and learning." I was a curious person and craved knowledge. There was always something new to learn, and knowledge was essential to survive as a paranormal hunter.

We both sat, and I reached for a box, and opened it. Inside was an old book, with handwritten text, titled *Angels in Hell: The History of Scheol.* The story began in the time of Adam and Eve.

After God created man, he sent fourteen angels to Earth to watch them. He called these fourteen angels the Watchers. God warned the Watchers to stay away from man, but, despite God's warning, the Watchers grew attracted to the women, slept with them, and procreated a race known as nephilim. Once God heard of the Watchers' deceitful act, he exiled them to the last realm of Hell for eternity. Then, he banished the Garden of Eden and cleansed the Earth of all its wickedness with a great flood. Satan, one of the fourteen Watchers, had foreseen the flood. Therefore, he had ordered Raziel, the angel of wisdom, to create a book of all divine knowledge and magic to give to his two sons.

I've learned about the nephilim before, briefly. There were sixty-eight of them; they were half human and half jinn, and they no longer existed. I knew Satan was one of the fourteen Watchers, but I didn't know he fathered two sons. Stunning how little I knew of the world in which I lived. This was the first time I'd read anything about the Book of Raziel, which was probably helpful, so I kept reading.

Due to the powers in the Book of Raziel, Satan's two sons survived the flood. For centuries, they kept out of sight from both man and the archangels. Until the younger of the two sons grew tired of hiding. He knew he was too great and powerful to hide within the shadows like a coward. To cultivate fear and gain power among the humans, he murdered thousands of men, women, and children. Eventually, the Arch Assembly seized him, held him captive, and tortured him. The eldest son begged the angels to release his brother, but they refused. Heartbroken by his brother's fate, he made a deal with the Arch Assembly: His brother's freedom for the Book of Raziel.

I flipped through the pages.
Is that it? End of story?
I was hoping to find a clue, anything to help us find Eden and get our hands on the Book of Raziel. With a deep sigh and a heavy heart, I looked up at Ezra. He was busy reading.

"Have you heard of the nephilim?" I asked.

Ezra raised his eyes to meet mine. "I have," he stated. "But that has nothing to do with finding Eden."

"I was reading a book you suggested. Anyway, I've heard of the nephilim, but I thought the entire race died in God's great flood, but according to this scripture, two of them survived. And not just any two: Satan's sons."

He tensed his jaw. "Don't say his name."

I lifted a brow. "Why?"

"Bad energy."

"I've never heard of that, but okay. What should I call him?"

"The devil, evil one, tempter, dark one, or my favorite, *father* of lies." He emphasized the word *father*.

"Anyway, I didn't know Sa... I mean... the Devil had sons," I said, shrugging my shoulders. "I just thought. I mean...what I'm trying to say is that I'm surprised I didn't learn about this sooner."

Does Sal know the Devil had sons? Does Winston?

"And I didn't know the book was created under the Devil's command," I continued. "No wonder it's so powerful."

"And evil," he muttered as he reached for a rolled document.

"Yeah, no shit. Do you think the two nephilim are still alive?"

He lowered his brows into a frown, and I wondered what he was thinking. He seemed to be fighting for words. "That's a long time to live, but if they're still around, they're probably tired of living."

We locked eyes for a moment without saying a word, and his eyes were a mask, hiding something, a *secret*. Yet, if I dared look more in-depth, I witnessed something else, a desire to be free from this *secret*.

Hmmm... what are you hiding, Ezra?

He softly shook his head. "We need to get back to work," he said, and slid the rolled document to me. "Read this instead."

The title: *The Circles of Hell*. "It's important to know our way around Hell before we go." I had to tear my eyes away from him. I wanted to figure him out, all his secrets, but he was right. We had to find Eden.

I unrolled the document he gave me and began reading.

Hell is divided into four realms: The Divide, The Shade, The Fields of Fire, and The Seas of Ice. The Divide is the first realm and is home to the disfigured souls who suffer leftover guilt, shame, or regret from their time on Earth. The souls are bent and deformed, stuck in darkness, never to see the light of mercy for a hundred years until born again with another chance at redemption.

At the end of The Divide is the River Styx, a black river

that divides the Underworld from Hell. The Underworld consists of the Astral Plane and the Divide, where souls have not yet met their final judgment. Charon, an all-seeing jinn like the Grim Reaper, can investigate a spirit's soul and decide their fate. He floats along the river, taking souls to their destination.

The second realm, The Shade, better known as Limbo, is home to those who died in common sin. These sins are less malevolent than those committed by the souls confined to the final two realms of Hell. Here, souls suffer mental pain, wandering for years in a melancholy world created by sorrow.

The third and fourth realms of Hell, Fields of Fire and Seas of Ice, are home to the deadly sins and the absolute damned. Here, souls suffer physical pain for eternity by fire, brimstone, gnashing of teeth.

The pictures were gruesome enough to turn any sinner into a saint. Souls were burned, beaten, raped, frozen in ice, or impaled. My stomach churned, so I closed the book and prayed that Eden wasn't too deep in Hell. I didn't want to travel to those last two realms. The torture there would haunt me forever, and I would not come back as the same person.

I remember Sal telling me that there was a lot of truth to The Divine Comedy, a poem by Dante Alighieri. After reading this, I could see how.

Ezra was hunched over a book, reading intently. I didn't want to bother him, so I grabbed a different box. Inside was an old parchment. I took it out and placed it on the table.

"What's that?" Ezra asked.

I ran my finger over the title. "I don't know. It's written in ancient text."

He leaned over and turned the parchment so he could see it. "It's written in ancient Aramaic." His eyes moving over the page. "It's about the Eda."

"What's the Eda?"

He leaned back and crossed his arms over his chest. "You haven't heard?"

"Obviously not, Ezra, or I wouldn't have asked."

"According to an ancient scroll discovered a few hundred years ago, there will come a human with god-like powers—an Eda."

I yawned. "Excuse me," I muttered. "How does a human become an Eda?"

"We only know what the scroll tells us, and according to the scroll, when the sacrifice is made, the Eda is born."

He paused a moment and stared at me, seemingly deep in thought. Finally, slowly shaking his head, he spoke again. "This world is full of mysteries."

Leaning back, I crossed my arms over my chest. "What were you thinking?"

"When?"

"Just now."

"I only hope this prophesied Eda is good. If you give a human 'God-like' powers," he shook his head, "Well, let's just say, I've never met a man who used power for good."

I scoffed at him. "What makes you think it'll be a man?"

He laughed as if what I had said was a joke. It was far from a joke. "Because women are too selfish to sacrifice themselves for someone else." I heard the pure distrust he had for women in each word he spoke. It made my heart hurt.

We stayed quiet, staring at each other. I moved my eyes over his face. His eyes were sad, his lips turned down, and his jaw muscles were tense.

"Maybe you're right," I said. Ezra lowered his brows, looking at me curiously. "But I'm pretty sure you're wrong."

Ezra folded his arms over his chest. "You disagree?"

I shrugged my shoulders. "I don't know, Ezra. I have faith in mankind. After all, you and I are going to Hell without greedy intentions."

He made a steeple with his hands and touched his lips. I tilted my head, unsure again what he was thinking. "Are you sure about that?" he asked.

I shifted in my seat, unsure where this conversation was going. "What do you mean?"

He leaned forward, and a few gold strands fell over his

strong cheekbones. "I sense a bit of regret in you."

I jerked my head back as I was caught off guard. I didn't think he'd say that. "Regret?"

"You're going to Hell to save a friend." I nodded. "Or are you going to Hell to ease your guilt?"

I narrowed my eyes, glaring at him. Yup, I totally wasn't expecting that. "And what guilt do I have, Ezra?"

His lips turned up into a cocky smile. "You tell me."

Was he right?

Sure, I regret not listening to Emerich when he said not to go on this last hunt, but who would go to Hell just to ease their guilt? That's a bit excessive. But I do believe someone would go to Hell to save a friend.

Right?

I held up a hand to ward off the truth behind his words. "You don't know me, Ezra. Not well enough to judge me like that, anyway."

"You're a strong fighter and damned skilled at throwing knives, but that isn't enough to survive Hell." What was he saying? I'm a trained jinn hunter. "I fear you're weak here." He pointed to his right temple. "That can make you weak here." He brought his finger to his heart.

I stood up and pushed a pile of boxes at him. "If I'm so damn weak, then find someone else." I was tired of everybody pointing at my weakness, telling me to hold back. *Damn it. I need people to point out my strengths!*

He caught the boxes before they slid off the table. Then, lightning-fast, he was on his feet and in front of me.

I formed fists and turned my head away from his prying eyes. I was breathing heavily, my chest rising and falling to the fast rhythm of my heartbeat. Ezra was close— too close. He had a clean, dangerous scent. I felt my knees tremble as his body heat seeped into me, and when he placed his finger under my chin, the shared heat and sensation thrilled me.

He gently turned my head, but I kept my eyes down. "Maeve," he whispered, getting me to look at him. I allowed my eyes to wander, taking in his beauty. His sheer maleness overwhelmed me, and every instinct I had said he was different. I couldn't put my finger on it. Still, there was something about him that was.... contrasting. I couldn't quite figure him out. It was a feeling of lust mixed with a feeling of fear. Like a jinn, he was beautiful yet scary. There was something dangerous simmering under his cool façade. I wasn't sure what it was, but I was captivated by that mysterious side of him. His eyes penetrated mine as if he were seeing into my soul. "I don't want someone else," he said, his voice husky.

Suddenly I was weak. His words sank in; I felt heat all over. I wanted him. I wanted a distraction. He was...

I can't.

I needed to be calm and collected—assertive. He just told me that my mind was weak, after all, and I couldn't allow him to get away with that. I was highly skilled in this sort of shit. I couldn't deny that I had issues, but my issues were just that...mine. They made me weak. They made me strong. They gave me a reason to hunt and kill jinn. And they were mine for me to worry about and fix when I wanted to fix them. They had nothing to do with him.

"I saved your ass from a Yomotuso-Shikome demon, so don't worry about me." I stepped around him, ready to leave. Ready for a break. "I'm tired," I said, reaching into my pocket. I pulled out the vial and peeled the label off. "In case you need to remember what it said," I handed him the label. "I'll be back in an hour or two."

I never slept longer than two hours, anyway. Not without having a nightmare. Plus, we don't have time to sleep for long periods.

I slid the vial back into my pocket and headed for the door.

"Can your knives save you from your own demons?" I heard him ask.

I paused, feeling my body heat rise to my cheeks. I opened and closed my mouth, wanting to curse him, but I couldn't fight the hurt and shame I desperately needed to hide.

So I left without answering him.

***

105

A sudden wisp of air swept across my skin, causing me to shiver and seek warmth. I cuddled deeper into the pillows, burying my head under my arm. There was a moment of peace that calmed me, soothing me as I sank deeper into sleep. Then, a strange feeling came over me, like a presence watching me as I slept. I opened my eyes, blinking until they adjusted.

A shadow, tall and built like a man, stood by the bed.

I tried to move, but I was stuck. My mind was awake, but my body was asleep.

The figure leaned over me. Closer and closer, he came. He had sharp, hawk-like features that radiated intelligence. He was predatory, primal, and without compassion. He was beautiful, like Ezra, but his eyes were reddish-orange like fire, prideful and sinister.

He opened his mouth, and I tasted sulfur on his breath. "Your blood is key," he said in a deep-seated yet hallowed tone that echoed in my ears.

He moved closer, cloaking me with his darkness. His skin chilled my skin, and when I exhaled, I saw a cloud of vapor in my breath. I tried to scream, but my tongue was too heavy, and it wasn't until a knock at my door that I woke.

I bolted upright, breathing fast as I surveyed the room. I held my hand over my chest, trying to calm my erratic heartbeat. I was alone.

What the fuck was that? A dream?

I was alone and going crazy. I wasn't sure what happened, but I didn't believe it was a dream. It was not like the many nightmares I'd had since childhood.

This was real.

Chapter Fourteen

EZRA

"Get your shit together, Ezra," I told myself, sitting down. I didn't have time to think about a woman. My late wife deceived me, cheated me, broke me. I would never let another woman into my heart again.

"Fuck!" The beast in me growled, clawed at the surface of my self-control. Breath, Ezra, just fucking breath. I closed my eyes and took in a deep breath. I must rein in my emotions before they damaged the job—my freedom.

The label from the vial caught my eye. It was on the table beside the book I had been reading. I picked it up and turned it over in my hand. She obviously didn't trust me with the vial. How could we work together if she didn't even trust me? I flicked the label. It fluttered to the other side of the table where Maeve had been sitting. I snatched another book from the pile, eager to bury myself in research. A distraction was needed.

Damn, the tiny print was blurring together. I blinked a few times to clear the muddle of letters. It didn't work. I was damn tired. How long had I been reading? Fuck, an hour, more? I closed and tossed aside the third or fourth book; I'd lost track. I rubbed my eyes, feeling tired. I had better get some sleep soon. The longer I went without sleep, the more I succumbed to the beast in me, and that wouldn't be wise around Maeve. She had woken the beast, and now he paces within me, eager to be set free. Eager to have his way with her.

Shit, there was no time for sleep. I grabbed another book and opened it, skimming over the headings when I spotted something interesting. I flipped ahead to that section, accidentally blowing the vial's label onto the floor. I leaned over and picked it up, running my fingers over the edges before setting it back down.

The section of the book that I had found interesting was thicker than the rest. The first page was folded in at the edges so that it didn't stick out. I unfolded the page, one corner at a time, and revealed a map of Hell: The Divide, the River Styx, and The Shade. I ran my finger across the map as I examined it.

"What's that," I whispered to myself, leaning closer for a better look.

At the end of the map, in The Shade, was a door, and on the door was a sun. Flames stretched outward, reaching all edges of the door.

I sat back, resting my hands on my thighs, shaking my head.

Was this the door to Eden?

I picked up the label and read it. *Find the Gate of the Sun, protected by blood; the Book of Raziel rests in the sacred land, guarded by Shamsiel, ruler of the fourth realm.*

The Gate of the Sun? I thought. It had to be what we were looking for.

The slow smile on my face grew wider as I connected the door to the scripture on the vial. Motionlessly, I sat to let relief sink in. This had to be the Gate of the Sun. *It had to be.* I leaned forward again, locking my eyes on the source of my relief. I let my head fall back and laughed.

"I found it. I fucking found it."

The gate. I found it. But damn, it was in Limbo where Cerberus lived; a three-headed dog with sharp teeth, poisonous saliva, and claws coated with flesh-eating mites. Awful, but still better than being in the last two realms of Hell.

I had to tell Maeve. I glanced at my watch. Was she awake? I shook my head. It didn't matter. I was going to wake her. I closed the map and book and slid them under my arm. I left the room in a hurry, and in a few short minutes, I was standing in front of Maeve's room. I knocked once when my cell rang. *Fuck.*

"Hello," I said, going into my room, which was next to Maeve's.

"Levi was spotted," said Dorian.

I slowly closed my eyes and squeezed the bridge of my nose. "Where?" I shut the door behind me. If Levi was spotted, it was intentional.

"Charleston," Dorian replied. "South Carolina."

I ground my teeth, feeling the tension in my jaw. I did not expect Levi to be so damn close.

What did he know? How did he know where I was? I need to be cautious. He would go after Maeve like he went after my ex-wife. He'd manipulate her like he manipulated her. Levi made Sky believe that power was better than love. *Would Maeve believe him? Yes!* Levi was a master of manipulation. It was his power. It was a power of mine as well, but I knew better. Manipulation was detrimental to my sanity. If I gave into that sort of greed, I'd risk losing myself to the evil that runs through my veins.

"Have you found the Book of Raziel yet?" Dorian asked, breaking me from my tirade of thoughts.

"No," I said matter-of-factly.

"And the location?"

"Yes."

"Where is it?"

I threw my head back and laughed. "Why would I tell you?" Levi could be listening.

"Does anyone else know of its location?"

"No." Of course, it was a lie. Maeve and Philip knew but not the exact location I'd just found. The fewer people who knew, the fewer people Levi could manipulate or hurt. God only knew what lengths that asshole would go to get his hands on that book. I had to warn Philip and Maeve. They must not leave this house.

Would Levi sneak into Philip's home, knowing I'm here? Yeah, he would.

"Are *you* in Charleston?" Dorian was prying.

109

"Goodbye, Dorian." I pressed the end button. He wasn't helping me find the book, so he didn't need to know more. I hung up before he said another word. I had other shit to worry about, adding Levi to that shit-list.

I had no more time to waste, so I went to show Maeve what I found. I rapped my knuckles on her door, and the second she opened it, I held up the book. "I found it," I said, making my way inside. The room smelled like her: strawberries and vanilla.

"Come in," she muttered, her voice still raspy from sleep.

I sat down on the rumpled sheets before looking at her. *Holy... shit.* She was in panties and a tiny tee that barely covered her, and immediately, I was stiff. Lust burned in my brain. I could think of nothing else. My fingers ached to touch her, my mouth to taste her. The beast in me screamed, demanding to be set free. He wanted his way with her, but I wouldn't allow that. Levi could be close, and if he noticed my feelings for Maeve, he would use them against me. Just like he used Sky to hurt me.

Wait, I don't have fucking feelings for her.

Maeve smiled a devilish grin and went into the closet. I shook my head, fighting the shivers of arousal.

She came back fully clad in cargo pants and a longer tee. "Sorry 'bout that," she said, biting her lower lip, making it red and plump.

She was playing me. I stood up and tossed the book to the bed. I strolled over to her. She didn't move away, not a budge. "Tempting me is a dangerous game, love," I said into the crook of her neck, noting the raw, coarse undertone in my voice.

She stepped back, lifted her chin, and faced me straight on. I couldn't tear my eyes from her slightly opened mouth, and the taste of her breath on my tongue drove waves of lust to my groin. "I like danger," she said, running the tip of her tongue across her bottom lip.

She was toying with me—purposely tempting me.

Would she have sex with me?

I shook my head to rid it of those thoughts, and instead of

grabbing two handfuls of hair, I pulled a tie from my pocket and tied it at the nape of my neck. I sat back down on her bed, ignoring the warmth of her body that lingered on the sheets. Clearing my throat, I opened the book to the map. "Look what I found," I said, getting back to the reason I came here.

"Did you sleep?" She was eyeing me with a single arched brow.

I met her arched brow with one of my own. "Worried about me, love?" She popped a hip and rested her hand there.

I was sure that my eyes were red with bags under them, but she didn't need to worry about me. We were in the middle of a stare-off, and who would win? That was the question with an obvious answer. She. It was always she. I went to pinch the bridge of my nose but stopped. I didn't want to remind her of another man. Who was it—Sal? "You're a stubborn woman. If you must know, I haven't slept in weeks."

"That can't be good for your health. And you look like shit," she said, her eyes sparkled with a twinkle of humor.

I clamped my lips together, swallowing my laughter. "We have work to do, Maeve, and we have little time. By the way," I reached into my breast pocket, "here's the label."

She snatched it and slid it into her pocket. "So, what's up?"

"As I was saying, I have good news. Turns out, you were right."

"I'm always right," she said, wiggling her eyebrows. "What did you find?" She pointed at the book. "And if you say it's a book, I'll kick you where it counts."

"It's a map, and…what the fuck…," I said, bringing the book closer for a better look.

"What?" She asked, looking at me and the book.

I flipped the page back as if to find it elsewhere. "Where did it go?"

"Where did what go?"

"The door; it was just here," I pointed to the spot I saw earlier. Maeve sat beside me and ran a finger across the map,

111

and it happened — the door appeared. She jerked her hand back, and the door disappeared. I squinted at her before observing the map. "How," I whispered as I ran my finger over the same place. Nothing happened.

Maeve touched the spot again, and the door reappeared. "It's only when I touch it. Why?"

"That's a good question. I saw it earlier." I thought for a moment. "The label…. The oils on your hands must have been on the label, and when I touched it, your oil rubbed off on me. Therefore, the map thought I was you."

She just stared at me like I had lost my damn mind. "That's crazy talk. The map isn't alive, Ezra. It can't feel oils. Maybe there's something special in you that the book senses. Maybe you're not as badass as you try to be."

I just stared at her. There was nothing special in me. I had no heart. "No. It doesn't make sense."

"Nothing ever does," she said. "Not when it comes to the paranormal. Take angels, for example. They're supposed to be loving, innocent, and protective beings, but I've seen with my own eyes that they can be stubborn, moody, and just as greedy as jinn. They're an enigma."

I gently shook my head. "You certainly are special." She touched the map again, this time in a different place, and nothing happened. Only when she touched Limbo did the door appear. It materialized at the very end of the page, close to the third realm. "And…if you look closer, you will see an engraved sun on the door."

She moved in for a closer look, and I felt her breast brush against my arm. "Is this…"

I nodded with a knowing grin. "I believe so, love."

She looked at me with her mouth slightly agape. "The Gate of the Sun?" She ran her finger over the door slowly. "And it looks like the door's in The Shade. Thank God! That's a good thing. I didn't want to go to the last two realms of Hell."

"Yes, but The Shade isn't going to be easy. Souls get lost there, wandering helplessly until they become confused and forgetful. Eventually, frustration and hopelessness set in and gnaw away at their sanity until they become trapped in their own minds."

"Trapped in their minds?"

"Spirits think they're reliving their past, a time that still haunts them, not knowing that what they're seeing and feeling is all in their heads."

"I don't like the sound of that," she mumbled.

"Who does?"

She looked at the map. "The door is at the end of The Shade. How will we make it?"

"Hell is a reflection of the mind, mostly of pain and sin, so a strong spirit is needed to keep the mind strong."

"How do we know if our spirits are strong enough?"

"Damn, Maeve. I can't believe you don't know any of this. It's like Winston purposefully wanted to keep your spirit week."

"He never thought I'd go to Hell either, Ezra."

I nodded, but was still unsure if her claim was valid. "Fair enough," I said. "You can tell the strength of your spirit by the energy field around you."

She threw her hands up and rolled her eyes. "Again, with the energy field?"

"Yes." I nodded. "The same energy I told you about when we were in the Astral Plane. Everybody has one, but only a few can sense them."

"Can you sense mine?"

"Absolutely. It's strong but not strong enough, and if I were to guess, it's because you're carrying too much old anger and guilt."

She moved away from me. "I'm sorry I asked."

"We should probably talk about it, Maeve."

"We should probably talk about Cerberus," she countered. "I heard he lives in The Shade to ensure nobody leaves."

"You have to face what's bothering you, maybe not now, but very soon. And to answer your question, we will have to get Cerberus to obey us."

"How?"

"You'll have to—"

"Here you are," Philip said from the doorway. "I talked to Bones, and he agreed to help. He'll be here tomorrow morning."

Maeve and I took each other in. I noted the fear in her eyes and the dread in her voice as she said, "That's not a lot of time." I couldn't agree more. Maeve wasn't ready. She needed to strengthen her inner spirit, and damn, I needed to convince her of that. She believed the pain she felt from her past gave her strength, but it was nothing but angry revenge. She needed to see her weaknesses to find her real strength.

I turned to Philip. "Can I use your gym?" I asked.

"Of course," he answered. "It's down the hall, across from the foyer."

I nodded thanks. "Maeve?" She lifted her chin, giving me her attention. "Let's go. I need to get you ready for Hell."

***

Fitness equipment lined the gym, and in the center of the room was a boxing ring. I didn't know why Philip needed a boxing ring, but the image of him fighting was hard to imagine. He wasn't a fighter. He was too soft-spoken and caring.

Maeve walked in, looking around, seemingly impressed. She had on cargo pants and a tee, looking like the hunter she was. "Hey," she said as she ran her hands over her damp hair, smoothing out the rogue strands. She had demanded a shower before meeting me, and her hair was still wet and tied back into a tight knot at the top of her head.

I also tied my hair into a knot at the nape of my neck. It's what I did when I trained, and right now, I was looking forward to it.

"So, what are we doing?" She unstrapped the belt securing her knives, and placed them on a chair beside the ring.

I jerked my chin at her knives. "Do you always carry those with you?"

She lifted a quizzical brow. "Uh...yeah, I do. One could never be too safe."

I shrugged because, honestly, I hadn't noticed. "You usually wear a vest with multiple pockets." She wasn't listening. She took out the vial and carefully placed it beside her blades, and she found some tape to stick the label back on. "So... what are we doing?"

I ducked under the rope and jumped into the boxing ring. "We're fighting." I was bouncing on the balls of my feet and rolling my head from shoulder to shoulder.

She jerked her head back and eyeballed me. "You look like a dancer, not a fighter."

I folded my arms over my chest and looked down at her.

She took in a cleansing breath, seemingly embracing a new mindset, and shrugged her shoulders. "Fine. If that's what you want, I will be honored to kick your ass." She hopped over the ropes and into the ring. She pivoted around in a circle, bouncing on the balls of her feet. "I still can't believe this gym...and a boxing ring?"

"Are you ready, love?"

Her lip curled. "Don't call me that. I'm not your *love*."

I grinned. "Whatever you say, ...*love*."

She rolled her neck. "Ready yourself because—"

Before she could finish her sentence, I blasted my foot into her stomach. The air whooshed from her lungs as I knocked her to the ground. She blinked a few times, catching her breath.

I stood over her. "Come on, Maeve. Get up." I snatched her arm and heaved her up, spinning her around until her back was flush against the front of my body. "You need to do better than that, *love*," I whispered into her ear.

"Don't. Call. Me. That." She spat the words out with venom.

I closed my eyes and ran my lips over her earlobe, speaking to her softly. "And why is that?" She tilted her head back and closed her eyes. I licked my lips and pushed my hip against the small of her back. "You're weak, Maeve."

"Don't forget. I have a nevus."

I was taken by her, mainly when her tongue darted out and ran across her bottom lip, making it plump and moist.

Mimicking her actions, I ran my tongue across my lips before finding my voice. "That nevus will not save you from your own demons." With my free hand, I swept her hair away from her shoulder, exposing her neck. I pressed my moistened lips to her skin and licked the sweat, savoring the sweet and salty taste. I could neither help myself nor deny my growing hard-on, so I let myself be distracted.

Senseless mistake.

She jabbed me in the gut with her elbow, freeing herself. She swung her body around and kicked. I ducked under her leg, but I didn't escape unscathed. She popped her fist out and hit me in the jaw.

I brought my hand to my chin to rub the ache away. It didn't help. She was petite, but damn, she had a good right hook. I darted my tongue out, brushing it along my now swollen lip. Her eyes locked onto my mouth, and that was my chance.

I slammed my foot into her chest. She flew back and landed on her ass. I love inflicting pain, and to be honest, this fight was damn fun, but a part of me—a big part of me—didn't enjoy hurting her. Even with her nevus, I still cringed when she groaned in pain. I'd prefer to leave her groaning in pleasure.

She sprang up. "What the fuck, Ezra," she shouted, rubbing her right ass cheek. "I can't afford injuries."

"You can't afford to be weak either…not in Hell."

"Fuck off," she snapped, her chest quickly rising and falling.

I sprinted at her and wrapped an arm around her neck, bringing her down. She landed on her back with a loud thump. I sat on her hips and held her arms over her head. She squirmed under me.

"Mmm…your squirming is a turn-on." She stopped moving, and I ran my fingers across her jaw and down her neck. "I thought you were a trained assassin…with a *nevus*."

She bucked her hips, pushing me back just enough to wiggle free. She jumped up and went for her blades, those silly toys of hers. They hindered her natural ability. When she sprang back into the ring, I was at the other end, watching and grinning. "And what do you plan to do with those toys? You can't bring them to Hell with you."

I had to give it to her. When she threw her blades, it was with great strength and accuracy, and she threw them straight at my legs.

I used the energy around me to do a butterfly kick. I jumped, twisted my body, and swung my legs around the blades. One by one, I snatched the knives and threw them back at her before landing on my feet. She didn't have time to react; the blades sped through the air too fast to see and stabbed the ground in front of her feet.

She stared at them with an open mouth and wide eyes. "How?" she asked.

"I trained for years to master my energy field, or better known as spiritual energy."

She tore her eyes from the knives and looked at me. "Great, so not only do I need a strong spirit to keep my mind sharp, but I need a strong spirit to fight like you?"

"That's right." I grinned and winked at her.

She put her hands on her hips. "And according to what you told me earlier, my spirit is strong but not strong enough because I have too much guilt and anger?"

She didn't look convinced. "You're distracted by your inner demons: anger, guilt, regret," I added. "Those weaknesses destroy your spirit and thus inhibit your ability to use spiritual energy, which you're going to need to defeat some immensely powerful jinn in Hell."

She scoffed at me and waved a hand in the air as if to dismiss me and my nonsense. "That's bullshit. I've killed many jinn, and I'm still alive. Plus, I have a nevus."

I pinched the bridge of my nose. This girl was damn stubborn, and I was getting tired of her using her nevus as an excuse for her strength. She was more than her nevus.

"Look, love. Your nevus works on Earth to give you strength and the ability to heal, but in Hell, in their domain, they will overpower your nevus. Using your spiritual energy is a much better tool. Now, don't get me wrong, you need your nevus. It will be our ticket across the river Styx."

I could tell by the look on her face that she was contemplating my words. Finally. "Okay, well then, how do I strengthen my spiritual energy?"

"By letting go of your inner demons," I shrugged, "figuratively speaking."

She rolled her eyes. "So, you're going to start preaching to me now?"

I ignored her remark. "You need to forgive yourself," I said as if it wasn't a big deal because it wasn't.

She folded her arms across her chest and eyed me suspiciously. "Forgive me for what?"

"The guilt you hold over your parents' deaths."

Her mouth hung open, obviously shocked by my words. "How do you know this?"

"When you talked about your parent's death, I saw the anger and guilt."

She smiled, but it appeared forced. "You don't know me."

"Maybe I'm wrong, but I'm fairly sure I'm not. You'll need to forgive yourself."

She brought her eyes to mine, and I saw her growing frustration. "My pain is a part of me!"

I turned my head down as I considered my following words. "I understand, but—"

"You're broken, yet you can still manipulate your energy. So why can't I?"

What sort of pain did she think she saw in me? Was I that transparent? Did I even feel pain because I was numb most of the time?

I turned away from her, keeping my head down as I snatched a towel from a small side table and wiped my hands. "Yes, I have my own demons, but that is for me to worry about."

"Answer my question!"

I looked skyward and silently asked the Gods for patience. "I learned to control my spiritual energy years ago. It's become second nature." She was digging for info, prying into my past, and that was why I wanted to leave. "Meet me here after six."

"So, you are broken. Who broke you?"

I still had my back to her, so she couldn't see my rising irritation. I ground my teeth, gripped the towel, and twisted it tightly. "I'm not talking about this with you."

She mumbled something under her breath and stormed out of the gym. The heavy door slammed shut, and the frame on the wall next to the exit rattled.

"Fuck," I mumbled, throwing the towel into a hamper beside the door. I wasn't looking forward to working with her later. What I had to do, she wasn't going to like.

I was going to make her relive the night her parents were killed. She would hate me and fight me, but she needed to face her fears and control her emotions before going to Hell.

The demons would use that night to haunt her, weaken her spirit, and trap her in Hell forever.

Chapter Fifteen

MAEVE

I closed the door behind me, trapping myself inside my guestroom, my haven away from home. Ezra's words about self-forgiveness drowned my mind, and no matter how hard I tried, they wouldn't go away.

What is my weakness, anyway? Fire. That's my weakness.

Hell had fire. Lots of fire.

Oh, God. Ezra's right.

I sat on the bed with an audible oomph. If I didn't find a way to get over my PTSD, I wouldn't make it out of Hell. What was I going to do, forgive myself? No! I couldn't. Forgiving was forgetting. I lived for their retribution.

I stood and rolled my achy neck around my stiff shoulders. Damn, I needed a hot shower.

What would Ezra look like naked?

I smiled and headed toward the bathroom. I turned on the shower and allowed the cold water to run over me before it heated. It was cold but felt good on my tender muscles. I lifted my chin, closed my eyes, and let the water run over my face, wetting my hair. Oh, how I wished I could wash away my past and start over again.

What would I have had done differently? Save Mom and Dad. That was what I would have had done. I rubbed my face and eyes and reached for the soap. I rubbed my hands together until a thick layer of sudds formed. I rubbed the soap over my entire body, hitting every curve and vital areas before rinsing. My body relaxed one muscle at a time. It felt damned good, so I stayed under the warm water for as long as I could, but time was running out.

I turned the shower off and stepped out. The glow from my cellphone. "Ah, shit! All ready." Groaning, I grabbed a towel. I showered longer than I had thought, and it was already time to go. I hardly had time to rest. I quickly dried and dressed, all while wondering what Ezra had planned for me. Are we going to fight again? God, I hoped not. Ezra was just going to kick my ass with his 'spiritual-energy' technique. I'd much rather watch *him* fight.

Mmm...his body, covered in sweat. Damn! I could really use a fun distraction. "Hell, we might just die in Hell. Might as well have a bit of fun before we go. Great, now I was talking to myself. I snatched my belt with my knives and strapped it around my waist. *But I really don't want to die a virgin.*

I took the vial, slid it into my vest pocket, and glanced in the mirror before leaving. I looked like shit. I wasn't a makeup girl, and even if I was, I didn't have the time to pack anything but my lip gloss. I pinched my cheeks, applied lip gloss, and put my hair into a bun leaving a few loose strands around my face for a softer look.

"There, that's better."

This ought to get some attention. I thought, smiling to myself.

***

Ezra sat in the center of the boxing ring, waiting for me. "You're late," he said.

I set my blades and the vial on a chair. "Hi to you too." I climbed over the ropes and into the ring. I sat next to him and tucked my legs under me. His eyes grazed my cheeks and lips. "Like what you see?" I winked.

He moved his eyes to mine. "Are you ready?"

A lamp glowed next to him, shining a light on a small silk pouch that lay on a tiny dish. "For what?" I eyed the silk pouch. What was it? A drug?

He seized the pouch, prompting me to look at him. "To meditate." He opened the little bag. Wow. He withdrew the most beautiful flower. Except for a hint of pastel pink that blushed the ends of the petals, it was almost entirely sheer.

"Why?" Meditation was foreign to me. Honestly, who had the time? At the DCU, we were trained to fight and use weapons, not meditate.

"Meditation is a tool to help people cope. During meditation, people focus on healthy emotions, and in your case, you'll focus on self-forgiveness."

I felt a tightness in my chest. "This isn't going to work." Forgiving is forgetting. I couldn't do that to my parents.

"Why not?" I went to stand, ready to flee, when Ezra caught my knee. Damn, his eyes begged me to stay. "Please, Maeve…let me help you."

I lowered my head. "You can't." My voice was nothing but a whisper.

"Yes, I can."

I shook my head. "No! You can't."

"Why?" he asked again.

"Because," I swallowed the dry lump in my throat, "I have PTSD. When I see fire, I get flashbacks."

There was a beat of silence. "I know," he said finally.

I placed a hand to my sick stomach. "You know? How?"

"Come on, Maeve. I wasn't born yesterday. I know the symptoms of PTSD when I see them."

I looked away, but I couldn't hide my shame. My face and neck felt hot. Damn, I was probably red like a pepper. I tried to hide my PTSD, but apparently, it didn't work. Ezra, Sal, Winston, Emerich, everybody saw through me, into me, as if I were made of glass, both translucent and breakable to them. *Damn!*

"Look, Ezra, one hour of meditation isn't going to be enough to clear my mind of all the shit in my head."

"Then, tell me, love. How do you plan to go to Hell? Because last I heard, there's lots of fire in Hell."

I threw my hands in the air. "I know, Ezra. Fuck! You think I haven't thought about that? I have." *Just minutes ago.* "But meditation? I've heard it takes years of practice, and I won't be able to forgive myself," I snapped my fingers, "like that."

He pointed at the flower. "That's called Angel's Breath. It has tranquility-inducing elements. Have you heard of it?" I shook my head. "It's called Angel's Breath because people who inhale its scent immediately feel at peace with themselves, making self-forgiveness easier."

I rolled my eyes. "Ezra, if you want me to relax, you'll need to use a damn tranquilizer."

"I don't want you comatose, love. I want you to be fully aware of your surroundings, your thoughts, and your feelings. Only you can let go of your inner demons."

I laughed, rolling my eyes again. "Come on, Ezra. This sounds too hippie-dippy."

"Hold up your hands like this." Ezra held his hands together. "Now, rub them." I did what he asked. I put my hands together and rubbed, but he shook his head. "No, Mave, rub faster."

"Geesh, okay." I rubbed my hands faster until Ezra grabbed my hands, stopping me.

"Now, slowly pull them apart," he guided my hands, "and bring them back together. Feel the energy flowing between your palms and fingers?"

Not at first, but then…I felt it—a light hum of energy. I nodded to him, feeling slightly overjoyed. The space between my hands felt warmer and thicker, prickling my palms like static electricity.

"That is your spiritual energy field. It's weak right now. The energy flow is fine and lightweight, but it will grow thicker and more powerful once you let go of your old guilt and anger. Then, you'll be able to contain it and use it. You'll even be able to use it to move objects without physically touching them."

I yanked my hands from his. "This is bullshit." I was shaking my head in disbelief. "I don't need this right now."

"You don't?" He lit a match, setting the beautiful flower ablaze. It sparked to life a kindled flame with an occasional glimmer of light, filling the gym with a golden glow and an intoxicating scent.

I froze; the tiny flame held me captive as my mind's eye

flashed back to my childhood memory. I saw two bodies, a bed, and men cloaked in darkness. The flashback was the same as always, and I smelled sulfur and burned flesh. The heat from the flames touched my face, and the screams billowed around me.

"Maeve," Ezra whispered. He lightly grabbed my chin, forcing me to look at him. His amber eyes had subtle streaks of gold, and I saw confidence and a hint of sympathy. They drew me out of my heart-shattering memories and into the here-and-now. "Let me help you?"

I wiped the sweat from my brow. The tiny flame from the flower died, leaving wisps of white smoke drifting toward me. I tucked my chin to my chest to hide my shame. Ezra was right. I had a problem I could neither hide nor run from. Hell had fire, lots of fire, and just the tiniest flame sparked by the flower gave me a flashback. If I went to Hell and saw all the fire and burning, my flashbacks would consume my mind and hold me captive. "All right, Ezra, you proved your point. What do I do?"

Ezra held the tiny bowl with the burning flower up to my nose. "Breath in the flower's perfume."

I inhaled. The smell was subtly sweet, like fresh herbs and spices in a garden. The wisps of smoke curled around my body like the soft caress of an angel, urging me to relax. My breathing slowed, my shoulders dropped, and I opened my hands and let my knees fall to the mat. The smoke had filled my mind and took over my thoughts, and just like that, my life flashed before my eyes, a rapid replay of events and people that mattered most to me. I saw Emerich sick in the alley. I saw Winston congratulating me on the night I became an assassin. I saw Sal carrying my young and fragile self out of my childhood home and away from my dead parents. I saw Ezra, his golden eyes staring into mine. Then, the spooling images slowed to a sudden stop at a time in my past. A time I never wanted to revisit but always did.

I smelled seared blood, charred flesh, and sulfur. My parents screamed, and five figures showed. They were cloaked in darkness. Their laughter filled me with agony.

124

The cloaked figures and their haunting laughter were nothing new, but one of them pulled his hood back, revealing his face. I'd never seen one of their faces before. He seemed to be the leader as the other cloaked figures stood behind him, submissively with their heads bowed. He was damn beautiful. Tall with long, black hair and eyes the color of rust...no, fire. They were like fire.

My heart pounded at the sight of him. He scared me—the look of him—beautiful yet powerful in a sinister way like a cult ruler.

The jinn, who appeared to be the leader, reached out his hand and grabbed my shoulder. I tried to pull away, but he dug his fingers and nails into my skin. He forced me to watch my parents burn to death; an image seared into my brain and heart for life.

Damn him!

That's why I hated being touched. I hated being grabbed even by those I knew meant no harm. My ears hurt as my parents' tortured screams scraped my eardrums...

"Breathe in, Maeve." Was that Ezra? Yes, it was.

I took a deep breath in and a slow breath out.

"Imagine your childhood memory is a ripple in a quiet pond."

I inhaled and exhaled. I did what he asked, and my vision rippled like a reflection in wavy water.

"As you exhale, imagine the outer ripple fade away."

I exhaled and focused on Ezra's words. They were magic, fighting against my flashback, and four of the cloaked figures disappeared, all except for the leader. He stayed, staring at me with a fixed smile that never wavered. It creeped me the fuck out.

"Control your breathing." Ezra inhaled and exhaled with me. "Imagine another ripple fading away."

The next ripple disappeared, and I no longer smelled burnt flesh or sulfur.

"Let them fade away. One by one, let them go."

I didn't hear my parents' screams. I didn't feel the heat from the fire on my face.

"Visualize a peaceful pond." Ezra walked me through this. His voice was comforting, and I had never felt comfortable during a flashback.

The jinn's fixed smile faded, followed by the rest of his face, then his arms, legs, torso, and head. He disappeared as an image of a small pond, surrounded by bright green trees and vibrant flowers, materialized in my mind. The sweet smell in the air and the soft breeze blowing through the trees took me to a calm place. Just me and the pond, so peaceful and quiet.

The air around me felt like static, like the zap you get from a sock fresh from the dryer.

"That's your energy. Don't fear it and its powers. Accept it, and you'll see it grow around you like armor."

I wasn't scared of my energy. Not in the least. I welcomed it, and it grew stronger and stronger. I imagined tiny particles moving electrons from one atom to the next, forming an electrical current. The current flowed through me, and a powerful sensation built and throbbed below my waist. Every nerve ending quivered.

Ezra moved closer, his body heat touched my skin, and I opened my eyes to see him. His eyes were a pool of amber, two golden orbs I could get lost in, and his perfectly defined lips begged me to touch them. Something in me changed. Lust mixed with relaxation made me rash— consequences be damned!

I leaned into him, moistening my lips with the tip of my tongue. "I want you," I said, running my bottom lip over my front teeth.

"Maeve," he whispered, sounding feral and thick with desire. "I can't.

I smiled a sultry come-on smile. My overwhelming need for him blotted out all other thoughts. I only thought of him.

Moving closer, I wrapped my legs around his waist and brushed my lips along his jawline. "I want to kiss you." I brought my lips to his. "Please."

His eyes were wild. I thought he would push me away, but he cupped my head and crushed his lips against mine. He took control, cradling my head in his hands. The kiss was possessive, rough, and deep, and his tongue invaded my mouth. Oh, how sweet he tasted, and I allowed myself to be wild, open, and willing. Only raw pleasure would sate me now, but then he broke the kiss, leaving me craving more.

"We can't do this," he said, panting.

I whimpered, rocking against his stiff shaft. He let out a frustrated growl as he reached around me and covered the flower with the palm of his hand, extinguishing the flame.

In a blink of an eye, as if a hypnotist snapped his finger, I awoke from my spellbinding state. I glanced around, checking my surroundings. What the hell just happened? I felt the heat rush to my cheeks, and I slid off Ezra and covered my eyes with my hands.

What had I done? I wanted him, and he told me no. I don't know why I felt terrible. I was trained to be a fighter, but damn, did my heart hurt, and the energy around me faded.

"A spirit is a component of our basic needs. You wanted sex," he shrugged his shoulders and stood up, "it's human nature."

If it was part of my nature, then why did my heart hurt?

"Look, Maeve," his voice was gentle and quiet, "I like you too, but…."

Why did he stop talking? But what? I needed to know. "But?" I urged him to continue.

He looked away. "But…not in that way." My heart sank to the pit of my stomach. He ran his fingers through his hair, seemingly frustrated with himself. "We have other things to worry about, Maeve."

I wanted to bring back the pond visualization to move away from the pain he put in my heart, so I imagined a tiny ripple in my peaceful pond. I accepted his rejection and didn't allow it to hurt me. The small wave faded, and I smiled when I felt the warm currents of my spiritual energy hum around me again.

Ezra reached for me, but I put up a hand, stopping him from touching me. I wasn't angry, I didn't need comforting, and I didn't want to be vulnerable. I needed to be strong, so

127

my spiritual energy exploded outward and pushed Ezra back like an invisible hand. He fell and hit the mat with a slap. I sat still, staring at him.

He didn't move.

"Ezra?" What just happened? Did I use my spiritual energy field like he used in fights?

Ezra's shoulders shook. *Wait, was he laughing?* He was fucking laughing. He sat up, rubbing his back as if it hurt.

"That hurt, love."

"Good, you deserved it," I said and stood with my hands on my hips. "What happened?"

"You knocked me back with your spiritual energy.*"

I lifted my hands, looking at them. My smile grew from ear to ear. "I like it."

Ezra laughed. "It's cool, isn't it?"

I nodded, still wearing a silly grin.

"You still need to practice making it stronger, but see how much you have accomplished with just an hour of meditation. I knew you could do it."

I waved a hand in the air. "That's because of the flower."

He made a sputtering sound with his lips, dismissing what I said. "Bullshit.

"And it was because you guided me. One ripple at a time, my flashback faded away." I thought about the jinn leader. "You said my spirit is the seat of my emotions and character, but what about memories?"

"Yes. In fact, spirits are keepers of memories."

"I saw something or rather someone I've never seen before —a jinn. He was tall with long, black hair and eyes like yours but more orange like fire."

Ezra narrowed his eyes. "His eyes were orange...like fire?"

I nodded. "Did he say anything to you? Did he tell you his name?"

"No. Does he sound familiar to you?"

"I don't know." Ezra scratched his temple. "Maybe."

"Really? Someone you—"

"I'm sorry to interrupt," Philip said from the other end of the gym. "Bones is here."

"Already?" I asked as Ezra cursed under his breath.

"He wasn't supposed to be here until tomorrow," said Ezra.

Philip shrugged. "He's early."

Ezra's shoulders visibly dropped. "Okay, Philip. Take Maeve with you. I'll be there in a minute."

I looked at Ezra. "What are you going to do?"

He shrugged. "I need to wash my face."

I lifted a brow. "You need to wash your face?"

"Come on, Maeve," said Philip. "Bones is waiting."

I left with Philip, but not without eyeing Ezra suspiciously. He was acting weird.

Chapter Sixteen

EZRA

The second they left, I fell to the floor, hitting the mat hard enough to crack my knees. I didn't need to wash my face. It was a lame lie. I needed a second alone to think.

I covered my face with my hands, not wanting to see the truth.

His eyes were fire. His hair was long and black. That jinn in Maeve's flashback was Levi. He was the only jinn with the same color eyes like mine but more orange-like fire. Maeve described them perfectly. Did Levi kill her parents, or was he somehow invading her memories?

I ran my hands down my face, pulling my chin. It stopped me from screaming. Maybe Levi would hear me, but that would only please him.

If Levi was using magic to invade her memories, then he must have felt her energy.

I was right. Maeve's spirit was strong. She controlled her thoughts, strengthened her spirit, and used her spiritual energy field in less than an hour. It gave me hope. She gave me hope. She had fight. If she held onto that fight, she'd be fine in Hell. Plus, I'd be there, helping her along the way. Together, we were strong enough for Hell and maybe even Levi.

I jumped from the boxing ring and headed to the door when I heard a voice whisper, "You can't go to Hell. Father will call for you." I spun around with my fists up, ready to fight, but nobody was there.

"Come out, you bastard!" It had to be Levi.

Silence.

I couldn't get angry. I couldn't get frustrated. Levi would see that and use it against me somehow, like a fucking puppet master to my weaknesses. I needed to keep my spirit strong, lift my head, and keep working until I got my hands on that fucking book.

Chapter Seventeen

MAEVE

Bones spoke with a soothing lilt, and I knew why they called him Bones. He was so skinny. Was he sick?

"Is this Maeve?" he asked, grabbing my hand and firmly shaking it. Wow, I was wrong. He was more than just skin and bones. There was muscle under that leathery skin.

"That's me. It's a pleasure to meet you," I said, smiling.

Just then, Ezra strolled around the corner. His hair was tied back into a clean knot at the nape of his neck. Did he run upstairs to change? Was that what the fuss was about? Obviously, he was dressed in clean slacks and a button-up. Geesh, what a bighead.

Ezra reached his hand out for Bones to shake. "Ezra," he said, introducing himself.

With a wide grin, Bones grabbed his hand and squeezed, but a heartbeat later, his smile faded. "Sorry, boy, I can't send you to Hell."

My jaw dropped, and Ezra stepped away, looking at Bones as if he had lost his mind. "Why not?" Ezra asked.

Bones lifted his chin with a stern glint in his eyes. "We won't talk about it now, but we both know why."

What the hell was that about?

Ezra grimaced and became unnaturally quiet. He tipped his head back and looked skyward, mumbling something under his breath. Then, hung his head, shaking it from side to side, followed by a long-drawn-out exhale. Finally, he looked at Bones. "Will Maeve be fine to go alone?"

If my life were a cartoon, my jaw would have hit the floor. "Are you fucking kidding me?" I turned my attention to

Bones. "Why can't he go?"

Bones slowly moved his eyes from Ezra's to meet mine. "His spirit is strong," said Bones. "But it's connected to something...evil."

I stared at Bones without blinking. Was he for real? "So, that's it?" I asked Bones. "You need to give me more than that."

Ezra held up a hand, stopping Bones from answering. "It's none of—"

Narrowing my eyes, I glared at Ezra. "Don't you want to know why?" Ezra opened his mouth to say something, but Bones cut in.

"Ezra's lucky. He was born with a strong spirit. One that can't be weakened, but it is also tied to something evil, probably a close friend or family member," said Bones.

From the corner of my eye, I saw Ezra flinch. "My fucking father was crazy," he uttered.

Philip choked and coughed, and Bones patted him on the back. Shit, I forgot he was here. "Are you okay, Philip?" I asked.

"Oh, yeah." He cleared his throat. "I'm fine." He flashed Ezra a quick look, one I couldn't quite read. Was it shock, uncertainty, fear? I wasn't sure.

"Okay, so I can't go, but what about Maeve? Can she go alone or not?" Ezra asked again.

Bones stopped patting Philip and reached for my hand, which I reluctantly gave to him. He squeezed it and closed his eyes. "Your spirit is strong too, like Ezra's, but it's—"

"Let me guess," I said. "Weak?"

"More like...suppressed," answered Bones.

Ezra folded his arms over his chest. "She's working on that."

Bones nodded before saying, "Meditation helps."

It wasn't cute, but I snorted and rolled my eyes. "So, I've heard." Ezra rocked back on his heels with a cocky grin on his face.

Bones clapped his hands together. "Very good," he said. "Connect with your spirit, and I'll send your soul to Hell."

I stumbled back a step. "What did you say?"

"I will send you," Bones answered, smiling as if this was him doing a good deed.

"No, no, no. Timeout." I held my fingers to the palm of my other hand, making the universal sign for a timeout. "Not that. The part when you said something about sending my soul to Hell."

"The physical body cannot go to Hell," said Bones. "I will need to send your soul— just your soul."

I jerked my head back and shook it at the same time. What was I expecting? I'd never thought about going to Hell or how I'd get there, but for some reason, the thought of removing my soul from my body made me sick to my stomach. "How will you send my soul and not my body? Last I heard, when a soul isn't in someone's body, it's because they're dead."

Bones rubbed his skeletal hands together as if this sort of talk excited him. "I'll stop your heart then call upon the Reaper to take your soul to Hell. But don't worry, we will keep your body on ice."

"Oh, okay...you'll keep my body on ice." I threw my hands in the air. "Everything will be fine. I have nothing to worry about." I rolled my eyes. "Everybody's acting like this sort of shit is normal. *Oh, I'll send your soul to Hell,*" I mocked in a deep voice. "*Then, I'll throw your body on ice until you get back.*"

"I understand this is overwhelming for you," said Philip, "But just know, doctors do stop a patient's heart before cardiac surgery. They pour cold water over the heart to keep the organ from dying."

"There must be another way," Ezra began, but I held up a hand to shut him up.

Looking upward, I prayed for my sanity. I was an inch away from losing my mind. Philip had the medical equipment to keep my body alive; I saw it all in the underground room. "This is getting weird. Okay, what if I can't free my spirit before I go to Hell?" I asked Bones.

Bones tapped his chin. "I think I might have a way to

help...but I'm not sure—"

Ezra hit the wall with his fist. "There must be another way!"

"Calm down," snapped Philip. "You can't go to Hell!"

My eyes followed Ezra as he stormed from the room without another word. "Geesh, why is he having a tantrum? He isn't the one going to Hell."

"He cares about you," said Bones.

A wave of heat burned my cheeks. I was speechless. *Does Ezra care about me?* He didn't want sex, but that doesn't mean he doesn't care. Right?

"Maeve," said Philip, gaining my attention. "I know you already decided to go to Hell, but I'd take a minute to reconsider because you'll need to go alone."

"Yeah, alright," I said, about to leave the room. "I need some time to think." The two guys nodded. "I'll be back."

I wandered aimlessly down halls and into open rooms until I came to a garden where I finally sat down to think. I took in the beauty around me. The air was fresh, with a hint of rose scent. Green and yellow brushed the garden, roses dotted the grounds with reds and purples, and above the lushness were swirls of orange mixed with splashes of purple and pink. I wondered if Eden would be this beautiful.

Was I ready to risk my life to find out?

Going to Hell was one thing, but going alone was terrifying. And stopping my heart so the Reaper could take my soul? Will I make it back? Sure, I'm strong, trained to fight and kill, but damn, going to Hell...alone?

I looked up to the sky as if I'd find an answer in the clouds when my cell vibrated. I groaned, and fished it out of my pocket.

Holy shit! I almost dropped the phone when I saw whose number flashed across the screen. Was this Heaven's answer?

I stood up, unable to sit in one spot. "Hello?"

"Maeve?"

I smiled at the sound of his voice. "Emerich, I can't believe it's you."

"The one and only," he said, followed by an ugly cough.

"How are you feeling? Better? Did Winston talk to the Arch Assembly? Did he find a way to help you? Please, tell me he did?"

"Whoa, Maeve." He coughed again. "One question at a time." His voice was hoarse but still kind.

I giggled, covering my mouth because it quivered. "I'm sorry. How are you feeling?"

"Well, I've been better." There was a pause, and I took that moment to wipe my eyes with the back of my hand. "How are you?"

I sniffled, then gave an awkward chuckle. "You're the one who's sick, and you're asking me how I am?"

"I'm always looking after my Mae Bear."

I smiled from ear to ear. "I'm...good." It was a lie; of course, I wasn't good. I was tired, stressed, and emotional.

"It's okay, Mae. Don't cry. I'm doing okay—really."

I wish that were true, but I could hear otherwise. Emerich wheezed with every breath and coughed after every word he spoke.

"Where are you?" he asked, and then came a bout of violent coughs, a whooping that sounded painful not just in his throat but in his chest. I placed a hand over my heart and grabbed a handful of my shirt. His pain was heart-wrenching, and I wished, at that moment, I could trade places with him.

I choked on a sob. "Charleston," I said, without thinking, immediately slapping a hand over my eyes. *Why did I tell him that?*

"Charleston." He cleared his throat. "Why are you in Charleston?"

I ran the back of my hand across my nose and sniffled. "I found a cure." My voice cracked.

"What?" Emerich choked, causing more coughs. He couldn't seem to catch his breath, sucking in the air between coughs.

"Hello," said another voice. "This is doctor Hemm."

"Is he okay?" I asked.

"I told him to rest, but he was persistent. He wanted to say…."

"To say what?" *Fuck, Hemm, spit it out.*

"I'm sorry, Maeve. He's dying. Getting worse each day. He wanted to say...goodbye."

I collapsed on the floor, and my eyes were swollen with emotion. "But...."

"I'm sorry," Hemm whispered.

I nodded as if the doctor could see me. "Just tell him...tell him that...that I'm sorry and to trust me."

"Yes, Maeve."

The doctor hung up, and guilt washed over me. Emerich's fate was in my hands. I heard a haunting ringing in my ears, and beyond that, all I could hear were the thoughts running through my head. If something happened to Emerich. If he didn't survive this disease...I couldn't stop the tears. I made my decision, a decision that, deep down, I had already made.

Emerich was dying, and I couldn't allow it.

I practically ran to the foyer. I pushed the doors open, and all three men stopped talking and stared at me. "I'm going," I said.

Philip eyed me suspiciously. "Are you sure?"

I walked up to Ezra. His stern expression softened as he reached up and rubbed away the tears on my cheeks. "I'm going to Hell," I said.

Ezra didn't smile. I thought he would be proud or relieved, but he wiped another tear from my eye. "Are you okay?" he asked.

"I have to save Emerich." That's all I said, and he nodded.

He picked a strand of hair that stuck to my wet cheeks and tucked it behind my ear. "We were just discussing with Bones —"

"Ezra... are you sure? I thought you didn't want—"

Ezra held up a hand, stopping Philip from talking. "I've been through worse," Ezra said. His tone was hoarse and sad but firm.

Bones stepped up to me. He reached out to touch my shoulder, but I took a step back. "What's going on?" I asked. Their expressions, all three of them, were forlorn.

Ezra gestured for Bones to continue, and Bones nodded

137

before speaking. "I can join your spirit with Ezra's."

"It will make your spirit stronger," Philip interjected, "connecting yours to Ezra's."

"This bond will also create a mental connection between us," said Ezra. "I'll be able to talk to you through this link—telepathically."

"Among other things," added Bones.

They bombarded me, talking one right after the other. My head was spinning, trying to keep up with what they were saying.

"Wait!" I yelled, looking at Bones. "Can you explain to me what the hell y'all are talking about? What is this link?"

Ezra and Philip stepped back, allowing Bones to explain. "A spiritual bond is made by taking two spirits and linking them together."

Was everybody around here so damned vague? "I don't understand what you're talking about."

Philip stepped up and moved to put a hand on my shoulder, but I stepped away. I didn't want to be touched— I never did— but even more, I didn't want anyone's pity. "Think of a spirit as having the same spiral structure as a double DNA helix," explained Philip. "Then, imagine pulling the strand in half and rejoining it with another strand."

Bones clapped Philip on the shoulder. "Great analogy. I will need to remember that one, Philip." Bones looked at me. "And, to make the bond, you will need to drink Ezra's blood."

I wrinkled my nose, disgusted. "Ew."

Bones waved a hand at me. "It isn't gross. Blood has a person's spiritual essence."

"This is a lot to process," I muttered, rubbing my eyes. I just got off the phone with a dying friend, and now this. My hand shook as I brought it to my forehead. I was feeling light-headed, so I sat down to keep from passing out. "Can everybody stop talking? Please. I need to think. Just for a minute. To fucking...think." I squeezed my eyes shut, thinking of all the possible consequences.

Bonding to someone else's spirit was...weird. I couldn't

138

even comprehend it. It was just unreal. "Everything in my life is like a fucking fantasy." I laughed, and the sound was the start of the madness. "I'm in a fucking dream," I mumbled, tapping my temples with my fingers. "Wake up."

Ezra grabbed my hands and put them to his chest. "I don't want to do the bond either," he said. "I was going to say no."

I looked up into Ezra's amber eyes. In their depths was a shadow of fear, but beyond that, I saw a light shine through, reflecting hope.

I reached up and ran my hand across the apple of his jaw. How thickheaded of me. I was so lost in my own feelings; I didn't even consider how Ezra felt. "What made you change your mind?"

He didn't respond straight away, but when he did, his words took my breath away. "I understand why you're willing to go to such great lengths for Emerich. You don't want to see him hurt." Ezra's voice was a soft whisper. "When you came into the foyer with tears and swollen eyes," he shrugged his shoulders, "I guess... what I'm trying to say is that I'm willing to go to great lengths for you too. I don't want to see you hurt."

I felt like I was falling. Ezra's words hit me hard, putting pressure on my chest that made it difficult for me to breathe. It was true. Ezra cared about me, maybe not romantically, but he cared. I said to Bones, "I need to know more about this bond. I drink Ezra's blood, then what? How do you link our spirits?"

"A spell," answered Bones. "I will gather herbs and stones to infuse the spell with energy. Then, I chant to focus that energy on the direct purpose, which, in your case, is to combine your spirit with Ezra's."

"Ezra said he can talk to me telepathically. Does that mean he'll know my thoughts? I mean... I have a lot of shit that I need to keep secret."

"Yes. After the bonding, you will experience something called spiritual sharing. Both of you will hear each other's thoughts and may feel each other's emotions," said Bones.

I bit my lower lip and ran it nervously between my teeth.

"Damn," I muttered. "Is there a way to control the spiritual sharing? A way to let him hear and feel me when I want him to?"

Bones smiled, showing me a row of stained teeth, and nodded. "Some can naturally close their thoughts and feelings, and they can do so almost immediately, but for most, it takes time. It also takes time to enter a person's mind. At first, the thoughts will come to you like a message from space. You might hear a word or two. Their voice may be choppy or staticky. You might even pick up a random sentence from time to time. Still, to have full access to the other's thoughts, to be able to talk to each other... both parties need to learn focus, patience, and trust." I listened in awe. I mean... I'd be lying if I said this stuff wasn't fascinating. "Also," Bones continued, "when a person is highly emotional, such as being intensely angry, sad, or scared, their thoughts and feelings are easily reachable."

Standing at the edge, my mind teeter-tottering on resignation. *Should I do it?* I had to save Emerich, but the idea of sharing my thoughts and feelings with someone? I was almost willing to make the bond just so I could rest— almost. It was easier to give in and make the best of the situation, but there were so many questions. "How long does the bond last?" I crossed my fingers. *Please say a couple of hours. Please say a couple of hours.*

"Forever," said Bones.

That one word shook me to my core, making my vision spin. I fell against the wall for support. The three men were talking, but their voices were muffled. Going back to a state of ignorance sounded nice, but that would get me nowhere.

Ezra will know my thoughts. He will know my feelings. What will Sal think? Oh, God. I don't want someone in my head, listening to my thoughts. I don't even like talking about my feelings or my past. I work for a secret government agency, for fuck sake. I have secrets, things to hide. He'll learn everything. Winston will kill me. I shook my head as if to shake the thoughts from my brain.

"Are you okay?" the three men asked at once.

"No," I said, running my sweaty palms up and down my legs.

Get your shit together, Maeve. The bond won't be all that bad. I would have Ezra to talk me through Hell. That was important. His spirit would strengthen my spirit. I needed a strong spirit. I would always be connected to him. *I like him.*

I smiled at the last thought, but to have him in my mind... forever! My smile fell flat.

"You don't have to make the bond to go to Hell," said Philip.

Ezra turned his attention to me. "Philip's right, but the bond will help, especially while you're in The Shade. If you get trapped in your mind, hearing my voice might be the only way to get you out."

"That's true," said Philip. "You'll relive your worst memory over and over on an endless loop, making it harder to differentiate between what's real and what isn't."

Yeah, and I'll probably relive the night my parents were killed, and knowing me, that would be my Hell.

I shook my head. I felt a sudden knot in my stomach. "Why am I doing this?" I asked myself, not realizing I said it out loud.

"Like Philip said, dear, you don't have to make the bond to go to Hell," said Bones.

"No, no. If I'm going to Hell," I said to Bones, "I'll need Ezra to keep me focused and strong. I think I'd prefer the bond."

"You don't have to do this. Any of it," said Ezra. "I can take you home."

Philip's eyes grew wide. "What about Levi? He plans to end the world."

Ezra looked at Philip and shrugged his shoulders. "I can find another way."

Philip sputtered. "By the time you find Levi, he'll already have the Grigori free from Hell."

I chuckled, a bit offbeat, considering the circumstances. "It's funny, isn't it? I accepted going to Hell easier than I'm accepting the bond. Damn, my priorities are skewed.

141

Anyway, Philip's right, Levi plans to jumpstart the apocalypse, and Emerich called ..." My voice cracked as my mind zeroed in on that single thought, giving me perspective. "I can't go home." I looked at Ezra.

"He called?" Ezra asked.

I let out an ugly sob. Hot tears streamed down my cheeks again. "Yes. He called to say goodbye." I wiped my eyes and nose with the back of my hand and cleared my throat. "I'm not ready to say goodbye." Standing tall, I pushed my shoulders back and looked at Bones. "Let's do the ceremony."

Chapter Eighteen

EZRA

Bones poked Maeve's pinky with a needle and squeezed the tip of her finger, pushing a tiny drop of blood into a small bowl he held. Fuck me. Maeve put her finger in her mouth and sucked. I licked my lips as I watched, feeling hot all over. Then Bones pricked my finger. "Fuck! Warn a man before you prick his finger."

Bones chuckled. "I did, but you were distracted."

Maeve giggled and watched me as I sucked on the tip of my finger. Bones turned to Philip, still holding the small bowls. "Where can I set up?" he asked.

"This way," said Philip, leading us to his office.

Piles of books and papers, both old and new, littered the floor and desk. Maps and globes of different sizes and heights covered the walls and floor. Philip didn't seem to notice the mess as he asked us to sit. I had to move a pile of books, with loose papers stuffed between the pages, from a chair.

"Should we do the ceremony somewhere else?" I asked, moving a coffee mug with cold coffee still inside. His office was a mess, with hardly any room to sit.

Philip sat at his desk with his hands folded before him on yet another stack of papers. "Yes, of course. Is there a problem with this room, Ezra? Not suitable for you?"

"No. No. It's fine," I said. "Bones?"

"Any place will do. Now, if you don't mind leaving me to set up, I will only be a few minutes."

The three of us left the office, leaving Bones to prepare, but what I thought would be a few minutes turned into an hour.

Finally, Bones opened the door and asked for me. I followed him into Philip's office and smelled the sweet scent of herbs and spices. The only light in the room came from a lamp set in the corner, and to my amazement, Bones cleaned the room and managed to make enough space to perform the ceremony.

"You undress and cleanse your body with this. It's freshwater with lavender oil," he said, handing me a bowl and a thin washcloth. "After you finish, put this on." He gave me a linen gown. "When you're dressed, step into a circle. I will be back."

I did what he asked. I undressed, washed with the water, and sat in one of the two connecting circles lined with what appeared to be a light grey powder. I've seen a few rituals and ceremonies in my time, and all of them called for human bones to burn to ashes. I was sure this ceremony was no different.

Bones opened the door, and Maeve came in after him, wearing the same linen gown. "Please, sit in the other circle," Bones directed her.

Maeve held her limbs close to her body and stared straight ahead with a blank expression. Was she scared? If I were to guess, I'd say she was freaking out—I was.

"Having second thoughts?" I leaned over and whispered.

She shook her head. "No."

"You look scared," I said.

"I am," she whispered, smiling softly with her hands clasped together on her lap. I had no reassuring words, and I fought to touch her, intertwine her hands with mine to give her comfort.

You seek her comfort. I untied my hair and raked my fingers through the strands. Fuck, this bonding shit was going to fuck with my head—it already had.

Bones crouched before Maeve, holding a small bowl to her lips. "This blood is of Ezra's essence. Drink." She froze, with her lips set in a flat line. I waited to see what she would do. Seconds passed. I thought she would run, but no. She opened her mouth, and Bones tipped the bowl. Talk about an

144

instant hard-on. Watching her throat work as she swallowed my blood, shit, it was raw and sexy as fuck.

That's why blood-drinking jinn liked women drinking their blood. There was something about it that was arousing, of course, but it was also…possessive.

Mine. The beast in me craved her—badly. I was supposed to be calm and relaxed, but I was the opposite of that. I was fucking wound tight: I ground my molars and clenched my fists. *Grow some fucking balls, Ezra. You don't need a fucking woman.* Damn, but this bonding was more than placing a ring on a newlywed's finger with a promise of marriage. A ring can be removed, but I claimed her with an unbreakable bond with my blood in her body.

Shit. My turn. Bones crouched in front of me, holding a different bowl. Shit. This was it. Was Maeve watching? Yup, she was. I opened my mouth and didn't look away from her when Bones brought the bowl to my lips.

"This blood is of Maeve's essence. Drink." I drank her blood. It tasted bitter yet sweet, like the smell of her skin and hair, a hint of vanilla.

"Now, close your eyes," said Bones. "Focus on the energy in the room."

I closed my eyes and followed Bones' orders.

"Feel the energy," said Bones. "Bring it into your body."

For me, sensing energy was easy, and right now, it was thick, pulsating around me and lifting the tiny hairs on my skin. I relaxed one muscle at a time, visualizing the energy and focusing on my senses. The electrical particles blanketed my skin, crackled, and buzzed, putting a copper taste in my mouth. The energy and I became one, penetrating my flesh and filling my mind, heart, organs, and blood.

Suddenly, Bones started chanting. "With this blood, I join your souls. With this blood, I join your souls." I opened my eyes to get a peek. Bones held another bowl above his head, and wisps of smoke swirled up from that bowl. "With this blood, I join your souls."

Then, without a word of warning, my vision went black. I was conscious but couldn't see. Adrenaline shot through my body, and I forced myself to calm my racing heart. The darkness cloaked me, consumed me, heart and soul. Bones' chanting grew louder, and with every word, the darkness swirled around me. Then, I saw flashes of light fly by me like a million falling stars, making the energy around me ripple as if I stood in front of a giant speaker that pushed sound waves through me. Then, the lights combined into one big ball of white power, pulsating and turning like a white star in the tiny universe that was in my mind. Our spirits were linked; I knew because I felt her.

It was hard to grasp what was her and what was the energy in the room. Suddenly my skin burned, not painfully, but more like a warm cover wrapped around my body. I knew it was her spirit fusing with mine. I wondered if bonding with Maeve would calm the beast, but instead, he grew possessive and caused havoc within me.

Shit! Not good. I'd have to meditate more.

"Thank you to the earth, to the oceans and seas, to the skies, and to the stars around us for combining these two spirits," Bones whispered. "Feel, taste, hear, and see. The ceremony is complete."

And just like that, my vision came back. I tasted Maeve's blood on my tongue, I felt her energy prickle my skin, and I heard her breathing in and out, slow and steady. I glanced over at her to find she was looking at me.

"The spiritual energy in the room is strong," said Bones. "I've never felt anything like it." Bones pointed up his index finger. "That reminds me... you two will feel each other's emotions through bodily-like sensations."

Maeve cleared her throat, getting our attention. "So, if Ezra is mad...."

She didn't finish her sentence. She was probably just as confused as I was.

Bones smiled and rubbed his leathery hands together. "If Ezra is mad, you might feel his anger through a heat flash or an icy sensation that prickles your skin. Understand?"

Maeve and I nodded. "Good, and in time, you guys will understand these feelings and connect them to the other."

Bones nodded, seeming pleased, and started cleaning up the items used for the ceremony.

Maeve was looking at me. I smiled at her, and she smiled back. "With my spirit linked with yours, you'll make it through Hell like a damn warrior."

She chuckled. "One step closer to getting the book."

I nodded. "Yes, one step closer to getting me…."

My smile faded. My heart sank. My gut fell to the floor.

The irony of my current situation hit me hard.

Here I was, working to gain my freedom only to have it taken from me in less than five fucking minutes.

I ran my hands up and down my face, groaning out my frustrations. Maeve's energy was everywhere, suffocating me. I felt my body tense. Every muscle fiber in my body was tight. Sensing someone so deeply caused me heartache. I was not prepared for this sort of connection. *This is too fucking much.*

I pushed myself up and darted from the room in a hurry. I didn't give a damn if I was half-naked. I headed straight to my room, ignoring Philip as he called after me.

I slammed the door behind me, turned my body around, pressed my forehead against the wood, and cursed out loud. With a tight grip on the handle, I screamed.

This had Levi written all over it. He always lurked nearby, within the shadows, compromising my freedom in some way or another. It was his fault that I lost my freedom to The Order.

I ran a hand down my face. I was an ass. The bond between Maeve and I was not Levi's doing, but in a fucked-up way, it was his fault. I don't doubt he manipulated the situation, so I would once again lose my freedom…and to a fucking woman. If it were not for his dishonor and greed, I would never have been in this damned predicament. My life was now hers. My soul was now hers. The thought—the truth —tore at me, my body, my mind…my soul. I slammed a fist on the door, causing it to rattle and crack.

And worse yet, the bond was permanent. Fucking eternal.

I let go of the handle and rubbed my temples to ease my

growing headache. I made a noise in the back of my throat as I ran a hand over the crack I left, cursing myself for losing control. Everything about Maeve made me lose control.

She owns you.

That thought wrapped around my heart and squeezed.

After she brings me the book, I'll kill her. She's dead. The bond's broken. Simple.

Fuck! What am I thinking? When Bones suggested the bond, I had said no, and I meant it. To be bonded to a woman... fuck that! Women are untrustworthy devils, but fuck, the second Maeve came into the foyer with teary eyes, I folded. I folded like a chump. Then, without another thought, I agreed to make the fucking bond. Just like that. It was true...something about that female made me irrational.

I pushed on my eyes with my fists and groaned. I knew damn well I could never kill her.

I fell back, wanting to get Maeve out of my head when I felt something that didn't make sense: a chill in my chest. Was it her I was feeling? Was I feeling her emotions?

Fuck! I pressed on my eyes with my knuckles. *She's just a female, Ezra. Get your mind back into the game. Focus on your job.*

Then, on the other side of the wall adjacent to the bed, I heard a door open and close.

It was Maeve.

I rolled to my side and listened.

Why did I have a sudden desire to shower? Seconds later, the shower's pipes in the walls hummed and cracked. *That's why.* Maeve's unconscious thought just crossed into my mind as if it were my own. I gritted my teeth and pictured her naked. Her breasts, perky and perfect in size. What a gift it would be to taste them, to caress her nipples with my tongue. The water probably clung to her most desired areas, begging to be pleasured. I would cherish her body, touch her like a goddess.

I adjusted my dick as the strain in my pants created an uncomfortable pressure, and the smile I had slowly faded as reality sank in. *What the fuck am I doing?*

I shot up from the bed, groaning. I went to the bathroom to rinse my face with cold water. Resting my hands on the smooth marble, I studied my reflection, something I'd often been doing. Choices and feelings have been riddling me, pushing me to evaluate myself and take a hard look at the real me. It was a way to understand myself as my thoughts, actions, and feelings seemed to be pulling me in different directions.

My thoughts were conflicted with both good and evil. Evil was my beast as he constantly tried to dictate my feelings and actions, pushing me to behave irrationally and ravish Maeve's body like a lust-crazed jinn. However, the good side of me wished to keep her away, knowing I'd break her heart. I don't do relationships.

I stood back to get a full view of myself. Usually, I would witness a tired, dull reflection, but today the man staring back at me was different. My skin was healthy. In countless years, far too many for me to count, I have not looked this human. My image reflected happiness, and I knew why. The truth that was hidden within my feelings of denial and resentment was now visible.

Maeve was…changing me. Before I met her, I had a wall constructed around my heart, but she slowly broke it down. Now, with the bond, I had a deeper, more intimate connection to her. It warmed me, and I loved the feeling. For the first time in a long time, I wanted to break that wall down myself, to blow it up. I wanted to embrace the warmth of her and let my heart feel again, with no barriers. But would she betray me? That was the question. That was always the question.

I held the edge of the counter as my mind bounced from one thought to the next. The possible outcomes overwhelmed me, flooding my mind, and the many emotions that swamped my cold existence brought forth memories. I thought of Sky, the dreadful woman who betrayed me for power and wealth. I squeezed tighter, and the counter cracked under pressure. Maeve said I was broken, and she was right. I was broken. Sky broke me. She broke my heart.

Fuck Sky.

The thought was more like a scream that echoed to my very core. As soon as Maeve returned with what I needed, I would find a way to break the bond. There was always a way. And indeed, the darkness of Hell would change her. She would lose her purity. Like the rest of the women in this world, she would become greedy and careless, like Sky. All women were like Sky.

I ran a hand across the cracked counter. If I did not calm myself, I would have to buy Philip a new home. Fuck, I was frustrated—sexually frustrated. I ran my fingers through my hair a few times.

Sex always helped. Sex would clear away these feelings, clear my mind, and aid my focus. Stepping back from the counter, I grabbed a hand towel and dried my face. I straightened my composure and grinned at my reflection in the mirror, liking what I saw.

I had several females to call, but there was only one woman that called to me. Maeve. And once I had a taste of her, I would surely lose interest—I always did. This one time, I'd let the beast win. But first, I had to get out of this fucking robe.

***

I didn't bother knocking, and she didn't seem to mind when I barged into her room. She lay on her bed, arms propped behind her head as she stared up at the ceiling. I shut the door behind me and leaned against it. "I can feel you," I said, referring to the chill in my chest.

"I felt you too," she said, still looking up, "inside of me."

I pressed my fist to my lips, hiding my smile. "Is that so?" My cocked jumped, practically begging for her.

She perched herself up on her forearms and glared at me. "That was until you bolted from the office," she blurted, and a sudden chill gave me goosebumps. Was I feeling her anger? I wasn't sure, and now wasn't the time to ask either.

"I was scared, love. Doesn't it scare you?"

She laid back down and folded her arms over her stomach.

"You scare me, Ezra." Her voice was low and soft to my ears.

She had changed out of the linen gown and into cotton shorts and a loose t-shirt. I prefer women in lingerie, but when the side of her shirt lifted, exposing the side of her stomach, I couldn't have been more turned on. I pushed myself from the door and sauntered over to her. Unable to stop, I ran my thumb over her bare skin just above her hip, where it dips at the waist. Her eyes settled on mine, and she didn't move away from my touch.

"I haven't felt this way about anyone in a very long time, Maeve, and that scares the hell out of me."

She swallowed a few times, and I was delighted observing her edginess, knowing I was the cause. "No one can live numb forever—life's too short."

I pulled my hand away. Her words delivered a hard punch. If only she knew I didn't have that sort of luxury. Men like me live numb forever.

"I don't know how to feel," I said. "I was robbed of my feelings long ago."

She sat up and crisscrossed her legs. "What's her name?"

I turned away from her. "Doesn't matter."

What did she do to you?

I was about to answer, but she wasn't looking at me. She was running her hands up and down her arms.

By the Gods. Did I just read her mind?

I wasn't going to tell her, but with the bond, she may find out nonetheless, and I preferred to tell her myself than for her to catch my thoughts. I turned my body away as I spoke. "If you must know, she cheated on me, and I couldn't be more thankful. Her greed made me realize that love is a fool's game."

The same chilly feeling from earlier hit me again but twice as cold, like ice packs on my skin. I connected the two moments of unexplainable chills with Maeve's actions, and I knew, without a doubt, I was feeling her anger.

"Bullshit," she spat, abruptly getting my attention.

I cocked my head, pointing an ear toward her as if I didn't hear her correctly. "Excuse me?"

She pushed herself off the bed and came towards me. She stood on her toes and held her chin up. "Bull. Shit." She was close enough to feel her hard nipples against my chest. "You don't sound thankful. You sound hurt. She hurt you so much, you refuse to love again. Though, I see your love for Philip."

I blew out a breathy laugh. "That's different."

"Bullshit!"

"That word is getting damn annoying, woman."

Her eyes suddenly soft and kind, her shoulders lax, and her energy suddenly wrapped around me like a warm blanket. If her anger made me cold, then her happiness made me warm. Why was she happy? She just finished cursing at me.

"I see your love for me," she whispered.

I laughed. "This isn't love." I leaned into her and inhaled her scent. "This is lust."

She brought her mouth to mine, ready to kiss me, but thought better of it and pulled away. Instead, she moistened her bottom lip with her tongue, making my cock jump. I ran my hand over her cheek before caressing the back of her neck. I could take no more. I pulled her to me, a rush of air escaped her lips, and I crushed my mouth to hers.

An intense wave of lust washed over me, settling into my cock with warm pressure that kept building and building until I was hard. I've been with many women. Still, with Maeve, everything was more intense. Was it our bond? Was I feeling her need mixing with mine? I was sure, but it was fucking perfect.

I brought my hands to her face, cupping her cheeks as our kiss grew desperate. She welcomed my eager tongue with her own. She tasted like mint and sugar. I sucked on her tongue and bit her lower lip before pulling back for air. "You're playing with fire, love," I whispered. "Can you handle it?" My mind warned me to stop, but my heart and body wanted more. I had lost all control. She was my weakness.

She shifted her waist until her stomach caressed my groin. "Fire scares me, but maybe you can take that fear away." Her raspy voice was a fucking aphrodisiac.

"When you see a fire, you'll think of me." I picked her up

and threw her on the bed. She yelped and giggled.

"No more flashbacks," I demanded, reaching behind my neck to grab the collar of my shirt, sliding it over my head. I tossed it to the floor and looked at her. She licked her lips, looking at my chest.

I moved to grab her ankles, but she moved away from me. "I thought you didn't like me in this way?"

I stood back, staring down at her. She was referring to what I had told her in the gym earlier, during her meditation.

I pushed my shoulders back and puffed out my chest. Maeve licked her lips, moistening them, as she stared hungrily at my body. Her energy, usually a warm blanket around my body, instead felt like electrical currents pulsating through my hard cock. I was starting to appreciate this bond. Sex before never involved the intensity of pulsating energy. With Maeve everything, every feeling was deepened, especially in my groin.

I bent over her, running a hand up the inside of her leg. "I like you, Maeve. I don't want to, but I do—so fucking much." Just then, her energy or her essence, whatever the fuck you want to call it, wrapped around me, filling me completely, penetrating every nerve in my cock. "Fuck me," I groaned.

"Mmm," she moaned, music to my lust. It drove me senseless. I needed her.

Kissing her inner thighs, I carefully pushed them apart to accommodate my shoulders. I traced her center with my finger. She was so fucking wet; her shorts were completely soaked.

"Ahhh...is it supposed to feel so...good?" She bit her lip and ran her hands down her stomach to the top of her shorts, "feels so intense." Was my energy also tickling her every sexual nerve into a lustful-induced frenzy?

She pushed at her shorts, seductively swaying her hips. The anticipation was killing me. Fuck, just the smell of her made my mouth water, but I couldn't be too eager. Not yet. I liked watching her squirm beneath me.

I kissed her thighs, inches from her wet center, getting

closer and closer. She ran her fingers through my hair and whimpered. I slowly pushed the end of her shorts to the side, revealing her wet center. I could feel her body heat on my lips, taste her sweet scent on my tongue, and I had yet to put my mouth on her.

"Mmm," she moaned while softly thrusting her hips, unconsciously begging for my touch, and who was I to deny her.

I caressed her folds with my thumb, slowly opening them to reveal her pink slit. She was wet—wet for me. I licked my lips before pressing her slick flesh with the tip of my nose. Fuck, she smelled delicious, sweet like fruit. I reached her clit and flicked her nub with the tip of my tongue. Wet heat flared between her legs, I was so hard it hurt, and Maeve sucked in a quick breath as she gripped the sheets tighter.

Then, sudden words entered my mind, thoughts that weren't my own, words like please, fuck me, yes, and Ezra. The fragments of her thoughts made me desperate. I ran my tongue slowly up her slit, sucking on her cunt until I could take no more. I slid her shorts down her legs, tossing them to the side, and groaned at the sight of her. She was the most amazing woman.

I pushed her knees apart with my shoulders and stroked her clit with my tongue. Her juices soaked the bed.

I want this. I need to feel him inside of me.

I heard the soft whispers of her thoughts in my mind, giving me reassurance. So, I used my thumb to massage and gently open her, and with my middle finger, I stroked her slit, slowly sliding it in. She was tight, so I took my time, sliding my finger in and out with smooth strokes. When she arched her back, pushing me deeper, I slipped in a second finger. I nearly came when I heard the wet thrusting sounds. She was so wet; my fingers were drenched. I bit my lip as I glided in a third finger, twisting and pushing them into her, stretching her more. She relaxed her hips, letting her knees fall open like an invitation, allowing me to go further.

I bit her clit, rubbing the nub between my teeth while sucking on it until it was swollen. That was her undoing. She

154

cried and moaned, digging her nails into my shoulders as she rode the waves of pleasure. I squeezed my eyes and bit the inside of my cheeks as a pulsating pressure that had been building and building finally erupted. I saw a burst of lights behind my eyes like the bright lights I experienced during the bonding ceremony. The feeling was so intense I thought I had come, but I didn't. It was her orgasm that shot through me.

Her pussy clenched around my fingers, soaking them. I replaced them with my tongue, thrusting the tip in and out, lapping up her sweetness. "Next time you cum, it will be when my cock is buried deep inside your cunt," I said, standing up.

She bit her plump lips. "I want you inside of me, Ezra."

I removed my pants, and my cock popped out, full and hard. Maeve inhaled a quick breath as she watched me stroke it, pinching the tip. Fuck me. Her pussy was wet and open, ready for me to take. My lips were still damp with her hot come, so I leaned down and kissed her, wanting her to taste just how sweet she was. She kissed me back with equal passion.

I slid her shirt over her head and tossed it to the ground with the rest of her clothes. Her breasts were so perfect and proud with tiny pink nipples. I squeezed and caressed them, gently at first, then rougher. I put one into my mouth and sucked. It didn't take much to make them tight.

Please. Her thought entered my mind, begging me.

I lifted my hips and held my cock at her opening. I grabbed her chin and kissed her hard while slowly sliding into her wetness. Her pulse beat rapidly with mine, her heat wrapped around my cock, and her skin was flushed and hot. I let my walls down, the walls I constructed around my heart, opening myself to her as I slid deeper. Then….

I jerked my head back until my eyes met hers. I felt her hymen, the thin tissue blocking my way. "You're a virgin?"

155

Chapter Nineteen

MAEVE

"I thought you knew?" I whispered like a ghost, leaving regret in its wake.

Ezra pulled back, and a coldness penetrated my bones. "I shouldn't have let this happen," he said as he crawled off of me.

My cold skin matched his sudden cold demeanor. "What's wrong? Are you mad?" I asked, running my hands up and down my arms to warm them. It didn't help. The chill reached my bones.

He closed his eyes and slowly shook his head. He may not have been mad but definitely frustrated. "I'm mad at myself. I should have known."

Okay, so he was mad at himself, but why? "Known what?" I asked.

"That you're a fucking virgin!" he snapped and punched the bed with his fist, right beside my head, making me flinch.

"Calm down, Ezra." I felt colder. The sharp chill stung my skin like frostbite. It was Ezra. I was feeling his anger, his ice-cold anger. "Your anger is making me cold." My chin quivered as I spoke. His eyes were soft as he nodded, looking as if he understood. *Did my anger chill him?*

He laid his forehead against mine. It was an intimate touch as our eyes met, and then, in my mind, I a voice enter like a phantom, softly whispering in my ears.

I can't do this. It was a thought not connected to how I felt. It was Ezra's. I hadn't heard him yet, so it caught me off guard, but it made sense.

"Because I'm a virgin?" To which he responded by sliding

off me.

"You're beautiful even when you frown." He smoothed the wrinkles between my brow with his thumb. *She's... special for... fuck-up like me.*

I shook my head. "You're not a fuck up, Ezra." He looked daggers at me. Was he mad that I had read his thoughts? *Yeah, like I could help it.* "What? You knew this would happen. Spiritual sharing, I think, is what Bones called it."

He groaned and turned away, and I wondered what he was thinking. "I don't do relationships. I don't do love."

You need someone to cherish you. His thought was loud and clear in my mind.

I flipped over, holding my upper body up with my forearms. "Okay, listen to me, buddy. I'm a virgin because I don't have time for relationships either, so hey... we're on the same page with that one. Also...normally...I don't like being touched," I whispered, taking his hand in mine, "but I crave yours."

Too pure. Too special. His thoughts entered my mind the second his facial features softened. A rush of warmth flooded me, and the goosebumps on my skin disappeared. So...his anger chilled me, and his happiness warmed me. Makes sense.

He turned and looked at me. His eyes were kind to my heart. I touched his cheek and ran my hand down the side of his neck until I found home at his heart. "I want this, Ezra. I want my first time to be with you."

He stared at me, his eyes searching mine, and for a second, I thought I broke him, believing he was going to have sex with me. "I am not the man for you," he said. "You don't know the person I am."

"You don't have the right to tell me who is or is not right for me, and besides, like it or not, I know exactly who you are." I crawled on top of him, his hard length snug between my folds. "You are the man I am forever bonded to." I slid my wetness along his erection. "Anyways, what makes you think the next person will be the man for me?"

He groaned before grabbing my hips and flipping me onto

157

my stomach. His large body, a solid wall of muscle against me, pinned me down. His body heat seeped into me, and his breath hissed a sound that was half-pain, half-pleasure. "I don't do love. I don't do relationships." He whispered to me in the crook of my neck, leaving trails of kisses along my ear lobe. His cock grew, positioned at my entrance.

I lifted my ass, daring him to take me. "Neither do I," I said, followed by a whimper. He spanked my ass, and I felt it ripple. If he was trying to make me run, it didn't work. Instead, I pushed my ass into his erection.

"Fuck," he groaned and flipped me on my back, and I squealed in surprise. He nudged his cock between my folds, pausing at my opening. "You want me?" he asked, rubbing the tip of his erection against my dripping wet opening. "You want this?"

"Hmmm," I moaned, wiggling my hips. "Can't you tell?" I reached down, ran a hand down my folds before stroking his cock with my juices. I was wet and ready.

He smiled, making his golden eyes glow like honey in the sun. He bent down; his warm breath tickled my neck as he nibbled my ear. "I need to know you're okay with this?"

I cupped his face in my hands and brought his lips to mine for a tender kiss. "Yes, Ezra. Thousand times… yes."

In one swift motion, he thrust into me, breaking my hymen and filling me completely. His girth stretched me entirely, and I gasped, causing him to pause. "Are you okay?"

Yeah, it hurt, but being connected to him made my heart soar high with bliss. I grabbed his head and kissed him. His tongue filled my mouth. The taste was minty sweet on my tongue. I felt my muscles stretch to accommodate his girth. I squeezed my eyes shut as he slowly pushed deeper and deeper, and when he was all the way in, he paused, moving his lips across my chest, caressing my skin with kisses.

"Ahhh…please…" His soft caresses were torture to my need.

He bit the tip of my nipple, holding it between his teeth as he flicked it with his tongue, and when the tip was red and swollen, he moved to the next.

I grabbed his shoulders and squeezed. His muscles flexed beneath my touch as he moved in and out, the friction penetrating every nerve in my core. His energy pulsated fiercely, pushing waves through my body until it reached my tender flesh. Like a thousand tiny electrical kisses, my clit swelled and throbbed, sending me into ecstasy. I threw my head back and moaned, a sound so raw and loud. Was this extreme sexual intensity typical, or was the bond making the sexual feelings more robust?

I locked my legs around him, gasping and groaning. His eyes held pure pleasure as passion burst where we were joined, and we climaxed together. All I knew was my release and his. My pussy clenched and rippled around him, drenching and clenching his cock. He forced himself to slow down as he spilled inside of me.

He kissed the tip of my nose before collapsing beside me. I snuggled into his chest and wrapped my arms around him. He pulled me closer, placing a kiss on the top of my head. His chest rose and fell in sync with mine, slow and steady. Our energy that had whirled like a tornado between my legs now settled into a calm, warming charge. The electrical particles stimulated my senses, arousing calm and relaxation, and sometime after, we both fell into a blissful sleep.

Chapter Twenty

EZRA

Maeve was safely tucked under my arm, close to my side, as she slept peacefully. I rested my head against the pillows and listened to the soft hum of the air conditioner slowly fading into soothing background noise. I closed my eyes. My limbs were heavy as my consciousness subsided, and my thoughts dissolved into sleep.

Sky was sat next to me. I tucked her pale hair behind her ear and kissed the skin at the nape of her neck. She tasted of honey and smelled of rosemary. Caressing the side of her breast, I wanted to bury my lust deep inside her, but she had pushed me away— a game she had been playing a great deal lately.

"Why," Sky demanded, rotating her body away from me.

I groaned and rolled over, facing the dark sky above us. "I told you why."

The moon was high and bright, providing us enough light to make love securely in the open air. I loved the way the light of the moon made her skin glow with a silvery hue. Gods, I was hungry with lust, but her mind was elsewhere.

She stood, taking her thin shawl with her and wrapping it around her tiny body, hiding from my hungry eyes.

"Why is this so important to you?" I asked. She didn't answer, which was not surprising. I stared at the ground. My thoughts shifted from her to Levi. It was hard to admit that they were so similar and in the worst ways. "You remind me of...." I dared not speak his name to her. She was defensive when it came to him. "His greed will one day be his undoing. You must not follow in his likeness."

Her face twisted with anger and disgust, and I cringed, not wishing to ruin this short time I had with her. If her father knew she was out with a man, he'd have her hanged, so before sunrise, she would have to return home. The leader of the Viking army, he was a ruthless man. He came into Britain and took over the island and established the Kingdom of England. He was now king and ruled with a rod of iron. "He doesn't deserve to be king," Sky said, speaking of her father. "If he dies, we marry, and you can be king." She only wanted me to be king, so she could be queen. She craved the title of power.

Attempting to ease the mood, pushing aside my frustration, I patted the spot she had left and begged her to return. "Please, lay with me, Sky."

She jerked her chin away and held it up. Her pride was unpleasant, marring her inner beauty. "You claim to love me, yet you refuse me a life I desire." She did not raise her voice, but her persistent manner was obnoxious.

Yet, my heart deceived me from what my mind knew to be true. No matter the motive, her tantrums had not once exasperated me enough to stay angry. I stood up and came to her, wrapping my arms around her from behind. "All we need is our love," I whispered, running my nose along her earlobe.

She usually leaned into my embrace, but lately, she had been moving away, adding distance between us both physically and emotionally. "I need his death."

I unwrapped my arms from her waist, letting her go as she had wanted, shaking my head at the audacity of her request. She stomped her foot and turned her face away from me like a child. She sought wealth and power, but this behavior proved she would not make a sound leader.

I grabbed her wrists tight enough to cause her pain. She bit her lip but refused to cry out.

"I cannot," I said. What she asked of me was not possible. Yes, I had the power to give her the sovereignty she so desperately wanted. Hell, I had the power to give her the entire world, but not without regret and consequences. I didn't want what Sky desired. I didn't want power or wealth. I had only needed her. If only she desired me, and me alone, but I wasn't

161

enough. I had no money. I had no power. I wasn't a king.

Angry, she spun around, her body distorted into something different, something...evil. Her skin was no longer a silver hue but black with fragments of ash that floated around her. Her hair was no more, and atop her head were blotches of burned flesh. Her fingers were thin like branches on trees, clicking and twitching of their own accord, and worst yet, her eyes... were gone, leaving in their place bloody, raw holes. She opened her mouth to speak, but smoke poured out like streams of black mist.

"Then I have no use for you," she said, followed by a scream that was joined by hundreds of other screams like the screams heard in Hell.

I bolted up, sucking in the air as if I were deprived of it. I was in bed, and Maeve slept beside me, her legs wrapped around mine. I ran a hand across my sweaty forehead, cursing myself. I hadn't dreamt of Sky in years. Was it because of Maeve and my feelings for her? My mind warned me to stay away. But my heart...

Fuck, this was a colossal mistake. I shouldn't have let it go this far.

I slid my legs out from under hers, and, as slowly as possible, I slid from the bed, careful not to make a noise as I reached down for my pants.

Emerich.

I jolted upright when his name sounded in my head. At first, I thought it was Maeve, but I realized it was her thought I heard when I saw her still sleeping. She must be dreaming about that prophet.

We just had sex. Why was she dreaming about him?

Pain in my palms from my fingernails digging into my skin surprised me. I didn't realize I clenched my fists. One finger at a time, I opened my hands, easing the tension, trying to rid myself of the sudden pang of jealousy. I pulled my pants on, not bothering with the zipper, before gathering the rest of my clothes. I cringed when my belt buckle clanked together, and I froze in place when Maeve mumbled something and stirred in

162

her sleep. When convinced she was not going to wake, I exhaled the breath I had been holding and crept to the door, which seemed miles away.

My hand was on the knob when…. "Where are you going?"

I lowered my head and ground my teeth. "I'm leaving."

"I see that. Why?"

God knew I should not have looked at her, but I did, and fuck me, she was beautiful. Her eyes were slack from sex and sleep, and the light spray of freckles across her cheeks made her look innocent. I felt terrible for having sex with her and then running, but I didn't want her to know that, so I mentally constructed a wall that blocked my thoughts and feelings from her. It wasn't hard. I was one of the lucky few that was naturally capable of blocking the bond. I figured controlling it was like controlling my spiritual energy. It took concentration and a clear mind. Plus, it helped that I already knew how to control and manipulate energy at my will. So effortlessly, I pushed my energy waves into my brain until I felt the sudden disconnection of the bond. A deep-rooted feeling of sadness came over me, my own sadness. The reason, I assumed, was because my body craved the person I was bonded to, and I just cut her off, but it was for the best. I didn't need her to distract me, and I didn't need her distracted by me.

I looked at her. Her features were sad but quickly becoming angry. "Meet me in the gym in thirty. Don't keep me waiting," I demanded before bolting from the room.

I stopped in the hall and fell against the wall, grabbing a handful of my shirt in front of my chest. I breathed in and out, and it burned like my heart was set on fire. Wait? I thought her anger chilled me. What was I feeling? Then, like a flash flood, my body was suddenly cold and stung like ice on my skin. I was hot on the inside, freezing on the outside. I realized what was happening. I was feeling her pain: a broken heart, and that pissed her off.

I turned to go back into the room, but… I thought about Sky. I ran my hand down my face, groaning at the fucked-up situation.

I can't deal with this right now.

Chapter Twenty-One

MAEVE

I threw my pillow after him as he exited. I wanted to fucking scream and give him a piece of my mind! I was pissed off, confused, and hurt, but what about him? What was he feeling? A deep feeling of loss came over me the second he blocked our bond. I hadn't felt such a loss since my parents died.

I threw the covers back and stormed to the bathroom. A bath sounded relaxing, especially before I met with Ezra, or I might just kill the asshole.

I bathed and dressed and headed downstairs, but I needed to find a certain someone—Bones before I went to the gym. I had to know more about this bond, like how to block it. He wasn't in the kitchen, not in the library, and Philip's office was empty. Where was that man? *Probably smelling roses in the garden.* I shook a finger. *Good thinking, Maeve.*

Bones was sitting on the grass in the garden. His eyes were closed, and his hands rested on his knees. Of course, he was meditating. I rolled my eyes. What was up with these guys and meditation?

"Maeve," said Bones. "What can I help you with?"

My eyes bounced around, seeking answers. How did he know it was me? "I…uh…." I wish he'd open his eye and look at me. He was sort of a creepy man but also kind. "I want to"—I sneezed— "excuse me." I rubbed my nose.

His eyes popped open. "You're allergic to the pollen. Shame."

What? Forget about allergies. "How do I control this bond thing?"

He pointed a bony finger at me and wiggled it. "I said it would take time."

"Not for Ezra. He can already block it."

He sat with his shoulders back, chin up, and his hands open and resting on his knees. He was relaxed, like a happy monk with not a single worry in the world. "It's like meditating and trying to connect with your spirit. If you want to connect with Ezra, then open your mind to him. If you don't, then close your mind." He shrugged his shoulders. "It's that easy."

My thoughts froze as I stared at him, shaking my head slightly. "No," I said under my breath. It was not that easy. Holy cow, I was running circles with this man. Bones was in dismay as he crossed his legs and closed his eyes. He was probably closing his mind as if it was as easy as slipping off a wet log. "When Ezra blocked our bond, it made me sad. I felt like he had died. Wouldn't that weaken my spirit?"

"Maeve, you listen here. You are in control of yourself. He cannot weaken your spirit. Only you can. Don't let him bother you. Learn to be better, to be above all the worry and stress, and you'll see, your spirit will grow strong and do things you didn't think possible like block the powers of a spiritual bond."

I squeezed my eyes shut and pinched my nose, growing more frustrated by the second. Didn't anybody speak plain English, free of clichés and needless jargon? The good thing about the DCU was that it was exact, with evident and direct answers and teachings. We trained to fight, to hunt, and to kill. I wasn't used to this spiritual well-being stuff. We never meditated.

I glanced at my watch. *Shit!* It was time to meet Ezra, so I thanked Bones for his help, though it was hardly that. He was so calm with a stupid grin that stretched from ear to ear. He opened one eye, peeking up at me with a look that said, I know what you're thinking. "What consumes your mind controls your life," he said like a calm bird on a Sunday morning.

I wanted to investigate his mind for the answers to

everything. His way of thinking was much more complex and intriguing than most people I'd ever met. "Yeah, well, I'd better go."

"Remember what I said...." Bones called after me as I jogged down the dirt path toward the house.

I threw open the gym doors and strolled in, shrugging off my vest as I made my way to the boxing ring. Ezra was standing with his back to me. "What took you so long."

"I was—"

"Talking to Bones," he interrupted.

"Did you just—"

"Read your thoughts? Yes."

What the hell? He blocked the bond, yet he was clearly privy to my thoughts. "How come I can't hear your thoughts anymore?"

He shrugged his shoulders as if it were a simple thing to do. "Everything, including your thoughts, is connected to energy. Once you learn to control the energy around you, you can control the bond."

I rolled my eyes. "Just fucking stay out of my head."

"Why? You have something to hide?"

In two short steps, I got up in his face. "Maybe I do, Ezra. What does it matter to you? My life is my business."

He took a step closer, so we were practically nose-to-nose. I could feel his breath against my lips. "Keep telling yourself that, sweetheart, but I can't help hearing your thoughts. It's up to you to block them from me." His voice was low and definite. "Which reminds me. About earlier…"

I turned my ear toward him and lifted a brow. I needed to know what he thought about earlier. Did he enjoy having sex with me or not? Was he going to say sorry for being a complete ass? That would be nice but unlike him.

"It was a mistake," he said.

Ouch.

His words hit me hard, and I swayed back on my heels, feeling weak. What could I say? I couldn't find the right words. Don't get me wrong, I had a lot to say, but they were not all *right*.

166

I rubbed my elbow and looked away, hurt and ashamed. I foolishly gave my virginity to this heartless man, and *that* was the honest mistake. I wasn't sure what he was thinking or feeling. He had the control to block me from his thoughts, and his face was blank and passive. I'm sure mine had shame and regret written all over it.

"I am a heartless man, and you should have run." His tone was rock hard, void of any emotion. "I did warn you, love."

My mind went from one thought to another, and my heart went from one feeling to the next. My mind was elsewhere, and my heart was in my throat. How could I train? I had to find a way to kindle the flame that burned for this man. If I couldn't train because of him, I would never make it through Hell.

I rubbed my eyes, wiping away the stupid tears that threatened to fall. *Learn to be better, to be above all the worry and stress.* I thought about Bones' words. *Whatever consumes your mind controls your life.* "You know what, Ezra. I'm not going to let you hurt me."

I closed my eyes and focused inward, visualizing a wall between Ezra and me. *I am better than him*, I said to myself. *I am above the hurt.* A calmness came over me. Then, I felt it like an umbilical cord being cut, leaving me without my primary source of life. I blocked Ezra from my mind and my feelings. It was heartbreaking, but I had to do what I had to do. I felt smug and smiled, knowing the incredible feat I just conquered. Ezra, on the other hand, didn't look happy. His expression was pinched as he glared down at me. "At a loss for words? That's a first," I said, winking at him.

He shook his head, slow and steady. "No... no. I am trying to hear your thoughts...but it appears you have blocked me. Congratulations."

I shrugged my shoulders and smirked. "It was easy."

"Well then, it should be easy for you to control your spiritual energy and fight like a real assassin."

I froze. "Uh...I guess."

His laugh had an edge that made me uncertain. "Well then, I won't go easy on you."

Before I knew what had happened, I was on my back, gasping for air.

Ezra stood over me, his chest rising and falling quickly. "You need to be ready. At. All. Times. Now, get up!" I held my chest, trying to catch my breath. "Get up! Damn it!" He grabbed my forearm and yanked me up.

I jerked my hand from his and pushed him. "That was a fucking cheap shot, Ezra." I was hardly able to get the words out. My chest hurt, damn it! He didn't want me using my blades during training because they were useless in Hell, but after that stunt, I wanted to fucking kill him.

"You need to be prepared for the unexpected. For fuck's sake, Maeve, didn't they train you at the DCU?"

"Fuck you," I spat. "I'm trained to kill and defend myself, and I've killed many jinn and demons, so tell me, why don't I have the strength to fight you? Something isn't adding up."

"I have my secrets." He winked at me.

"Not for long," I said, running at him. I felt his energy waves pushing against me, and when he lifted a leg to kick me, I slid under him, grabbing his ankle at the same time.

He yanked his ankle free from my grasp. "You fight well," he said before thrusting his leg into the air. I ducked under him, barely dodging his foot, but the bastard predicted my move and swung his leg back, kicking me in the nose. "But not well enough."

I fell sideways. My teeth rattled as my shoulders and head hit the floor. Blood exploded from my nose. Even he flinched when he saw red splattered across the floor. I hoisted myself onto my forearms, wiping my nose with the back of my hand.

Ezra folded his arms over his chest. "You should have predicted that move, Maeve. You should have blocked me. Pay attention to the energy around you. It'll help you fight."

I spat blood onto the floor and ran a hand across my mouth. "Fuck. You." I jumped up and lunged at him, throwing punches hard and fast. He closed his eyes, and I laughed, but then he blocked and dodged every one of my hits. My face was warm, and my chest burned, but I didn't stop.

"When your brain sends messages to your body, it pushes your energy around." Ezra leaned back, dodging another hit. "I feel that energy and can predict your movements before your body receives those messages."

I kicked my leg out, but he ducked under it. He popped back up and grabbed one of my fists, twisting it behind me, forcing me around. He wrapped an arm around my neck and pushed my wrist up between my shoulder blades. My back pressed flush against his chest.

"You're weak," he whispered in my ear, sending shivers down my spine.

"You're broken."

He pushed me away from him, and I stumbled forward but didn't fall. "If you think I'm hard on you, wait until you're in Hell." His temper rose by the second. A faint growl traveled from the back of his throat. It didn't sound human, and his face showed anger, regret, and...pain? I wasn't sure, but whatever it was, it was making him weak. It was my chance to act, but a sudden thought crossed my mind, a thought not my own. *Their deaths deserve more.* Ezra's internal voice echoed loud and clear in my mind. Was his mind easy to access due to his growing anger, or did he purposely open his mind to me?

I clenched my fists, believing in the latter. "Say it out loud," I demanded. "Say. It. Out. Loud."

His look was so intense, I prepared myself for another hit. "Their deaths deserve more than your weakness," he said, instead.

Hearing him say it out loud was a punch to my gut. My shoulders slumped. Was he right? Of course, he was, but I couldn't forget what happened. That was something my mind, heart, and spirit would never do, but maybe I could push my memories to the back of my mind. "Fine," I whispered

"Fine?"

"You win." The words fell from my lips so effortlessly, and I felt lighter. *What consumes your mind will control your life.* That's what Bones said, and he was right. I held my past at the front of my mind, close to my heart, never allowing myself to move past it. I would neither forgive nor forget what happened, but I needed to stop thinking about it and let it rule me.

"My anger and regret gave me purpose, but now and while in Hell, I will do my best to keep my past in the past."

"That won't be enough. Suppressing your past and the emotions that follow will only leave you numb inside."

"You would know," I muttered.

His energy pushed against me, and he jumped at me. I pushed out my hand and shoved the energy back at him. He fell, landing on his ass with a thump.

My mouth fell open, but I covered it with the back of my hand. Momentarily, I was speechless. *Did I do that?* I looked at my hands as a smile slowly grew, reaching ear-to-ear. "Nice...." I giggled at my subtle reaction to something so... cool! "Ha," I barked, pointing at Ezra, "I did it!"

Ezra stood, rubbing his ass. "You're getting stronger, and eventually, you'll be able to run faster, jump higher, fight harder, and move objects."

I was running my tingly hands up and down my pants, still smiling like a fool. "So, I guess suppressing my past is enough?"

He shook his head with a grave expression on his face. "Hell has a good way of taking what you suppress and bringing it to the forefront of your mind."

"Well, good thing I have you" — I tapped my temple— "in my mind to keep me focused."

"Don't be ridiculous, Maeve. I can't physically go to Hell and fight the demons and jinn. You will have to fight them, and the only way to do that is with your energy. There is no way around it, love. You'll need to forgive yourself." He rested a hand on my shoulder.

A burst of electricity boomed as the energy pushed outward, hitting the walls and filling the room with thick static waves. "That was...interesting." My eyes were big around. Was that normal?

Ezra's hand slid from my shoulder. "I guess our energy is

strong when we're together."

I smiled as a thought popped in my head. "When this is all over, we should partner up. Hunt demons together. They wouldn't stand a chance against us."

He shook his head and looked toward the door. "I work alone."

I rolled my eyes. "You work alone because you can't or because you don't want to have a partner? Is it The Order? Do they want you to be alone? Or is it Sky?" I blurted out the last question. I wasn't even sure where it came from.

He froze. "How do you know her name? Did you...." He pointed a finger to his head.

"No, you said it in your sleep." I stepped closer, seeking acceptance and trust. He crossed his arms over his chest, closing me out.

In the depths of our bond, I could feel the distant pain he battled. It was a hot sting to my heart, and I realized his mental walls were weak, probably because he was upset. His past had weakened him too, and if he was weak, then I was weak.

"Our spirits are bonded now. Because of you and our bond, I can easily grasp my energy, but I'm afraid that the past you still hold on to will weaken me."

"My spirit can't be weakened. Even Bones told you that."

"Why can't yours be weakened, but mine can?"

He shrugged his shoulders. "Some people are lucky and are born with indestructible spirits."

I rolled my eyes again. "Yeah, maybe angels are born with indestructible spirits, but you're only human."

"Maybe I'm part angel," he said with a wink.

I eyed him, playing with the idea in my mind before shrugging off the notion. "You wouldn't be such an ass."

There was a twinkle in his eyes as he smirked. "I know plenty of angels who are total assholes."

Yeah, he was probably right about that, but we were getting off-topic. "So, who is she?"

Fuck? Why does it matter? His thoughts invaded my own, followed by another stabbing pain in my heart. "She is

171

nobody important." He jumped down from the boxing ring.

"Then, what's the big deal. Just tell me about her. No harm in that. It might help loosen the tension between us and strengthen our bond."

He was quiet. I thought he wasn't going to tell me, but then he cleared his throat, his eyes vacant, as he slumped into a plastic chair by the door.

"She cheated on me. She was the only woman I ever loved, and I thought I knew her. I was blinded. She wanted money and power, something I didn't care for. So, in her eyes, I wasn't worthy enough, so she slept with…."

I slipped under the ropes and down from the boxing ring. "Who?"

His eyes met mine. They no longer had a twinkle in them. "My brother."

I sucked in a quick breath. *Did he say brother?* I didn't know he had one. That must have been a blow to the heart, and I hurt for him.

Ezra stood up so fast the chair fell back, and in two long strides, he was in my face. I had to lean back to add a safe distance between us. The look on his face was wild. I had never seen him so angry. He pointed his finger at me, and I couldn't help but notice his chest rising and falling like a wild cat after a chase. I opened my mouth to speak, but he cut me off. "Don't feel sorry for me." Did he feel my emotions through our bond?

A sudden sadness fell over me, the same melancholy feeling I had when he blocked me from his thoughts. At first, I didn't want to make the bond because of the mind reading, but now, I craved his thoughts.

"I'm glad she cheated on me. She saved me from being weak. I will never trust a woman with my heart again."

"But you're still hurting. Doesn't that—"

"Enough," he yelled.

I stepped back, staring at his eyes. Did they just flash orange? I blinked to clear my vision. It was probably the lighting.

There was no openness to him, no wedge to access his

heart, and his expression was blank. I went up to him and placed my hand on his chest over his heart. I wanted to meld into him, but the look on his face kept me still. A storm of emotion passed over his usually impassive face.

His face was predatory, primal, but not without compassion. I raised my hand and ran my fingers across his square jaw and up to his high cheekbones. His golden eyes, not orange, watched me. I lifted onto my toes and lightly ran my lips across his before kissing them softly. He didn't kiss back, but I wasn't dissatisfied. I felt his cock rub against my belly. I teased him, stroking his bottom lip with the tip of my tongue.

He grabbed the back of my neck and crushed his lips to mine. His tongue eagerly moved against mine, and he tasted like whiskey and mint. He cupped my face and kissed me harder. My front teeth grazed his, but I didn't care. I was lost in his embrace, moaning into his mouth. He slid his fingers into my hair, grabbing a handful and yanking my head back. I yelped in surprise.

His mouth hovered over mine. "I agreed to the bond to help strengthen your spirit. I didn't agree to a relationship." He stepped around me and left. I looked after him, hoping he'd come back. He didn't. And the moment he left, he took a piece of my heart with him.

Chapter Twenty-Two

EZRA

Stepping outside, in Philip's garden, I gathered my thoughts.

Dreaming about Sky brought out the worst in me. Now I was adding Maeve into the mix.

I gave into the beast's desires, as well as my own, and had sex with Maeve.

Bad fucking mistake.

The last person I opened my heart to was Sky, and she broke it. Dreaming about her was a harsh reminder of why I don't do love.

My heart pounded, and my head hurt from grinding my teeth. My beast was clawing at the surface, wanting to get out. I needed to meditate before that part of me got out of control, and I risked the beast staying indefinitely.

I ran my fingers through my hair and tied it back into a knot before sitting in the grass. I crossed my legs, tucking my feet under my knees. Inhaling the fresh salty air, I closed my eyes, breathing in and out.

My chest rose and fell to the calming rhythm of my heartbeat. The beast fell silent, no more nagging in my mind. The energy around me hummed and kissed my skin, giving my soul strength.

"Hmmm," I quietly hummed.

My mind drifted to a quiet place in the woods. It was dark, and I could see all the stars in the sky and hear the crickets' soft chirps and...

"Your energy is buzzing around like a swarm of angry bees."

I opened my eyes and saw that Bones was looking down at me.

"Is there a reason you're here," I asked him?

He pointed with his thumb to the house. "I just ran into Maeve."

"She's ready. Her spirit is strong enough."

Bones shook his head. "Not if you keep weakening it."

"How am I weakening it?" I closed my eyes again, hoping he'd get the fucking hint and leave.

"Yes, your spirit is strong, one that can't be weakened… thanks to your father." But Maeve isn't so lucky. Her spirit is vulnerable, like the rest of the average human population. Your words can damage her."

Did Maeve tell him I was an asshole? Or did he feel her negative energy like he felt mine?

"Alright, then…I'll leave you." He walked toward the house. "Oh, before I forget, Maeve leaves after sundown."

Shit, that was in a few hours.

Damn! I can't believe I told her that having sex was a mistake. *I'm a fucking asshole.* She was going to Hell, partly for me, and she might die. Having sex with her wasn't a mistake. Truthfully, it was special…something I'd never forget. That's what scared the hell out of me, turning me into a certified asshole.

Bones was right. I need to put my shit aside.

I better talk to her and apologize.

Chapter Twenty-Three

MAEVE

It was getting dark, but there was just enough time to catch the sun and soak in the beauty around me. I sat on the lawn between two birch trees. I was surrounded by pink, red, and orange flowers. Butterflies fluttered around, and dragonflies zipped by. *Will Eden be this beautiful, so full of life and color? Will I make it there to find out?*

The moment was peaceful, and I could use those few minutes of peace when...

My cell rang.

Well, there went my few minutes of peace. It was Sal. *Should I answer?* He was probably going to demand I come home and tell me I was childish. But I missed him. Oh, to hell with it. I hit answer.

"Hey, Sal."

"What are you doing?" His tone had bite.

"Hi to you too. Oh, I'm fine. Thanks for asking. Shit, Sal, do you always have to be such a—"

"Cut the shit, Maeve. Don't make me drive to fucking Charleston and drag you back home."

How did he know I was in Charleston? Oh, that's right, I told Emerich. I slapped my forehead. I really needed to watch my mouth. "I wouldn't allow you to drag me home, but you are welcome to come to Charleston."

"You're ridiculous."

"Stop treating me like a child, Sal."

"Then stop acting like one."

"Stop acting like my father!" I bit my lip, immediately regretting what I said. When my parents died, Sal took care

176

of me. He was like my father, but he wasn't. Sal took over after I watched my own father burn to death.

"Where you're going...I can't protect you."

Did he know I was going to Hell? "How do you know where I'm going?"

"You took the vial, Maeve."

Oh, yeah. Forgot about that. Damn. "I'm strong, Sal. I'm not a child. You can trust me."

"You don't understand. You will die." Sal sniffled as if he was holding back tears. "And I can't save you."

Was he crying? Sal doesn't cry. He's invincible. He's my rock. I swallowed the lump in my throat. "I don't need your protection anymore." It was true. I was learning new things and becoming strong. I didn't need him or Winston like I did before. I had grown a lot in just a few days, more than I had in the past fifteen years.

He choked on a sob. He *was* crying, and my heart broke. "I have to protect you...always."

Tears raced down my cheeks. He wasn't going to let this go, and I couldn't let him talk me out of it. Emerich's life was in my hands. "I have to go, but...I love you."

We said goodbye and hung up, and I covered my face with shaking hands. I might not come back, but I knew Sal would be waiting for me if I did.

Soon, I would leave this world and enter a realm where beauty doesn't exist, a place of eternal darkness, full of pain and evil. Shadows crept over the landscape, erasing all the vibrant colors as the sunset behind the horizon.

"It's time to go," I muttered to myself, standing up. I took one more look at Philip's garden before walking through the front door into his house.

Bones, Philip, and Ezra waited for me in the foyer. They talked amongst themselves, but all I heard was wah, wah, wah, like the adults in a Charlie Brown cartoon.

"It's time," said Bones. I heard that loud and clear. "I need the Earth's elements, so we'll be going to the ocean to conduct the ceremony, but don't worry, we'll bring your body back safely."

"Yeah, I'll try not to worry. How far are we from the coast?" I asked.

"A short walk from here," answered Philip.

I nodded. "Let's just get this over with."

Ezra approached me. "Do you have the vial?"

I needed the blood in the vial to unseal the Book of Raziel —of course, I had it. "Will I be able to bring it with me?" I asked Ezra.

"Winston hid the Book of Raziel in Eden, which is in Hell," he said. "So, if this blood is really meant to unseal the book, then I'm assuming he placed a hex on the vial so it can travel between realms."

"I hope so," I whispered, feeling doubtful. Why? I wasn't sure, maybe because luck hadn't been on my side lately.

"Just in case, hold onto it tightly and focus on it. Maybe you can bring a spiritual version with you."

"Vials don't have spirits," I said with a chuckle.

"No, but blood does," he said. "Come on, let's go."

Philip was right, the beach was a short walk from his house, but I wondered how they planned to get my body back unnoticed. As it was, Bones seemed to struggle with his supplies, even with Ezra and Philip's extra hands.

I sat down in the sand. My body was on cruise control, just going through the motions with little thought or feeling. To be honest, I wasn't scared. I wasn't worried. I felt completely numb. I wasn't sure how long I sat watching and listening to the waves when a soft tap on my shoulder told me it had been long enough. Ezra looked down at me.

"Is it time?"

"Almost." Ezra sat down beside me, staring into the dark abyss. "Let's go over your mission."

I gawked at him. "Well, you better make it quick, Ezra. I'm about to go."

"I'll be brief." He looked over his shoulder. "Bones is still setting up."

I looked behind me too. Bones was pushing a torch into the sand.

I looked back at Ezra. His amber eyes were a darker

brown. "Better now than never," I mumbled.

"The first thing you'll need to do is find the River Styx. You'll see spirits wandering the edge of the river, but they're harmless."

"How do you know?"

"They're lost and confused souls that died before their time."

"What do you mean by 'died before their time'?"

"If a soul dies before they're meant to, they'll wander the river, waiting for their final judgment."

"So, if I die, I'll be stuck wandering the River Styx?"

He shrugged his shoulders. "Probably."

"Who determines when we're supposed to die?"

"God."

I looked up at the blanket of stars twinkling above us. "Then why do we die before our time if our life is already set by God?"

"We have free will to do what we want, and sometimes our choices lead us down the wrong path."

A crab crawled out from under the sand and scuttled over to the ocean. "We're in charge of our own destiny," I muttered, watching as the crab let the tide take him away. I could relate to that little ol' crab as I would let Hell take me away from this world.

"Anyway," Ezra continued, "when you get to the river, you will have to wait for Charon. Do you know who Charon is?"

"Yes. I read about him at Philip's underground room."

"He'll come floating in on his boat and take you to The Shade."

The lights on a ship twinkled in the distance. "What if Charon doesn't let me on his boat?"

"Show him your nevus."

I looked at Ezra. "How do you know all of this?"

He smiled; his grin was devilishly sexy. "Like I told you before, love. I know a lot of things." He said the same thing the night we met in the graveyard. Wow. That night seemed so long ago. "When you get to The Shade, remember to keep your spirit strong. That place can be damn depressing, wandering around alone. It's no wonder souls retreat into their minds. It's a way to escape the gloom of The Shade."

"I don't want to get trapped in my mind, Ezra. I would relive the night my parents were killed over and over for eternity. I just know it."

He rested his hand on my knee. "Calm down, Maeve. What you think you're experiencing is in your mind— a memory. Just remember, Hell is like a dream."

"If Hell is like a dream, then will I feel pain?"

"You will feel pain. You'll bleed, see, hear, and talk too. You'll even be dressed."

"Okay…that's weird. But how? I mean…how do I feel pain?"

He grabbed a handful of sand and let the grains slip through his fingers. "When you're in Hell, pain is a reflection of your memories. What you remember pain to be on Earth. It's complex." Ezra shrugged his shoulders dismissively, "but what would Hell be without pain?"

"Pain is a state of mind?"

"Yes, pain is a manifestation of the mind. Monks set themselves on fire and don't feel any pain."

"Mind over matter?"

"Some call it a mind. Some call it a soul."

"Wait, so when Bones said he'll send my soul to Hell, technically, he meant he'll send my mind there?"

"Pretty much. Just remember, to survive Hell and the pain you'll feel, you need to remind yourself that it isn't real— it's all in your mind."

"Good to know," I said under my breath.

"I know. I should have prepared you better." He gazed out into the night. "I was caught up in my own shit." There was a moment of silence. We both stared ahead at the waves. "Philip told me something else, right before we walked here.

"What?"

"When you reach the Gate of the Sun, Philip believes that it will take you to a cave, and according to some old manual, your journey is far from over. The cave will be pitch black," he glanced up, "darker than a sky without stars." He looked

180

at me. "You need to hurry and reach the end before sunrise."

Sunrise in a cave that is situated in Hell, how was that possible? I wanted to ask, but given the situation, it was necessary. "What happens when the sun rises?"

"If the light from the sun touches you, you will turn to ash."

A shiver ran down my spine. "I hurry... or burn?"

"Philip isn't certain, but that's what he believes to be true."

I looked inward, thinking about the cave and its mysterious deathtrap of fiery doom. "Or burn?" I felt a subtle heat brush across my face. Just thinking about burning to death brought forth symptoms of a flashback. Thankfully, Ezra kept talking, a well-needed distraction.

"Yes, Maeve, you might burn, but let's move past that. Philip and I discussed Eden a little. We don't know much, but we both agree the book will probably be by the Tree of Life. It's a powerful tree and guarded as well."

"Okay, so how do I find the Tree of Life?"

"You'll need to find the heart of Eden."

"And how do I find the heart of Eden?"

"Follow the rivers."

"Rivers?"

"You'll see when you get there," he said.

"What do I do when I get the book?"

"Hold the book close to your heart and say, *Mans darbs šeit tiek darīts.*"

"What does that mean?"

"My work here is done," he said with a smile followed by a wink.

I lifted a curious brow. "Why are you nice to me all of a sudden?"

"I was dealing with my own shit, but someone reminded me that being an asshole isn't necessary or helpful." Ezra winked at me again. His hair was tied at the base of his neck, but a rogue strand escaped the knot and hung over the apple of his cheekbone, making him look as sexy as hell. I couldn't help myself. I reached up and tucked it behind his ear. He closed his eyes, and I saw his jaw muscles tense. I let my hand fall to the cold sand, feeling I had upset him, but then he opened his eyes and looked at me. I saw within the depths of his golden eyes a reflection of love and respect. "Having sex with you wasn't a mistake," he said. "In fact, it was an extraordinary moment, which scares me, and like always, I ran from my feelings." He was making tiny circles in the sand with his finger.

I sat a little straighter. "What feelings?"

He dusted off his hands. "We can't have a relationship, and when this is all over, we will have to go our separate ways, but...I'll always think of you."

A sudden rush of warmth settled in my heart, lifting my spirit. I was feeling Ezra's emotion. An emotion he most likely denied having, but there it was for me to feel.

Ezra loves me.

I felt it in my heart. I was sure of it, but I'd wait for him to realize it.

I bowed my head to hide my growing smile. I didn't want him to see my sudden happiness for fear he might run again. However, I couldn't hide the sudden burst of my energy that vibrated around me in thick waves, pulling the tide in until it touched my boots.

Ezra followed the wave with his eyes. "Do you see that? Your energy pulled the tide in."

We smiled at each other, and I shrugged my shoulders as if it was no big deal. "You made me happy." *Because you love me.*

"Earlier, after I was an ass to you, Bones came to me. He said my actions would weaken you," he shrugged his shoulders, "He was right."

"Oh," I said with a sigh. Okay...so, Ezra may not love me romantically, but he did care. I guess...that's good enough.

"Are you okay?" Ezra asked, and thankfully, as I didn't want to answer him, Bones called us over.

Ezra sighed. "It's time. Are you ready?"

I kicked the sand and lifted my shoulders. "As I'll ever be."

Philip and Ezra stood by the ocean's edge as I walked up to Bones. He was dressed in a black cloak that blended into the darkness. He stood by one of the six wooden unlit torches he had pushed into the sand. Ash was sprinkled between them, forming a pentagon shape into the center of which he directed me to. Then, he opened a thick book that looked heavy and old. "One thing you need to know," he said. "You have an hour to do your thing."

What the fuck! "Why?" It didn't seem possible.

"Your body starts to die after an hour."

"Time is different in Hell, Maeve," said Ezra. He moved closer, standing next to the ash on the ground. "Time moves slower in Hell. A minute here is an hour there."

I opened my mouth to say something, but Bones threw his arms up, and all the torches lit up at once. I was surrounded by flames. They whipped around in the air, taunting me. My eyes zeroed in on the one closest to me. *No, Maeve. Not now.* I clenched my hands into tight fists until my nails dug into my skin. It was coming, a flashback.

Bones started chanting, and thank the good Lord, he distracted me from my consuming thoughts. I couldn't understand what he was saying, but his voice was loud and demanding. The ocean grew fiercer, pushing the waves into the sky. They looked like claws trying to grab me. Ezra and Philip stood beside a rock for shelter.

Hot tears stung my cold skin, and I shivered uncontrollably. Everything was a greyish hue, and there was a buzzing sound in my ears. I tried to stay standing, but my limbs were heavy. I hunched over as a burst of pain shot through me, and I crumpled to the ground. Usually, my nevus healed my pain, but not this time because I didn't have any physical wounds. Something was pulling my soul from my body, and it hurt. An electric shock exploded through me, under my skin, in my veins, attacking my organs. The neurons in my brain fired angrily as they fought to stay connected to my body. It didn't work. My heart stopped beating, and I struggled to breathe.

Then, I saw him. He appeared to be ten feet tall and

carried a scythe. Like the jinn leader in my flashbacks, he wore a heavy hooded cloak that covered his head and hid his face. I shielded myself, scared and in pain, as he approached. I curled into a fetal position, waiting for him. He got closer and closer until finally, he stood over me.

The Grim Reaper.

Chapter Twenty-Four

MAEVE

Shaking uncontrollably, he stood over me—the Grim Reaper. His large hood shadowed his face, and his black coat swept over my trembling hands. Red glowing eyes stared into mine like a promise to bring me pain.

Move, Maeve. Run.

I couldn't move. My bones were like jelly.

Closer and closer, he got. My heart raced. Nowhere to go, to run, to hide, so I sank deeper into the sand, chanting to myself, words of hope: *please, help, stop, leave.* But nothing could change what was about to happen.

I covered my head with my arms. Still, I could get a peek between the gap under my armpit. Ezra was yelling, but what was he saying? I wasn't sure. I couldn't hear him over the ringing in my ears. Philip held him back by the arms, and damn, I've never seen Ezra look so pissed and desperate. He fought Philip, struggling to what, to come for me? Bones... he stared past me, at the Reaper. I saw his mouth moving, but I couldn't hear what he was saying either.

The ground shook, and I started sinking into the beach. "No, no, no. I change my mind. I don't want to go." But it was too late. I was being pulled into the sand as if I were inside an hourglass. It didn't take long, maybe seconds, and I was up to my shoulders in sand. The Reaper reached for me with a long-crooked finger, touching my forehead, right between the eyes.

The sand swallowed me whole.

***

Cold.

I was cold, yet the air around me was hot as if I was lying by a fire, making me sweat and shiver at the same time. There was no fire as all over was darkness, and it was quiet —too quiet.

I wasn't at the beach anymore.

I was in Hell.

"Hello?" I croaked, coughing and wincing from soreness in my throat. I inhaled or at least tried to. My lungs wouldn't expand. Breathing was an instinctive reflex of the mind, but I didn't have a body. Ezra said Hell would be like a dream, and maybe it was a manifestation of my mind, but I felt my body: limbs, eyes, chest, lungs, hands, fingers, and feet, just the same as I felt pain.

My legs wobbled. I could hardly stand. Damn, I was right, everywhere was darkness, no light to be seen. Oh, good, Lord. What was out there lurking in the darkness? Demons and jinn, closing in on me.

What's that? A shuffling noise followed by a sad moan sent shivers down my spine.

What the fuck?

I wasn't alone. More moans and cries echoed all around me, some near and some not so near.

I crouched and reached for my blades.

Fuck! No blades. *What do I do?*

I couldn't stand here, hoping the gate would come to me, and of course, I didn't have much time to waste. Reaching out in front of me, I felt around, slowly shuffling forward. A trail of moans orbited around me, getting closer and sounding sadder. I froze. *What do I do?* I had to find the River Styx, that was what I had to do, but it was so damn dark. I couldn't see an inch in front of me.

Sss.

I jumped. *What was that? A snake?* It sounded like one.

I turned my head left and right. Nothing. It had to be behind me. Inch by inch, I slowly turned. "Holy…" I covered my mouth with the palm of my hand. A cloud of glowing red vapor floated right in front of me. It stood out against the

186

blackness and moved with purpose as if it had a mind of its own.

I cocked my head like a curious puppy and reached forward. *Touch it. No!* I stepped back, adding a safe distance. It followed me, moving closer and closer. Wisps of heat brushed my face. I wasn't sure what to think of it. It wasn't scary and didn't seem threatening, but something about it didn't feel right either.

It grew longer, stretching into a snake-like shape. I kept my eyes on it while shuffling backward. *Should I run?* I jerked my head right. *What was that?* Something swept across my hand, but it was too dark to know for sure.

I kept a steady eye on the mist. It grew longer and longer. What was it doing? In a sudden whip of motion, too quick for me to follow, it slithered down my throat, spanning outward and down my entire back. I fell to my knees and grabbed my throat.

Oh, God, it's inside me. It was moving under my skin and in my body like a million tiny spiders. I slapped my legs and arms with a smack. "Get out!" Smack. "Get out!" I collapsed to the ground. The mist was heavy, and I crumbled. Shit, how could vapor be so heavy?

"The weight of your sinsss pushesss hard, Yesss?" I heard a stream of hissing voices. "Your sinsss consume you."

Was the vapor a manifestation of my sins? Were the demon voices coming from the vapor inside of me?

"We know your sinsss," the voices said in unison. "Your anger is red like blood, and your guilt is heavy like stone."

Get up, Maeve. I tried, but each time I fell.

"Your anger isss red like blood, and your guilt is heavy as stone."

"Shut the fuck up," I screamed, and a surge of moans and cries that were different from the voices — less malicious — resonated around me.

"Your anger isss red like blood, and your guilt is heavy as stone."

Why do they keep saying that? I started humming, a weak attempt to drown out the voices. It didn't work. They got louder.

Maeve?

Go away! I thought.

Mae…it…Ezra…open…me…

"Ez…Ezra?" Oh, thank god. He was talking to me through our bond. It worked, but…his words were choppy.

"We know what you suffer," hissed the voices again. "Your anger isss red like blood, and your mind is heavy with guilt."

"Fuck," I cried, pushing on my ears with the palms of my hands as if I could force the voices out of my brain.

…Ma…focus… voice…

Ezra? Can you hear me?

He didn't respond. Shit. Shit. Shit. I was confused, so confused… did he want me to focus on the demon voices?

"Your anger isss red like blood and thick with guilt."

"Shut up," I whispered.

…list…en…my…voice…

A light bulb sparked to life in my head. I knew what I had to do. Ezra said to listen to his voice and his voice only. The demon voices were feeding me lies, trying to weaken my spirit. I had to block them out and concentrate on Ezra's voice.

I focused all my energy on the bond I had with Ezra. I thought about our connection, forcing my brain to open to him.

Maeve? Can you hear me? Listen to my voice.

Ezra?

Maeve?

Oh, Ezra…. I closed my eyes just for a second, allowing relief to flow through me. *Ezra…oh, God…I don't know what it is, but it's inside me.*

What's inside you?

A cloud or something… Maybe a vapor or a snake. I don't know for sure, but it slithered down my throat. It's so heavy and pushes me down.

"We know what you suffer," sang the voices.

It isn't a physical weight, said Ezra. *It's a reflection of your inner demons weighing you down.*

"Your anger isss red like blood, and your mind isss heavy with guilt." The voices repeated the same line over and over on an endless loop.

I can feel your anxiety through our bond, Maeve. You need to calm down. Focus on the mission. Tell me where you are.

I don't fucking know. I thought. *It's too fucking dark.*

Listen, Maeve, your inner demons are also blinding you. You need to strengthen your spirit. Self-forgiveness, Maeve. It's the only way to ease the weight and see what's around you.

I couldn't forgive myself, not so quickly, but I could focus on my positive traits like my strength, courage, and desire to save Emerich. Immediately, I felt lighter.

This time not collapsing to the ground, I stood and looked around. I was able to see, and my jaw dropped at the scene before me.

There were bodies everywhere spread out forever in all directions, some moaning and crying.

The bodies were bent into unnatural positions. Their eyes were open but lifeless, their backs curved into U shapes, their heads twisted backward until their chins rested between their shoulder blades, their mouths were open wide enough to fit my foot, and their legs were bent like grasshoppers.

A field of crumpled souls, I thought.

You're in the first realm, said Ezra, *The Shade.*

The crippled souls, probably those around me, stay stuck in darkness for a hundred years until they are reborn for a second chance of redemption. Yes, this was good. In this realm was the River Styx. I had to find it.

Maeve? Ezra's voice echoed in my mind.

"I'm here," I said aloud, and a handful of crippled souls turned their heads and looked at me.

Shit!

What's wrong? Asked Ezra.

The souls just stared at me with a desperate look in their eyes. They seemed harmless, yet I stood, ready to fight, just in case they attacked. Sal taught me to always be on my guard. No matter what or how innocent a person or thing appears to be.

How do I find the River Styx? I asked Ezra, eyeing the souls who were looking at me.

Close your eyes and listen.

Okay, I thought.

I closed my eyes and focused on my hearing. He was right again.

I hear it, Ezra. A faint sound of flowing water. Just up ahead.

Good. Follow the sound.

I stepped around the crippled souls, careful not to step on a hand or foot. I wasn't sure it mattered since we weren't physically in Hell, but stepping through them seemed rude and simply weird.

As I made my way through the maze of souls, I had to stop to refocus every so often. The cloud of vapor still stirred within me, trying to push me down. I wouldn't let it. I kept reminding myself of my strength and will to help Emerich. My positivity kept the cloud light.

After what seemed like an hour of walking, the sound of rushing water became louder. I was getting closer, and it was to my right. Excitement rang in my heart, pumping adrenaline to my muscles. With the sudden burst of strength, I sprinted forward, taking advantage of my body's energy, stepping around various body parts.

The river was just up ahead, and I didn't slow down until I saw it.

Orange flames flickered behind the mountains at the edge of this realm, adding depth to an otherwise wide river of blackness.

I've found the river, Ezra.

Is Charon there? he asked.

I pushed my way past the weary souls that walked along the river's edge. Ezra told me that they were harmless, so I didn't fear them. I looked up and down the river. There was no sign of Charon and his chariot.

Not yet. The river was murky and thick, and more souls

floated along with the sluggish current. They also seemed harmless, much like the souls on land.

I sat on my knees, right at the edge of the water, and watched all the different souls drift by. Some were old, some young, and they were all from different parts of the world. So far, it seemed that Hell was a melting pot of different ethnicities. Not one soul was the same, and the only things that brought them together were death and sin.

One soul caught my attention. A young girl in an antique dress and apron captivated me, and for some reason, I reached for her. I was desperate to pull her free from the black water, but she shook her head. A frantic look strained her dull-colored face, and I yanked my hand back.

"Do you want to become one of us, stuck in this river for eternity?" asked the girl.

I shook my head. "What happened to you? How did you get here?" I asked her.

"I tried to save someone from the river too. Now, look where I am. I float in this damned river forever." She blew out of her nostrils like a little angry bull.

I couldn't help but smile, though her situation was not something to be happy about. The girl was cute and a refreshing break from all the hell around me. "So, tell me how a kind girl like yourself ends up in Hell?"

"What makes you think I'm kind?"

I shrugged my shoulders. "You just saved me from becoming stuck in the river forever. That's something only a kind person would do. Don't you agree?"

I saw her slender shoulders rise and fall as she slowly exhaled. "If you must know, I was murdered."

"You were murdered?" I slowly shook my head. "You died before your time."

"That's right, but I'm not worried. I'll get out of here one day. I'm sure of it." She smiled a grin that reached from ear to ear. "My judgment will come soon."

As the girl swam away, I watched her go until she disappeared into the darkness. She was obviously a good person. She had enough consciousness to save me, but I wasn't sure if she would ever meet her judgment. Once you're in the River Styx, you're there for an eternity, but she didn't deserve to be in there. Maybe something Bones could do, use a spell or some sort of voodoo magic, free her from Hell.

I sat and wrapped my arms around my legs, resting my chin on my knees as I watched in a daze at the poor souls passing by. Their reflections and clothing told their former stories, and I imagined who they were in their past lives. If I died in Hell, I would end up here. The thought made me cringe, but I imagined it would be better than the last two realms of Hell.

It was hot and dreary but also peaceful. The spirits, both on land and in the water, didn't bother me, and the river's current was slow and calm. But that didn't last, like the calm before the storm passed.

The souls in the river grew frantic. They darted to the top of the water, reaching for nothing, and then my nevus burned.

"He's here," said a soul. I shot up with a burst of energy. The chariot floating our way.

Charon is coming.

Chapter Twenty-Five

MAEVE

I was gazing down the waterway when I spotted an old, ghostly soul pointing at me with a shaky hand. He was tall and wore tattered clothes.

"Always knew I'd end up here. Never good enough," the old soul said. "You'll go to Hell, boy, actin' like that. That's what my ol' man would tell me but never did listen. I didn't believe in the ol' Heaven or Hell thing." He had a toothless grin. "I was wrong."

I smiled back at the old, toothless soul. That was all I could think to do. After all, what could I say? 'Yep, your ol' man was right.'?

I shook my head and looked toward the river. Charon was getting closer. He was tall, bone-thin, and dressed in a long, black cloak like the Reaper, but he sported a long, white beard. The souls in the water clawed at the boat, angrily and helplessly, and I cringed when Charon flung his whip down upon them. *Snap.* Oh, Lord, please don't hit the poor girl. I searched for her, but there were too many floating souls.

When Charon came to a stop, the souls on the land rushed past me, moaning and crying. They were like a pack of sad dogs. What was up with all the moans? Did they suddenly lose their ability to speak?

"Your toll," Charon demanded, his voice low and lifeless.

The toothless, old soul passed his token to the ferryman. Charon held his boney hand just above the coin until the metal absorbed into his flesh.

What I didn't understand was why these souls wanted to pass to the next realm. What if they were placed into a more painful situation? Did they think that there might be a better life beyond the mountains? Maybe it was an uncontrollable drive to find their place in Hell. Either way, I dreaded what was beyond those mountains. I knew my journey was only going to get worse.

Hey, Ezra. Charon is here, I thought. *What do I do? I don't have anything to give him.*

Show him your nevus. Ezra answered right in time as Charon pointed a long, crooked finger at me.

Please work, I silently pleaded to myself as I held my breath and lifted my wrist to show Charon my nevus. Holy shit. How was I just seeing this? My flesh was see-through, just like the wandering souls at the water's edge, and it was like I didn't have any innards. I couldn't see my bones, muscles, and veins. I was a ghostly reflection of my body, and my nevus glowed a faint red.

Charon zeroed in on my nevus, scrutinizing it, and images of "what could be" flashed through my mind. What if he rejected me? I would fail, and Emerich would die, that's what, and the apocalypse would destroy the world. I had a lot riding on me, but to my relief, Charon nodded his approval. I blew out the breath I was holding and stepped on board.

I settled into the back of the old, wooden boat. The wood was rotting, dozens of bent and rusted nails stuck out, and there were holes, too many to count, dotting the entire floor. I could see through to the souls swimming underneath. It was a wonder how this boat stayed floating, but then there wasn't anything solid in Hell—right?

Charon cracked his whip, and the sound echoed above all the groans and moans of the miserable souls in the water. He whipped their hands and faces, and they retreated into the abyss. The boat pulled ahead, taking me to my next destination. The souls on the shore continued to roam the water's edge, and I couldn't help but wonder how long some of them had been there, wandering and waiting for Charon's return. I was thankful my nevus worked, and I got on the boat as quickly as I did, as I only had a few short hours to finish my job.

***

As we floated deeper into Hell, heat from the flames whipping angrily behind the jagged mountains stung my ghostly skin, and my nevus burned more than usual like a dozen bee stings. I forced myself to focus inward, deep within myself. The pain was in my mind, and with that thought, eventually, the burning faded. Hell was fucking weird. It was like a dream, just as Ezra said, but with real pain and the fact that I couldn't wake up.

After what seemed like an hour, the boat started to slow, and my eyes bounced around, taking everything in. Charon stopped before a bridge made of what looked like bones and sheets of thin leather.

Where were we? Was this the Divide?

The toothless, old soul stared at me with wide eyes.

Was this my stop?

I looked to Charon for direction, and he pointed his bony finger, ordering me off the boat. I swallowed my fear and stood, nodding bye to the toothless soul, and the moment I stepped onto the bridge, I choked.

Draped over the bones wasn't leather. It was skin. The smell was putrid, and I could taste the rot on my tongue.

I could feel pain, feel my body, and now I knew I could smell and taste. I thought back to an old dream I had as a child. A spider fell and landed on me, and though it was a dream, I distinctly remember feeling the spider's hairs on my skin. That shows how much our brain manifests what we believe we feel, hear, taste, and see relating to our environment.

I bolted forward and fell the second my feet touched the soil. My palms dug into the dirt. "Mother fucker," I spat, pushing myself up while rubbing the mud from my hands. I turned to see what made me fall when I noticed Charon, his boat, the river, and the bridge were gone. A sickening feeling settled in my gut as I felt alone, and once again, I had to adapt to a new realm and find my way through this part of my journey.

Ezra? I called to him, hoping our bond still worked.

Where are you? he asked, and I breathed a sigh of relief. Hearing his voice brought me comfort.

The Divide. I think.

All around me were nothing but tall trees as far as I could see in every direction. A blanket of heavy mist settled on the mossy ground, and every shade of grey painted this landscape murky. But it was better than a field of deformed souls.

You need to find the door. Ezra's words echoed in my mind.

I'm on it, I thought.

According to a map Ezra had found at Philip's, the door appeared at the other end of The Divide. So, I started walking in the opposite direction of the River Styx.

There were so many trees towering over me. Tall and thin, they reminded me of white birch but with little branches and no leaves. I walked and walked and walked. The mist, cold and damp, swirled around me, leaving me disoriented and confused. Still, I walked.

Deeper and deeper, I went into the shadowy forest where the mist was thicker. I could hardly see. Not that it mattered as everything looked the same.

Doubt was slowly sinking in. I did my best to push it back, but the more I walked and walked and walked, the more pissed I became. The darkness that tunneled down my throat in the last realm grew heavier and heavier as doubt finally settled.

How can I save Emerich if I can't fucking save myself?

Defeat, gnawing at my will to keep going.

I pressed on my temples, attempting to clear my doubts and push forward, but it was getting tough as a haze seemed to cloud my brain. At times, it took a colossal effort just to remember my mission.

Maeve? It's Ezra. You need to settle down. I can feel your anger. Remember, The Divide is meant to drain your spirit and make you doubt yourself. Focus on your strength and stay confident.

I sputtered like an old water faucet as doubt still lingered. The darkness inside of me pushed down, adding weight to my back, and the more steps I took, the more exhausted I got.

I had to find the Gate of the Sun, and according to Ezra, my blood would be enough to open the door. "But what fucking door?" I held out my hands and spun around. "There is no fucking door!"

I had been walking for hours.

The trees...were they getting taller? Maybe I was shrinking.

I rubbed my temples with my fingers, frustration gnawing on my judgment. I was officially losing my mind. I looked ahead, wishing to see something—anything— I saw nothing but miles upon miles of trees and mist.

I sank to the ground, feeling hopeless. *Why? Why? Why?*

Maeve? A voice sounded in my mind, but it was distant.

"Who's there?" I asked, popping up with hope, literally spinning in a circle to find someone—anyone.

There was no one. I frowned and slumped back down, holding my head between my knees.

Maeve? It's me, Ezra. Speak to me.

My thoughts froze. *Ezra?*

Yes, he said.

I stood up again. *How did you do that?*

Do what?

Read my mind?

What? Fuck, Maeve, it's me, Ezra

Ezra? Oh, shit. Like a slap to the face, I remembered.

Where have you been, Ezra? I've been wandering for hours, but everything looks the same. I don't know where I'm going or what I'm doing.

Time is different in Hell. A minute here spans hours there. Listen, love, The Divide is draining your spirit, making you forget the reason you're there. Focus on your mission.

How's that going to help?

Focusing on your mission like finding the door, getting to Eden, saving Emerich. Those thoughts will keep your mind focused and prevent you from forgetting.

"What was that?" *Did the mist move?* I asked myself.

What? Asked Ezra.

I held up a hand and felt no wind, yet the mist swirled, became thicker, and wrapped around me.

Maeve, don't lose sight of who you are. You're a strong fighter, and you're in Hell to save—

Who's there? I listened.

"We are dead," said a voice.

Suddenly my nevus seared my ghostly flesh, and I cried out in pain. "We are dead because of you." It was a woman's voice.

Mom? It sounded like her.

It's a trick... Ezra's words faded as I tuned him out. I didn't want to hear him. I wanted to hear Mom.

"You were a curse," the voice said again, scorning me.

"Mom?" I choked on a sob. The tears that had gathered on the rims of my eyes fell, leaving wet trails down my cheeks. I was desperate to know. Was it her? My heart swelled with hope. It had to be her.

I pushed the burning pain to the back of my mind, willing it to fade away by focusing on one thing—my mom. I went running toward her voice but fell forward, landing on my hands and knees.

"Fuck," I spat. "What's going on?" I tried to stand, but my legs were rooted in the ground like two tree stumps. I hoisted myself up with my hands until I was standing.

"Hopeless," whispered another unknown voice, a man's voice.

"No!" I screamed, yanking and pulling my legs. The roots started to snap and break, so I pulled harder and harder. One last sharp yank and I was finally free.

I sprinted forward, desperate to find Mom, but faltered, skidding to a stop. Where was I? The trees were gone. The fog was gone. I wasn't in The Shade. I stood in a hallway that expanded on and on with no end, and all was quiet and still.

I cocked my head like a lost pup. "This place looks familiar." I scanned the area, searching for answers: pictures hung on the walls, an old Persian rug with a stain by the top of the stairs, green trellis wallpaper, and decorative mahogany crown molding. "Oh, no…." My words faded away as the memory popped into my mind. I knew where I was.

My home from childhood.

"Mom!" It was her. I knew it. I sprinted down the hall and ran and ran, but the farther I ran, the longer the hall grew.

"Hopeless," said the man's voice.

I slowed but didn't dare stop. "Dad?" It was my dad's voice. It had to be him. If it was Mom, then it had to be my dad too.

"Hopeless," he said again.

I wiped away the tears that blurred my vision. "No," I whispered, running faster. My thoughts scrambled to understand. I was in Hell. Why was I hearing my parents? Were they doomed to Hell? Did I doom them to Hell?

A scream echoed, bouncing off the walls like thunder. The glass from the pictures on the walls and the light bulbs under the lamps exploded. I faltered, covering my head with my forearms. The shards were sharp, cutting my skin. I had no choice but to stop and pull out a piece of glass when another scream sounded.

I jerked my head up, ready to run, ready to help them, but the hall was gone. I was somewhere else. I knotted my hands in my hair and pulled. "No, no, no." It was like I was in a dream. My surroundings kept changing without warning or reason.

I stood in a room. A bedroom, to be exact.

At one end of the room was a bed and at the other….

I fell to my knees as nothing could have prepared me for the chilling sight that materialized before me.

At the other end of the room were five figures cloaked in ash. Their faces were shrouded by large hoods. Tall and menacing, they stood towering over a very frightened and younger…me.

My breathing stopped as things were happening too quickly for me to process. "No, it can't be." I rocked my head back and forth with my eyes closed, taking a moment to deal with what was happening.

You can do this, Maeve, I thought to myself. I needed a mental push—some encouragement. After all, here in Hell, I was my only hope. *You're stronger now and wiser. You got this.*

With a deep breath in and a slow breath out, I took a hesitant step forward. "Oh, God. No." I bit my trembling lips to stop myself from crying. How much more could I take before I collapsed, defeated? The sight caused me pain— physical pain. My eyes stung, my head throbbed, and my chest felt torn from the inside. I reached deep within myself and pulled all the strength I had, but damn it, I couldn't believe my eyes. Standing still and quiet, looking away from the cloaked figures and at the bed Mom and Dad were tied to was my younger self.

With unsteady feet, I managed to squat before her. She didn't see me. I was invisible to her. Poor thing was fragile, and her big, round eyes reflected fear. The pain in my heart brought tears to my eyes once again. I wanted to hug my younger self and tell her it would be okay because, in a few short minutes, her entire life was going to change.

Mom and Dad were going to die, and I was going to be forced to watch— again.

I stood with tight fists at my sides, and I glared at the jinn. Their cloaks were black, and smoke swirled from the ends of their robes. Each wore a hood, hiding their faces, except for one. He reached up and pulled back his hood, revealing his face.

The one I referred to as the leader looked the same as he did in the flashback I had in the gym: tall, with black hair and fiery eyes. He reminded me of Ezra. He had the same sharp angles, square jaw, and straight nose. He was handsome and mysterious.

"Please, don't hurt her," Mom cried, pulling me from my thoughts.

"If you lay a hand on her, I swear to God..." yelled Dad. The look on his face was wild. I'd never seen him so upset. He yanked at the ropes, trying to free himself. It was a futile attempt.

The leader held up a hand. "Now, now, now. We all know God can't help you here," he said with a hiss.

My younger self stood, frozen in place. Her young mind was too innocent to understand what was happening. The leader glared down at her, smiling like the grinch— greedy and evil. He didn't see me either, I was invisible to everybody, but I wondered, could I stop him from killing my parents?

I would undoubtedly try. That was for damn sure.

Screaming like a wild animal as all my old pain and pent-up emotions rushed to the front of my mind. Adrenaline pumped through my veins, and I ran at the leader. I was ready to wrap my hands around his neck and strangle him, but instead, like a glitch in a video game, I ran through him.

My arms swung around in large circles as I skidded to a stop, a foot away from hitting a wall. "FUCK," I screamed, punching the wall with a crack. My heart dropped as reality sank in. I couldn't stop him. All I could do was watch like a hopeless child.

The leader leaned over and whispered into my younger self's ear. I don't know how, but I heard what he said. "You can save them. All you have to do is come with us."

"No," I whispered, "That can't be true." I slapped my hand over my heart and stumbled back. The sheer shock from his words stunned me. That bit of information was new. I had never heard the leader tell me that before now. My flashbacks and dreams only showed bits and pieces of that night. The rest of the details I had repressed or pushed to the back of my mind, but in Hell, those memories were free to haunt me.

I could have saved them. I knew it. I fucking knew it. Deep down, somewhere lost in my subconscious mind, I knew I could have saved them. But I didn't.

I. Did. Nothing.

But what about now? I slapped my forehead, feeling stupid. I couldn't touch anything without going through it. But... my younger self could.

I ran over to her and fell to my knees, disregarding the pain that shot through my legs. She stood still, watching the horror play out before her.

I wanted to grab her shoulders and shake some sense into her, but I couldn't. "Please. Go with them," I begged.

She did nothing.

I balled my fists until my nails dug into my skin. I wanted to fight. I wanted to kill. I hated being useless— unable to help. "Do something," I yelled, hoping that somehow, someway, I'd be able to reach my younger self, to penetrate her mind. Maybe on a subconscious level, I didn't know, but I was willing to try anything.

I opened my mouth to scream, but my mom yelled instead. "Don't listen to them, Maeve. Runaway."

"Run, Maeve. Go hide," Dad screamed.

I punched the floor with my fist. "NO," I screamed. Fresh tears gathered in my eyes, and my chin fell to my chest. It was hopeless. I was hopeless. I collapsed to the ground, unable to bear my body's weight.

Time seemed to slow down, and a sudden feeling of heaviness expanded to my core. For my entire life, I wished I had saved them. I felt guilty because I didn't, and now I learned they never wanted me to.

"No. Don't listen to them. Please, save them, please," I mumbled, tears and snot wet my face. I sat back on my heels, lifted my arms to the heavens, and screamed.

I refused to believe what Mom and Dad were saying.

I sprang to my feet, waving my hands in front of my younger self. "Look at me!" I shouted. "Why can't you see me? Damn it." My face was warm as blood rushed to my head. "Don't fucking listen to them. They're lying," I screamed so loud my throat burned. "Save them. Go with the jinn. You can save them. You can save Emerich."

If she went with the jinn, Mom and Dad would live. I would never end up at the DCU. I would never meet Emerich, and he would never get sick. Everything would change, including my past, my present, and my future.

"End this now." I choked on a sob.

My younger self trembled. Fear consumed her.

The leader's face changed into something evil. His eyes

turned red, and his teeth grew long and sharp. My younger self didn't notice him. Her eyes were glued to Mom and Dad.

"All you have to do is come with me, little one," said the leader.

"What's the matter with you. Don't just stand there," I yelled at my younger self again. I was fueled by anger, trembling just like her or more. "Save them...please," I whimpered helplessly.

"No!" yelled Dad, and for a second, I thought he was talking to me, my older self.

I turned toward him and my mom. "Why, Daddy?" I asked. Tears were pouring from his eyes too.

"Don't go with him. We'll be okay, love bug," said Mom.

She was looking at my younger self, begging her to run, but it seemed as if she was talking to me too. It shattered my heart. Oh, how I wished I could speak to her again. I would tell her I loved her. I would tell her that I would save her. I would find a way.

My younger self stood, frozen with fear and confusion. I knew because I was her.

"Take us instead," screamed Mom.

"Take us," repeated Dad.

I fell to my knees next to my younger self. I couldn't believe what I was hearing.

A shadow crept forward, shrouding us in darkness. The leader stood tall, looking at my parents. "As you wish," he said, snapping his fingers.

"No," I screamed, jumping to my feet.

Mom and Dad's bodies lit up the dark as flames engulfed them.

My younger self screamed. She tried to run, but the leader placed a hand on her shoulder, forcing her to stay in place.

"Mommy," my younger self cried. "Daddy."

I pointed a shaky finger at my younger self. "She's a fucking child," I yelled. "Just take her." I jumped in front of the leader's face, yelling at him. It was hopeless. Nobody heard me.

The leader smiled an evil grin that spread from ear to ear.

"We'll meet again, little one," he said before disappearing.

"I'm here now. Come and get me, fucking asshole." I turned around with my arms up and out.

Maeve, talk to me. What's wrong? Ezra tried to reach me, but I didn't care to hear him. I wanted to save Mom and Dad.

I ran to the bed, reaching for the ropes to untie them, but my hands went right through them. I tried again and again. It was hopeless. I was hopeless. I couldn't save them again.

I watched in horror. It was all I could do.

Every detail was clear and accurate, more so now than ever before in my dreams or flashbacks. Their skin sloughed off in flakes. Their eyelids burned quickly, but their eyeballs boiled first before bursting. Once their skin and surface tissue melted, their muscles caught fire, exposing their organs. They exploded and burned away one by one, and after what seemed like hours, Mom and Dad were skeletons with carbonized tissue.

I wrapped my arms around my stomach, feeling nauseous. My younger self walked past me and climbed into bed with Mom and Dad. I held a shaky hand to my mouth as a sob escaped my trembling lips. I shook my head and closed my eyes, failure consuming every inch of my soul. My younger self laid in a fetal position next to Mom and Dad and cried.

That was the worst three days of my life. I had slept between them without food, water, and sunlight for three days. The memory choked me, making it hard to breathe. I remember being so hungry, my stomach ached, but I refused to leave their side. I had to use the bathroom, but I didn't leave the bed. My younger self was scared they would disappear, leaving me alone.

One night, I tried talking to them, hoping they would talk back. They didn't, and my younger self cried some more. I think deep down inside my tiny mind and body, I wanted to die too. I had no reason to live.

Emerich wouldn't allow that to happen. He had a vision of me lying between my burnt parents. The thought brought more tears to my eyes. When Sal came to rescue me, I was nothing but skin and bones. Too weak to move. Too weak to talk. Too weak to even open my eyes. I was nearly dead.

I ran the back of my hand across my eyes to wipe away the tears. What now? Would I relive the night again?

Slowly, the scene faded away, and again I stood in darkness.

"Why didn't you save us?"

"What?" I asked, looking for Mom. I turned around and saw her standing behind me. "Mom?" My voice shook as my lips trembled.

She looked at me with one charred and bloody eye, while the other was nothing but a black hole. "You didn't save us." Hatred seemed to seep from her very core, making her look evil. My dad appeared out of nowhere, standing by her side.

"Daddy?" I stammered.

Unlike Mom, he had grief instead of hatred. His skin melted off his bones, dripping to the floor. His scalp had patches of burnt hair, and his eyes were all white with no pupils. I reached for them, but they backed away from my touch.

"I-I'm so, so sorry." I held my palms flat together, pleading for their forgiveness.

Mom held up a hand, cutting me off. "We suffered because of you." Her words drilled a hole in my chest, leaving me empty inside. I whimpered uncontrollably.

"I...I..." I didn't know what to say. I hung my head, ashamed of myself. I could have saved them, but I didn't. That night, the jinn wanted me, and for some reason, they couldn't take me unless I agreed to go. By the time I did agree, it was too late.

It all seemed so unreal, like an evil plan, carefully constructed, leading me here to this exact moment. None of it made sense. Nothing ever made sense. Not in my life. I wished I were like the rest of the world, blissfully unaware of the supernatural that lived among us.

"They didn't want us. They wanted you," Mom and Dad spoke to me in unison. Tears of blood dripped from their eyes. "They wanted you!" they screamed, and suddenly my nevus burned so badly I thought it caught fire.

I squeezed the wrist that had my nevus and nodded. The jinn wanted me, not Mom and Dad. *They can have me,* I thought. Then, as if I called them with that single thought, the hooded jinn appeared again.

***

Who can have you, Maeve? Ezra was talking to me, but I was lost in my regret and shame.

One of the jinn stroked my mom's head as if to praise her for a job well done. She looked up, gleaming with pride just before she and Dad caught fire.

"No. Not again," I screamed, darting toward my parents. I wanted to save them. I tried to save them, but the jinn leader appeared and held me in place, forcing me to watch Mom and Dad burn again. "Please," I begged. "Don't do this." Mom and Dad's skin burned, revealing bones and muscles. I sank to the ground, feeling vulnerable. "Stop! Burn me instead. Take me," I whispered. I'd prefer to burn than be doomed to watch my parents die over and over.

Like a switch being flipped off, the fire disappeared. All that was left were my parents, shriveled and charred. Their mouths hung open as they died, screaming for help. Their lips burned away, leaving nothing but teeth. The smell in the air was of charred flesh and burnt hair. It was the smell of death.

"You for them?" asked the leader.

My chest was empty and heavy at the same time. I slowly stood, keeping my eyes on my parents as I said, "If I stay here, will you free them?"

A jinn stood behind the leader, snickered and hissed, but the leader held up a hand, quieting the laughing jinn. "Yes," said the leader.

I stood taller and held my head high. "Then, take me," I said. "But, before you do, tell me one thing. Why me?"

"You don't realize how strong you are," said the leader. "I wanted you on my side. You would have made a great weapon to use against those who try to ruin my plans."

"What plans?"

The leader shook his finger. "You asked me to tell you one thing, and I did."

Maeve, what's happening? Ezra sounded desperate, but the jinn leader interrupted.

"You're out of questions, puppet," he said, opening his mouth, revealing rows of pointy teeth. I closed my eyes and tilted my head, exposing my neck. The jinn leader grabbed my shoulders and pulled me closer to him.

Stabbing pain in my neck caused my skin to burn as if fire flowed through my veins, reaching every inch of my body. But I refused to cry, scream, or run—it was my turn to die.

Chapter Twenty-Six

EZRA

Maeve, talk to me.

Fuck. Why wasn't she answering?

I took great care of her body while she was away, carefully placing her on a bed of ice, but damn, it wasn't easy seeing her in such a way: cold, pale, and stiff. The sight brought me pure pain.

Fuck, Maeve. "Will you hurry!" I was talking to her soulless form, praying to the Gods that she would answer.

Philip and Bones were in the room with me, but they stayed back, giving me space. It was a good idea as the beast in me grew anxious every second away from Maeve.

Please, love, tell me what's happening. I froze, listening and waiting for her to respond. Nothing. Not a single damn word.

"Fuck!" I punched one of the wooden desks in Philip's basement. He and Bones looked up at me. Philip was concerned, and Bones...well, he always had a fucking smile on his face. I waved, letting them know that I was okay. Bones continued talking, but Philip eyed me closely like I was some ticking time bomb—I was.

"Argh. Fuck!" I crumpled to the ground, hitting my fists on the floorboards, cracking and denting the surface. My body burned as if I caught fire. What the fuck was happening? Bones and Philip ran over to me, but I pushed them away.

I ground my teeth as pain gripped every nerve in my body.

"It's the bond," said Bones. "Being connected to Maeve, he is feeling her pain."

"She must be in trouble," said Philip. "Ezra, you need to

focus. Think past the pain."

"She...AHHH..." The burning was so fierce. I could hardly talk. "She... isn't... listening to me."

"You have to do something before you both die," Philip shouted, grabbing hold of my shoulders and giving them a firm shake. "Say something that will get her to listen."

I gritted my teeth and worked past the pain, focusing on the bond. *Maeve, please...I'm hurting...what's going on?*

For...them, she said through the link.

Her words penetrated my mind through the sharp pains in my head. "I hear her," I whispered.

I don't...understand, Maeve. I talked to her while clenching my fists and pressing them to my aching eyes.

I...can... free them, she said. Her words were broken from pain.

Free who?

Mom and Dad.

Free them from what?

Death.

No. No, love. That isn't possible. You...you can't free anyone from death.

I was prepared for this moment. I knew, if Maeve got lost in her mind, the guilt she still held over the death of her parents would be her weakness. I was in awe of her devotion. She was sacrificing herself, longing to save her parents, but she couldn't. She had a false hope, and I kept repeating the word *no* in my head.

She was pure. Too pure for someone like me.

A tear slid down my cheek.

I pushed myself up, stood on my knees, and caught the tear. The tiny drop of liquid rested on my finger. I closed my eyes to savor the moment. *So many years.* So many lonely years, and this was my first tear in over a century. I cried once in my life. It was both heartbreaking and pathetic.

When Sky cheated on me and broke my heart, I cried. I cried over a worthless woman, a sign of weakness. From that day forward, I closed my heart and grew hard. I wasn't necessarily mean to women. I'd sleep with them, and they would want more, but I'd refuse them. I broke many hearts, including Maeve's. I thought I was protecting my own. I was rude and refused to let her into my life. I foolishly thought all women were the same— greedy.

But not Maeve. She was different. She was kind and pure and worth my tears.

She was worth giving my heart to.

I kissed the tear away and closed my fist, holding it to my heart. I cried for Maeve; because of her. It wasn't weakness; because of her, it was strength. I was no longer scared to open my heart to a woman, and that took strength.

I tilted my head back, facing heavenward, with my eyes closed, smiling like a fool. I allowed my heart to swell. My nerve endings tingled, drowning the burning in my veins. My spirit grew more robust than ever because of my newly found happiness.

Maeve, listen to me. Your parents sacrificed themselves to keep you alive.

My jaw dropped, and my arms went limp as understanding sank in. How did I not see this before? The answer was right in front of me.

It was at that moment, it all made sense.

Maeve's parents sacrificed their lives for her.

And, when the sacrifice is made, the Eda is born.

Was it possible? Could Maeve be the prophesied Eda?

Maeve's spirit was naturally strong. And though she kept it weak because of the pain she held over her past, it was naturally pure and thus, according to Bones, had great potential.

I held still as the truth washed over me.

One day, soon, she will obtain god-like strength.

Maeve will save the world. She will stop Levi.

She was the Eda.

Your parents sacrificed themselves for you, and when the sacrifice is made, the Eda is born.

She still didn't respond.

Damn it, Maeve. Are you listening? You can't let them take you. Levi will end the world, and only you can stop him.

Chapter Twenty-Seven

MAEVE

I'd given my life to free my parents. Me for them; that was the deal.

I would finally be brave and save Mom and Dad, but then Ezra said that I couldn't free someone from Hell through our bond.

He was probably right.

But I was still going to try. *Me for them.* I thought of nothing else. I was going to free my parents. Save them from death.

Ezra spoke to me again. This time his words *Levi*, *world*, *end*, *Eda*, and *stop him* penetrated my grief-stricken mind.

I wasn't sure if Ezra was passing his energy to me through our bond or if it was his encouraging words that gave my spirit strength. Either way, I knew one thing for sure.

If I was the Eda, then Emerich, the world, and even Ezra depended on me.

I couldn't let them down.

Whatever remorse I had felt faded away and was replaced with an incredible urge to fight.

My energy hummed with power and strength just under my skin and around my body. The charged particles moved violently, just waiting to explode, and, like the sun, I could gather all that charged energy and use it.

I jumped into the air, the charged energy propelled me, and when I landed—sleek, demanding, and vengeful—the energy exploded out like a bomb, and the jinn flew back. I didn't have my blades to use, but I had another weapon.

Me.

I stood before them, my skin crawling with energy and humming with power.

The leader's face turned back to normal, making him attractive again. "You could have saved them," he said. His tongue slithered out like a snake's as he licked the last drop of my blood from his lips.

"You're lying," I snapped, wiping the blood from my neck.

He backed away from me and wrapped his arms over his puffed-out chest. "I refuse to fight you. Wouldn't want to ruin that beautiful face."

"Fight me, you bastard!" I couldn't free my parents, but the least I could do was avenge them by killing their murderer.

I threw my hands up, pushing my energy outward like a sonic boom. All the jinn flew back, except the leader. He stood firm, unaffected by the waves of my powerful energy.

The leader shook his head and chuckled. "He taught you well."

Was he referring to Ezra? Did he know him? It made sense. After all, Ezra was a jinn hunter. "Fuck you!" The ground beneath me started vibrating.

He spat on the ground. "I don't fuck humans." His eyes rested on my breasts. "But I can make an exception."

Pieces of rock and other debris floated up and around me as if I was their center of gravity. I wanted to stop and stare, but that would make me look like a pupil in the eyes of a leader. "Shut the fuck up and fight."

He popped his knuckles, eyeing the floating rocks around me. "I don't want you dead, puppet."

I stood on the balls of my feet, ready to kill. "Why?"

He smiled, and I licked my lips, lusting over the sensuality that oozed from him. "I want you to be mine."

His words entered my ears and sent a shiver down my spine. I wasn't sure if I was disgusted or turned on. Regardless I wanted him dead. "Ha. I'll never be yours."

Mimicking me, he licked his lips, and I hated to admit it, but flashes of him kissing me entered my mind. "Maybe not today, but one day, you'll be mine." He vanished into a cloud of black smoke, and I was left facing the other jinn.

Why did he keep disappearing? He was just about to drink me to death, and then he refused to stay and fight. Was this some sort of sick game to him?

"Where'd you go? Stay and fight like a man, you coward." Low, sexy laughter drifted in the air, making me hot all over, but he didn't come back.

The other four jinn stood in the shadows until their leader disappeared, and now they crept closer, circling me.

"Come on, assholes. Bring it," I spat. With my spiritual strength and Ezra by my side, I was ready.

I swung my body around and kicked my leg out full force. The floating rocks and debris shot out, hitting the jinn like bullets. I froze, dumbstruck. *Did I do that?*

Another jinn snuck up behind me. I side-kicked him, and his head jerked back with such force that, if he had been human, the impact would have snapped his spine.

The other two jinn charged me, and I jumped just in time to kick one in his face, breaking and smashing it. I felt the crunch and grimaced at the gruesome sight. The other one punched me in the gut, and I fell on my ass. He jumped on top of me and slapped my face.

Whack. I saw a flash of lights behind my lids.

I ground my teeth, pissed off. The jinn dared to smile down at me, showing me his sharp fangs.

"I don't think so, fucker," I said, bringing up my legs and wrapping my thighs around his neck. Growling, he grabbed my ankles, trying to pull my legs apart, but I was strong. I managed to fling him off me with just my legs.

I bounced back up, with my fists raised and ready to strike.

One of the jinn I had kicked down jumped back up and attacked. The fight continued. I would hit, kick, punch, and they would keep getting right back up. I was proud and powerful, and my energy held me steady, but I couldn't last forever. I didn't have time.

How do I kill them? I asked Ezra.

You can't, he said. *You can only make them disappear.*
How?
By focusing on your task. Focus on the door.

It was hard to focus on anything between kicks and punches, but I focused on my mission.

I thought of Emerich.

I thought of Ezra.

I thought of my parents.

I closed my eyes and spoke softly to myself, hoping that somehow Mom and Dad heard me. "Mom, Dad, you sacrificed your lives to save me, and I will not let your sacrifice be in vain."

They gave their lives to save me, and for that reason, I was sorry. I had been sorry for a long time, but it couldn't be forever. I couldn't let their sacrifice be lost by my guilt. I had to let it go— I had to forgive myself.

When I opened my eyes, the jinn were gone.

Instead, I was looking at a massive door.

It was thick, tall, and it floated a few feet above the ground. I ran my hand across the intricate carvings. In the center was a sun with flames flaring out in golden swirls. There were also rivers, trees, and angels carved between the flames.

I pumped my fists into the air and danced around in a small circle, too giddy to control myself. *I found it, Ezra. The Gate of the Sun.*

Maeve, I forgot to tell you. If you see—

Thwack.

Something hit me. I flew backward and hit a tree.

Lungs or not, my chest burned like the air was pushed from them.

With my hand on my chest, I pushed myself up, catching my balance when something dripped onto my shoulder. It was wet, gooey, and foamy. I lifted my head and saw the beast that hit me.

Cerberus, the guardian of this realm, was a three-headed dog. He was slightly taller than me, but he was a mass of pure muscle. All three heads moved independently, had eyes that glowed red, and a mouthful of sharp teeth. They snapped their jaws, exposing rotting gums that smelled like spoiled fish. All three licked their dagger-like teeth and zeroed in on me. Strands of sticky foam dripped from their mouths. I doubted my spirit would have enough strength to fight this demon—the most unnerving beast yet. And I'd seen a lot of disturbing demons.

I wanted to run but had to fight, and the charged energy still within and around me made that possible.

After a few heart-stopping moments, Cerberus lifted all three of his heads, closed all six of his eyes, and howled. That was my chance.

I lunged forward with as much strength as I could muster. Cerberus stood on his hind legs, and when I got close enough, he came down on me, shoving me with his front paws. I flew backward and landed on my ass hard. Pain shot down my back.

"Fucking dog," I spat, pushing myself up. I could feel the energy around me. It was thick and vibrated with power. I used it to propel myself into the air. I swung my leg out, ready to kick Cerberus, but I wasn't fast enough. He lifted a paw and slapped me on the arm. His claws sliced my skin, and this time I landed face-first on the hard, cold ground. I was injured badly, making it a considerable effort just to stand.

I grabbed a handful of dirt and jumped into the air, using my energy to give me strength. All three heads turned toward me, and before I landed, I threw the dirt at them. The soil didn't fly like bullets like last time, but it slowed the beast down.

The hound wiped the dirt from its eyes using its paw. It was my chance. I spun around, ready to kick the closest head, but I was too slow. Another head bit me with his rotting teeth, tearing into my flesh.

Lifting my free arm, I hit the head with my fist, scratching and pulling its ears until it flung me. I slid across the dirt, gravel digging into my flesh. The bite burned as if the dog's saliva was poison. I held my arm and clenched my teeth,

215

rocking back and forth like a baby— it hurt that bad.

"Fuck!" I screamed, knowing I had to get up. Now, I was easy bait, lying on the ground like a dog treat.

With my good arm, I hoisted myself up, stumbling around. I hid behind the nearest tree. My head was spinning, and my stomach was queasy. Closing my eyes, I tried to even my breathing until my vertigo stopped.

A few seconds later, when I felt better, I examined the damage. Holy shit. It was worse than I thought. There was nothing but muscle and bone, and I bled severely. That's why I was feeling lightheaded. I was losing blood.

What do I do, Ezra? He's too strong.

Show him your nevus.

Why? It doesn't work. It only glows.

It glows so jinn and demons can see it.

What the fuck! What he said sounded insane.

What's my nevus going to do?

Do it, Maeve.

Fuck!

I stepped around the tree and stumbled toward Cerberus. I could collapse at any minute, so I had no other option than to listen to Ezra. I lifted my hand, but it fell limp at my side. I was weak and could hardly move, let alone hold up my arm. I had to do it. I refused to fail this far into my mission. With all my might and a loud scream, I swung my arm up with my nevus facing out.

My nevus glowed red, and all three of Cerberus' heads saw at it. Oh no. I was seeing dots and hearing a buzzing noise.

I was going to pass out.

I fell to my knees and tried to focus on my breathing. "This isn't real," I whispered. "It's just in my mind." I can't bleed without a physical body. It was in my mind.

Understanding that my pain was nothing but a manifestation of my mind seemed to help. I didn't feel like passing out anymore, but damn, it still hurt. The pain felt so real. It was hard to convince my mind otherwise.

Showing Cerberus my nevus had better work because I

didn't think I could fight anymore. He was going to destroy me, and even with a strong spirit, his strength overpowered mine.

"Please," I whispered. "Just let me go." Then, as if he heard my plea, the dog sat and bowed all three of his heads submissively, as if I was his queen.

I sat still, gawking at the dog. It worked. How? Did my nevus give me some sort of authority of him?

I clenched my arm and stood up. Cerberus didn't budge.

Why is he bowing to me? I asked Ezra.

That night in the grave, I told you that a nevus is a marking spell meant for the elite inHell.

So, he thinks I'm a powerful jinn?

He thinks you're related to the Grigori.

Remind me to remove this nevus when I get back.

Don't be ridiculous, Maeve.

He was right. I was thankful for my nevus. It had saved my life numerous times.

I crept forward, one tiny step at a time, until I reached the door. Along the way, I kept an eye on Cerberus. If he attacked me, he'd kill me. I was too weak and tired to fight, and I lost a lot of blood from the cut he gave me.

Okay, I'm at the door, but there's no handle. What do I do?

Your blood, Maeve. Your blood will open the door. Remember the map?

Yes, I remember.

I had blood— a lot of it.

With the hand I used to cover the bite, I reached for the door. I bit my lip as doubt kicked in. I couldn't believe that I had made it this far. Something was bound to happen— something terrible. What if my blood doesn't work?

I closed my eyes, my breathing slowed, practically came to a stop, as I placed my bloody palm on the door, right in the center of the sun. Not a sound. Not a movement. I slowly opened one eye, peaking at the door.

I let the breath I was holding out and opened both eyes as relief sank in. The door opened. Inside was so dark, I couldn't see a damn thing, but the door had opened, and I was about to enter the next realm. The final realm.

According to Ezra, I had to pass through the cave before sunrise or burn to ash. This was my last task before reaching Eden. With my arm throbbing and bleeding, I prayed I made it that far.

It worked, Ezra.

I knew it would, he said. I could sense his joy and relief.

I didn't bother looking back at Cerberus. I just wanted to put that dog behind me and never think of him again, so I stepped through the door and into the darkness. I flinched when I heard it close behind me. This is it; I'm stuck now. There's no turning back— not that I would.

I felt around, trying to get a sense of my surroundings. The ground was uneven, and parts of the rocky wall jutted out. Damn it. If I weren't careful, I could trip or walk right into a protruding rock. I rolled my eyes. *As if the bite wasn't enough.*

I held my wounded arm close to my chest and started walking. With my other hand, I felt my way around. Every so often, I would trip over a rock or a hole in the ground, but nothing slowed me down. Until…

Smack. I ran into a wall.

I felt around blindly, first to the right and then left, until I found an opening. I continued like this for what seemed like an hour or more. The throbbing in my arm caused a throbbing in my head.

I wished my nevus worked because I could really do without the pain.

How are you, Maeve?

I need to rest.

You don't have time to rest.

I leaned against the wall, breathing heavily. *Just for a minute,* I thought. I was moving slowly, yet my lungs couldn't keep up. It had to be the bite. It still bled, dripping blood all down the front of my body.

No, Maeve. Keep going. The sun will be coming up soon.

My arm hurts.

Mind over pain. Keep your spirit strong, love.

I let my eyes close, j*ust for a minute.*
Move, Maeve! Keep going!
Oh, no... I thought.
What's wrong?

I leaned forward to get a better look. I saw the outlines of rocks and the rough terrain at my feet. I turned and glanced over my shoulder. A light shone at the opposite end of the cave. A sudden burst of fear sprang to my chest.

If the sun touches me, I turn to ash. I thought.

Move your ass. Now! Ezra screamed in my head, activating my fight-or-flight reflex.

I was hurt. I was losing a lot of blood. I was tired. But I ran as fast as I could. I kicked up dirt and tripped over a rock, falling to my knees.

Keep running, Maeve.

I forced myself up but stumbled over my feet and fell again. This time, I scraped my knees, hands, and forearms on the gravel. A pain shot through my wounded arm, forcing a scream from the pit of my stomach. I started breathing heavily, like a pregnant woman in labor. "Come on, Maeve. You got this. You got this." I tried to get up, but my legs gave out, and I collapsed to the ground.

"The bite is. Not. Real. Damn it" — I tried to get up again — "Aww... come on. Get. Up. Fuuuck!" I can't. My limbs were too heavy to lift. My vision was dimming, and the buzzing noise was back.

Death seemed more appealing as the light behind me grew brighter. I didn't know how much more time I had.

Ezra? I said.
What?
I'm not going to make it.
Keep moving, damn it! Desperation crept around the edges of his words.

I clutched my now pulsating arm. *I can feel the sun on my back. The warmth feels good.* There was silence for so long I thought I had lost our connection. *Ezra?*

I'm here, love.

Talk to Emerich for me. Tell him I'm sorry. And tell

Salazar that...that I love him. And...and...I'm sorry, Ezra. I failed.

Keep going. Don't give up.

He must know that I couldn't, yet I heard the desperation and felt his sadness and regret through our bond. It chilled my skin.

I can't.

Damn it, Maeve...

The sun's light shone brighter. *It's too late, Ezra.* There was a long moment of silence.

Please. That word was like a soft whisper in my head.

I closed my eyes, listening to Ezra's desperate cries until they faded away.

Chapter Twenty-Eight

EZRA

A sudden chill freezing my insides, and a wave of loss swept over me. My spirit died a little as the energy around me dwindled to a soft tremor.

Maeve? Maeve? Answer me. Nothing. *Please, Maeve.*

She was dead. If not, she was a breath away.

Maeve. Please, love, please.

She didn't answer. She was gone.

I fell to my knees and cupped my head in my hands, wailing for the first time in my life. I cried, begging someone to help. I was clutching myself when Bones and Philip stepped behind me. I shook my head, trying to tell them to leave, but I couldn't form the words.

I shouldn't have let her go. I should have stopped her, found another way to get the book. I stood, nearly stumbling over my feet as I stepped to her body. "She's gone," I whispered, gently sweeping her hair away from her face. "She's dead."

"How do you know?" Philip asked.

"The bond," answered Bones.

"I shouldn't have let her go," I said.

"She wanted to go," said Philip.

"No! I should have found another way to get the book." Pain raked my body, and I trembled everywhere.

Philip stepped up behind me. "There was no other way, Ezra."

I swung around, stepping into his face. "There's always another way," I growled. My voice, laced with anger and anguish. The beast was breaking the walls of my sanity. I didn't bother to stop it.

"Not always, boy," said Bones in his calming voice.

"She's too good for death," I said, flexing my fingers into fists. I started hitting my chest harder and harder with every punch until I fell to my knees, coughing blood. I wanted to feel numb, but no matter the pain I caused myself, I could not relieve the hurt in my heart.

I thought of possible ways I could bring her back. I cupped my hands and looked up to the heavens. "Please, please, please. I'll do anything. Just bring her back." I was willing to try anything. Bones, the witch doctor. He could help.

I sprang to my feet and spun around, eyeing the one man who could save her. "Do something." There was a reflection of sadness he held in his eyes, but I didn't give a fuck. "Bring her back."

Bones muttered a line of words, but all I heard were no, can't, sorry. I didn't buy it. I walked to him in two giant strides. The beast in me wanted to scare and fight, and for the first time in a long time, I embraced the darkness. "Bring. Her. BACK!"

I screamed the last word, making the walls shake. My anger and desperation were beyond any sort of rational control. In my vision, I saw red and orange.

I was lost.

The beast was out.

Bones didn't waver. He stood taller and looked me dead in the eye. "It. Is. Not. Possible. She is beyond my reach, boy."

Faster than Bones could probably comprehend, I seized him by the throat, holding him up until our eyes were level with each other. "You should have told me this before sending her to Hell!" I yelled with an evil growl.

"You knew that already, Ezra," said Philip, trying to calm me, but his words were lost to me.

The beast didn't listen.

The veins in Bones' eyes were breaking under my strength, yet I squeezed his throat tighter, choking him. He clawed at my hands, struggling to breathe. I didn't care. I was going to break his neck.

The beast was high on anger, influenced by the pain I felt in my heart.

Maeve was mine. She was the calm to the beast that lived within me, constantly clawing at my will and rationality. She was calm. She was the balance. She was the one I needed to tame the beast inside of me. I needed her. The beast needed her.

If I didn't calm myself, the beast would take over indefinitely.

Philip stood beside me, calm as always. The beast growled, warning him to stay away. "There is a way to save her," said Philip. "Through the bond, you can give her your life— your spirit."

At first, his words didn't sink in, but when they did, the beast calmed. The orange and red in my vision faded, and one finger at a time, I let Bones go. I stepped away, letting him collapse to the ground. The poor man clutched his throat, unable to speak, gasping for air.

Philip squatted beside Bones, resting a hand on his shoulder while still looking at me. "Are you willing to give your life?"

His words drifted through the still air, embracing my broken heart. I regarded Philip, noting the grief in his pale eyes.

Thanks to Philip, I knew what I had to do. It didn't occur to me sooner because grief and anger prevented me from thinking clearly. I was going to save Maeve.

Even if it meant giving her my life.

"Leave me," I whispered.

Philip nodded and helped Bones from the floor.

I closed my eyes and breathed in and out and long and slow to calm myself.

Philip said there was a way to save Maeve. Mere words had never calmed the beast. Never. It took extreme focus and spiritual strength. But, as soon as the idea drifted from Philip's lips, I opened my eyes, and the beast was gone. Submissively, the beast retreated to the back of my mind, where I mentally keep him at bay.

I looked at Maeve. I had better hurry before it was too late. "Philip," I called. The door opened, and Philip stood in the doorway. I placed a hand on his shoulder. "I have to do this. She's the prophesized Eda."

Philip didn't look surprised as he nodded his head. "I had a feeling she was."

"She needs to kill Levi. Will you tell her that?"

"Yes," he answered as he sniffled and wiped his nose. "You're willing to sacrifice your life for hers?" I nodded, and he smiled. "You love her."

"I do."

"Okay," he said, grabbing one of the blades that I placed beside Maeve's still body. Then, he pulled me into a tight embrace. "You're a great man, Ezra. You always had a big heart," he whispered right before he slid the blade between my ribs, hitting my liver.

I stumbled back, holding my side. Philip wore a somber expression before leaving the room. Blood gushed out, making my heart beat faster, leading to more blood loss. I stumbled over to Maeve's body; my vision was fading in and out, followed by a loud white noise ringing in my ears. I moved Maeve over so that I could lay next to her. I grabbed her hand and held it to my heart. Then, I closed my eyes and focused my mind on her as my blood and soul spilled from my body.

Chapter Twenty-Nine

MAEVE

A light charge of electricity hummed over my skin, awakening my nerves. I opened my eyes and blinked.

Is that...? Were my eyes deceiving me? It wasn't possible...was it?

"Ezra?" I was hardly audible as my life was a breath away from death. I felt it in my lungs, the heaviness and ache from a single word.

Ezra knelt before me, caressing my cheek. His fingers left a crackling sensation in their wake. "It's me, love." He kissed my lips with the softest caress. A delicate halo outlined his body as energy radiated from him, prickling my skin. I reached forward and touched his collar bone. The energy gathered around my hand, shining brighter as ripples of it, absorbed my fingers and palm. I felt stronger.

"Am I" -I swallowed the dry lump in my throat- "on earth?"

"No," he whispered into my mouth.

I licked my lips, and I could taste his breath on my tongue. "How are you here? I thought you couldn't come to Hell?"

"I'm here for you, love," he said, rubbing his lips along mine. "I couldn't leave you in Hell, not in this dark and God-forsaken cave."

We were in the cave. Ezra had come to me because I was tired, weak, and ...

Dying.

I smiled, it was weak, but I still grinned. *I'm not going to die, not anymore. Ezra came to save me.*

Between our bodies were thicker waves of energy. They

crept up my arm and into my skin. My body took what he was offering like a starved animal, greedy for more.

"You're saving me. Your energy is going into me." He nodded. "How?"

The smile on his face was big and bright, reflecting happiness, but his eyes were somber. "My love for you is strong."

I wrapped my arms around his neck and pulled him closer to me. "Then, I must thank you."

He used his tongue to open my mouth, and I tilted my head, letting him kiss me deeper. His tongue caressed mine, slowly and passionately. I ran my fingers through his hair, pulling him closer.

His energy, like a static charge, stimulated my nerves. It hummed and moved like a billion different atoms, ready to explode. I nearly lost my breath when he pushed his energy through me in waves of pleasure and warmth to my center, causing it to swell and wet. I threw my head back and moaned.

"That's it, love. Take from me. Take my spirit. Let me give your body life again." His words didn't make sense, but I was too lost in my lust to ask.

Ezra moaned into my mouth, sucking on my tongue just before pulling back. His lips were moist and swollen. "Make love to me?" he asked.

I bit my bottom lip, running it between my teeth, as I removed my shirt. I couldn't get it off fast enough, so Ezra helped me pull it over my head. He tossed the piece of clothing to the ground and sat back, looking at me.

His eyes wandered over my body from my eyes to my lips until they settled on my breasts. He wiggled his fingers at me. "Come here," he ordered.

Standing on his knees, I walked over to him. He placed his hands at the small of my back and pulled me closer. Then, he took one of my nipples into his mouth and sucked. I let my head fall back and moaned. He sucked harder, pulling until my nipple was stiff and sore. He let it go with a pop and moved to the next one.

226

I could take no more. I had to have him. "Please, Ezra." I was breathless and desperate. "I need you inside of me."

He bit my nipple gently before standing up. He reached behind his back and whipped off his shirt while I tugged at his zipper. His abs clenched as I ripped open his jeans. His hardness sprang free, and I licked my lips, staring at it hungrily. I wanted to taste him.

I wrapped my fingers around his erection, and he grew even thicker in my hands. I was anxious to take him into my mouth, but I wasn't sure he would fit. His girth was thick and grew, filling my hand, as I made a fist around his shaft and began stroking him. His moan echoed around us, and I enjoyed the power I had over him. My dripping wet center throbbed, desperate for release... but not yet.

I gripped the base of his cock and peeked up at him. He stared down at me with hungry eyes as I lowered my head and took him into my mouth.

He groaned and pushed himself deeper. "Fuck, Maeve." He slid his fingers through my hair, working my head up and down his shaft. I deep-throated him, moving up and down his erection until he came. I watched his face as I sucked, loving his reaction.

He cupped my face, running his thumb over my lips before leaning down and kissing me. "My turn," he whispered, lightly pushing me down until I laid on my back before him with my knees up.

He stared down at me as he kicked off his pants, tossing them aside. "You're so beautiful. Perfect in every way."

I whimpered as his words alone sent shivers of pleasure to my center. Rubbing my swollen nub, I wiggled my rear, urging him to hurry. "Make me yours, Ezra."

"You're already mine," he said. His voice was husky and full of lust.

He fell to his knees and pushed my thighs apart with his hands. A sound from the back of his throat came out like a growl, and he mumbled "mine" before swiping my hand away and replacing it with his warm, wet mouth.

My eyes rolled back as he licked my throbbing clit,

working it until it was tight and pulsing. Just as I was building, ready to explode any minute, he moved his tongue to my opening. I had to bite my lip to stop the scream from escaping. Oh, God. My muscles felt like they had melted, and my legs fell apart.

He used his fingers to spread me wider so he could effortlessly suck on my wet flesh. The sound of his tongue working my wetness was enough to make me come. I bit my lip to stifle the moans. I wanted to slow this moment, savor it. Ezra ran his other hand tenderly up and down my thigh. The touch, maybe simple, was so much more to me.

This wasn't sex; this was lovemaking.

His hand sent kinetic energy down my leg, setting my center ablaze with pulsating tension. It was his spiritual energy. It wrapped around me like a security blanket, pushing me to the edge, making me quiver and pulsate.

God, I needed this moment. I needed Ezra.

Who was I kidding? I need him forever.

He pushed the tip of his tongue into my core, and I couldn't hold back the cry that escaped my lips. He moaned too, but it came out as a hungry growl. He darted his tongue in and out and up and down my folds. I gripped his shoulders tightly, digging my nails into his skin.

"Yes," I cried.

I could feel the blood building, my nub was throbbing, and with one bold swipe of his tongue, I went spinning into pleasure.

He sucked and licked me as I quivered beneath him. My folds were swollen, and he lightly kissed my clit before kissing the soft patch of hair above my core. He made his way up my stomach, leaving trails of soft pecks until he came to my breasts.

He watched them as they rose and fell. "Your breasts are so round and full." He ran a finger over one of my nipples before cupping it and putting it into his mouth. He flicked the nub with his tongue, making it even harder, as he sucked on it, tugging on the peak. When that breast was swollen and red, he moved to the other one, flicking his tongue over the swollen tip.

I arched my back, begging for more, but he pulled back. "I'm going to make love to you," he said, settling himself between my thighs. His cock pressed against my wet opening. "Are you ready?"

"Hmmm," I moaned.

In one swift move, he was inside of me, filling me completely. He didn't pause like last time to see if I were okay. No, this time, he thrust in and out, faster and faster. The tendons on his neck stood out as he continued to push into my core.

He kissed me and intertwined his fingers with mine as we moved together. I felt my muscles begin to swell and grip him tighter. He moved faster, plunging into me like a fierce animal.

The tiny particles of our energy vibrated and hummed. They zapped my skin, sending tingles to all the right places.

As the sexual sparks began to build, I wondered...how could I feel this pleasure? After all, we're in Hell. But Ezra said Hell is like a dream, and I've had orgasms in my sleep before.

I wrapped my legs around his waist and raked my nails across his back.

He thrust deeper, faster, and then...stopped. His pulsing cock exploded, a blast of hot cum filled my core. Every nerve ending in my body quivered, and the tension inside exploded.

We came hard, each fueling the other's climax. It was then, I felt Ezra's energy explode into pulsating power. The halo around his body flowed to me like a stream of light, soaking into my skin and giving me more fuel to continue my journey. Ezra held my face and kissed me hard, his tongue exploring every inch of my mouth. Then, he lifted his head and stared into my eyes.

"I love you," he said.

I smiled and kissed his lips. "I love you too." My chest grew warm and tingly because Ezra's love for me was intense.

Ezra slid out of me, sat up, and pulled me into a hug. "I have to go now," he said, kissing the tip of my nose.

I shook my head. "No, go with me. We can get the book together."

He moved away from me. "I can't." His voice was like a distant whisper, and looking at him, I noticed that he was transparent.

"What's going on? Why are you disappearing?"

"He is calling to me." The warm feeling in my chest was consumed by a freezing chill.

I tried to grab him, but my hands passed through him as if he were nothing but an illusion. "Who's calling you?" He was fading quickly; I could hardly see his limbs. "I don't understand?"

The spiritual energy that glowed around him dwindled down to nothing. My body took it all, and I was now encased in a ball of light. "What's going on?" I whispered, looking down at my body.

I shook my head in disbelief. "No, Ezra. This isn't happening. I have enough strength now. We can go to Eden together."

He shook his head. "I don't have enough time."

"No!" He came to Hell to save me, and now he's leaving. "Ezra, damn it! Don't leave me!" Tears streamed down my face.

"I'm saving you."

I wiped my tears away with the back of my hand. "I'm okay now."

I bit my lip, thinking. *Okay...* I said to myself, trying to make sense of the situation. Bones said Ezra couldn't go to Hell, but he had. Maybe it was because he couldn't stay long. That had to be it.

"A sacrifice is an act of love," he said. His voice was like a whisper in the wind. I could hardly hear him.

I bolted up, holding fists at my sides. "What the hell are you talking about?" He also stood, standing in front of me. I could barely make out his fading features. He raised his fingers and ran them down my eyelids, making them close. "Sleep," he demanded.

And I did.

Chapter Thirty

MAEVE

Wake up. A voice penetrated my sleep.

I blinked a few times, allowing my eyes to adjust to the brightness. Sitting up, I shielded my eyes and took in my surroundings. Colors everywhere: green, pastels, gold, and peach. I was surrounded by a lush landscape filled with exotic flowers and fruit. Insects hummed, birds sang in the background, and a gentle flow of water somewhere behind me. Was this Philip's garden. No, this place was too... beautiful. Everything seemed to be dusted with a diamond coat, sparkling, and reflecting all the rainbow colors. And the smell. Oh my. I closed my eyes and inhaled, letting the scents invade my senses. The air was fresh, earthy, and floral, like soft rain in a lush meadow filled with tropical flowers and fruits, on a warm summer's day.

I stood up, feeling the soft ground as the grass tickled my toes, and turned toward the sound of moving water. I rubbed my eyes. *Was this for real?* Or was I still dreaming? I'd seen many bodies of water, some clear and bright blue, but nothing like the stream flowing a few yards away from where I stood.

Lights reflected in every direction, adding a silvery shimmer to the water, and the stream swirled with every shade of blue, purple, and turquoise. I approached until my toes touched the water. Despite the rainbow of colors and sparkles, the stream was clear and brimming with gold, red, and white fish swimming above a riverbed of gold pebbles.

I looked down the stream both ways. How far did this paradise stretch?

Paradise. After traveling through Hell, that word alone

warmed my heart.

I inhaled a sudden breath as it occurred to me. Paradise….

Was I dead?

My arm, where Cerberus bit me, the wound was gone. I was completely healed. Was this Heaven?

No. I thought to myself.

Only the archangels know what Heaven looks like, but they refuse to tell us. According to Sal, Philip, and the Arch Assembly, if this were Heaven, I would have been greeted by God before coming into his kingdom.

I knew where I was.

I was in Eden.

This had to be Eden. It was too beautiful not to be.

Ezra? I made it. I'm not dead.

I hummed and spun around, holding my arms out wide and turning my face to the sun. The rays warmed my skin, and I giggled. I squeezed my toes into the grass, enjoying the softness as I waited for Ezra to respond.

Ezra? Where are you?

Why wasn't he answering me?

I froze, my arms fell limp by my sides. I had been dying in the cave, or I thought I was dying. But Ezra came to me. He helped me get here before he went back to Earth.

Ezra?

He still didn't answer.

A heavy feeling grew in the pit of my stomach. Something wasn't right, but I didn't have time to worry. I had a job to do. Besides, maybe our bond didn't work in Eden.

According to Ezra, I had to find the heart of Eden, and there, I would find a massive fig tree with expanding roots, otherwise known as the Tree of Life. The heart of all ancient cities was almost always settled by water, so I followed the stream.

I strolled the water's edge, enjoying the scenery. It was nice not having to worry about jinn, demons, voices, or dense vapor and dark caves. After what seemed to be about an hour of walking, the stream opened to a lazy river. I picked up my pace and didn't slow until I came to the mouth of the river.

I gazed upon four other rivers joining to form one body of water. The force from the joining currents created a mist. *Was this the heart of Eden?* I could see why a tree would flourish here, with constant sun and water. But there was no Tree of Life.

"Your time on Earth is not finished," said a male's voice.

I drew in a swift breath and whirled around. A man, at least two feet taller than I, stood before me. His golden-brown skin was perfectly smooth and flawless and stretched tightly over his enormous muscles. I followed the square line of his jaw to a pulsing vein along the side of his neck that dipped down into broad and defined shoulders. His black hair was in a braid that was hung over one shoulder. He wore loose linen pants, no shirt, thick leather bands around his wrists and ankles, but no shoes.

"Tell me, young girl, why are you here?"

"I'm—"

"Do you seek eternal life?" He wore a smug smile, showing me his deep dimples. His eyes reminded me of Sal. They were clear blue with specks of green, but unlike Sal's, his reflected anger.

"I'm looking for—"

He held up a palm the size of my face. "You seek the Book of Raziel?"

"Yes. How did you guess?"

"It is not accessible to you."

I squared my shoulders. "Normally, someone of your size would frighten the hell out of me, but," I lifted my chin, "I've been through Hell, faced my own demons, and nearly died by the claws of Cerberus just so I could save a life."

"Do you believe that your sacrifice is enough?"

"Absolutely."

He laughed and lifted his arm, pointing behind him. "You can try." I lifted a brow, eyeing him suspiciously. Was he baiting me?

I bent to my right, looking around him. If I were a cartoon, my jaw would have hit the ground for up ahead, clouds of mist swirled around the Tree of Life. And nestled among the

233

thick roots and spongy moss rested the Book of Raziel. It was easily recognizable, a massive book with an emblem on the cover with two snakes wrapped around a DNA helix.

Wait…if that was the Book of Raziel, then this massive-bodied angel was…Shamsiel.

Winston said that Shamsiel would kill me if I tried to take the book, and according to the label on the vial, Shamsiel had a sword with blue flames. I looked around for the sword, expecting to see it leaning against a tree, lying on the ground, or strapped behind his back. I strained my neck, trying to peek around him, but there was no sword.

He glanced over his shoulder and back at me, probably wondering what I was looking for. I let the air I was holding out in one breath. Thank God there was no sword.

"Who sent you?" he asked.

"Nobody."

He had a cynical brow. "Did Winston send you?"

I shook my head. "No." Winston didn't try to stop me either, but I wasn't going to tell him that. I wasn't sure Shamsiel wouldn't tell the Arch Assembly, and I didn't want to get Winston in trouble.

"Who told you about the book?"

I was getting anxious. This was the last thing left to do, and I was sure I was running out of time. Bones said that I had an hour before my body tissue would start to die. Plus, I just wanted to get this shit over with. "I'm sorry, but I don't have time to play twenty questions."

"Answer me!" His voice boomed, yet, I shrugged.

"I don't want to."

"A human cannot come into Eden without being sent here by some other higher power."

I thought about what he said. Initially, Bones sent me to Hell, but I got into Eden...or had it been Ezra? Nevertheless, I wasn't going to give him any names, and regardless of who sent me, I made the decision to go through Hell, and it was my strength that got me here.

I lifted my chin and pushed my shoulders back. "I sent myself."

"You can't have the book."

"I literally went through Hell to get that book. I fought jinn, my inner demons, and Cerberus."

"You said that already. Still, I'm unimpressed."

I didn't falter under his stare. Instead, I eyed him as if I were his equal though I was not. I was far below his status in our world, according to the heavenly ranking given by the Arch Assembly.

Shamsiel stepped toward me, and I took a tiny step back. I tried to be brave, but I was nothing but an insect compared to his brute size. "I must protect that book. It is my duty," he said, holding out his hand, "and I swore to kill all who try to take it." A sword, framed by sapphire flames, materialized in his hand.

And, there it was, in all its glory, his sword. Big, shiny, and silvery. The blue flames covering it flickered out in all directions as if waiting to strike their next victim.

I closed my eyes and lifted my hands, feeling the energy around me. The tiny particles clung to my skin like static electricity. For the first time, I gathered that energy until it formed a protective shield around me.

Shamsiel laughed. "Your energy isn't strong enough," he said, right before he lunged at me.

He swung his sword, aiming for my neck, but I jumped and rolled clear, barely dodging it. That was close. Too close. He almost took off my head.

I sprang to my feet and placed a hand on my chest, trying to calm my racing heart as reality sank in; Shamsiel was right. My energy didn't compare to his strength, and his fiery sword would slice through my energy like butter.

Plus, did I really want to fight him?

He was an angel, a divine being, and I was about to steal something banned by the Arch Assembly.

"I need it," I shouted. "I'm sorry."

I ran toward the book as fast as my legs could carry me. I didn't bother looking back until a sharp zap sounded. Looking over my shoulder, I saw a blue flame shoot from his sword like a lightning bolt. A crack vibrated near my temple, creating a thunderous boom that made my eardrums hum.

I stumbled over my feet, falling face-first to the ground. My chin hit the dirt hard enough to scrape my skin, but the fighter in me didn't waver. I pushed myself up, ready to run again, when another flame shot out like a whip on fire, hitting my arm.

Suddenly, my muscles tensed, causing my body to fall back like a ragdoll.

"That's a taste of what my sword can do," yelled Shamsiel.

I stood up on wobbly legs, holding my hurt arm. "Fuck you," I rasped, barely able to catch my breath.

That hit weakened my muscles, and if that was just a taste, I was doomed.

Where was my energy when I needed it? Why did it always fade in and out? I tried to focus on my spirit, my inner peace, to give me strength. In my mind were ripples in my pond, but what could I do? I couldn't sit down and meditate. I would die.

Shouldn't I have complete control of my energy by now? I used it to fight in Hell because I forgave myself. Right?

I no longer have guilt.

I have a will.

A will to save Emerich.

And when there's a will, there's a way.

For the first time, everything in my vision changed— I saw the energy. It was colored like a gradient rainbow and pulsed in spherical waves.

I lifted my hand, and the energy gathered in my palm like a ball of electricity. It sparked and glowed a bright white, and it zapped and hummed angrily, ready to explode.

Shamsiel lifted a brow. "Who are you?"

"I'm not sure of the context of your question, but I'm Maeve, and I am here to save my friend."

I threw the ball of electricity. It flew like a ball of fire, causing ripples in the spherical energy waves.

Shamsiel lifted his sword, and…

Crack!

236

He smashed the ball, causing it to explode. A blast of light burst violently due to excessive internal pressure, followed by a glimmer of sparks.

I held up my hand, gathering more energy, but I wasn't fast enough. Shamsiel thrust his sword out, sending out another blue flame that slapped me across the face. The force spun me around in a full rotation, making my knees gave out, and causing me to collapse to the ground.

My muscles contracted, and I started to thrash and shake uncontrollably. Every nerve in my body begged me to surrender, but my spirit wouldn't give up. I absorbed the energy through the pores on my skin, giving strength to my muscles until I could stand.

Looking at Shamsiel and his fiery sword, hot tears gathered at my lids, partly because of the pain but mainly because I anticipated failure. My chest rose and fell quickly to the rhythm of my heart as I spotted the book. It was only a few yards away, but I couldn't run fast enough. My spiritual energy was powerful, but Shamsiel's overpowered mine.

I was giving up— ready to beg him to stop when another crack sounded. I fell to the ground, shielded my head with my arms, and squeezed my eyes shut, bracing myself for the agony.

But nothing happened.

I opened my eyes, hoping to see mercy in Shamsiel's face, but there was none. Instead, his eyes reflected shock and anger as he stared past me. I sat up and turned to see what he was staring at.

I couldn't believe my eyes.

Was my mind imagining things?

Maybe I had gone mad? Going through Hell would make a person crazy, right?

Because what I saw was impossible.

He stood tall, taller than Shamsiel, and was dressed in his usual jeans that hung slack on his hips. He was shirtless, revealing a solid chest and abs.

I wanted to run into his arms, bathe in his protection, but I was stuck, shocked to the core.

He was pissed.

Honestly, I wasn't sure who to fear most. Shamsiel? Or…
Sal?

Chapter Thirty-One

MAEVE

How did he get here? Did Winston send him?

Sal glanced down at me; his eyes were soft for a moment before turning hard again. A vein on his temple became engorged and pulsed, a sign that he was upset, and as he lowered his brows, his eyes appeared darker.

Sal was facing Shamsiel because of me. Waves of guilt flooded me, followed by a sudden onset of vertigo. Was it my wound? It had to be.

My world started spinning, and I lost my balance. Stumbling forward, I reached out for something to hold onto. Sal cursed under his breath and tried to catch me, but Shamsiel whipped his sword, releasing a blue flame.

I waited for the hit, but instead, I felt a whoosh of air, moving the ends of my hair in all directions. Then, a pair of strong arms wrapped around me.

I expected pain, but instead, warmth from Sal's healing power soaked into my wounds, healing me before he unwrapped his arms.

"You challenge me, Salazar." Shamsiel's voice thundered through the air.

"Back down from this, Shamsiel," Sal warned.

They know each other?

"Keep your human under control," Shamsiel said.

His human?

"Remember your place, cherub," said Sal.

Shamsiel pointed his sword at Sal, but he didn't flinch like I did. "I am only doing my job, guardian, and that human—"

"She is my fledgling," Sal interrupted.

239

Fledgling?

"Take her away," snapped Shamsiel.

Oh no, I don't think so. I'm not leaving without that book. Maybe I could sneak over to the book and take it before someone gets hurt. Slowly placing one foot behind the other, I tried to slip around Sal unnoticed, but my head hit something soft yet firm.

I turned to see what it was, and everything I ever thought about Sal blew to pieces. I'd been through Hell, seen some crazy shit, yet… what I saw blew my mind and sent it whirling with a million questions.

Sal had wings.

Sal was just...Sal. The man who raised me. He wasn't supposed to have wings. Sure, it was possible, but...how could I not have known this? How? All these years, and he had wings? And they were as big as a truck, black and shiny, dense and powerful, and they formed an arch that towered over him.

Holy shit, it all made sense: his power to heal, his obsession with my safety, and his uncanny ability to show up out of nowhere, as if he could sense my danger.

"Take her away from here this instant," Shamsiel said, "or I kill her."

Looking at me, I saw the question in Sal's eyes. *Would I leave without the book?* He knew the answer.

I shook my head and mouthed sorry.

Sal formed fists and shook his head, obviously disappointed. Yes. I was stubborn, and yes, sometimes I do things without thinking, but I had come this far.

I'm not leaving without the book.

A gust of air twisted into a small tornado of dust where Sal had been standing, followed by a deafening crack. The ground trembled beneath me as Sal landed inches from Shamsiel. Out of thin air, Sal drew a sword of his own. It was massive, thick, shiny, and outlined with petite sapphires, but it didn't have flames.

"We need the book," said Sal, "to save a prophet." My cheeks felt warm as my heart swelled. Sal chose to fight with me for Emerich's life.

"You can't have it," answered Shamsiel.

Sal lifted his sword, wielding it with two hands. "Then we fight," he said before swinging his sword with blinding force.

Shamsiel leaned back, dodging the sharp end of the blade. "Is that all you got," he asked, cracking a smile.

Sal was waving his sword in figure eights while circling around Shamsiel. "You're about to find out."

I saw a flicker of doubt in Shamsiel's eyes as he charged Sal.

Swing.

Sal met Shamsiel's sword with his own. The weight of it sent Shamsiel's blade backward. Sal swung again, slicing Shamsiel's shirt at the midsection.

Swing. Clank. Sparks flew as their swords hit. They held their swords in an x-shape, eyeing each other.

"End this now, Shamsiel, and I may let you live," yelled Sal. He pushed forward with his sword, and Shamsiel stumbled back.

Earlier, Sal had called Shamsiel a cherub. According to the ranking set by the Arch Assembly, Sal, a guardian angel, ranked higher in command than Shamsiel. But did that give Sal the right to kill Shamsiel?

Shamsiel flew into the air, leaving a cloud of dust in his wake. "You will be punished!" Shamsiel's voice boomed from above the clouds. The ground shook from the vibration.

Sal was looking up. "And if you kill her, what of you? She is my fledgling," Sal said, his voice just as loud. "Do you not know who she is?"

A blue flame shot down from the clouds like a lightning bolt. I clamped my hands over my mouth, holding back a scream. Sal's death flashed in my mind. I held my breath, expecting the worst when the feathers on Sal's wings turned into fire. The blue flame hit the tip of Sal's wing and evaporated as if it was nothing more than a drop of water on a bed of hot sand.

Shamsiel shot down from the sky with his wings tucked behind his back. He landed behind Sal, causing the ground to crack and split under his feet.

Sal spun around, swinging his sword. Shamsiel raised his and blocked Sal's strike.

Clank. Clank. Clank. Strike after strike, Sal kept swinging his sword, and Shamsiel blocked each blow.

Shamsiel saw an opportunity and stuck out a leg. Sal stumbled backward and fell, losing his sword. Shamsiel stood over Sal and pointed the tip of his blade at Sal's heart.

"No," I whispered.

If I didn't do something fast, they were going to fight to the death.

I sprinted toward the book and didn't slow until I reached it.

I had to work quickly. I knelt beside the book and tried to pick it up, but it wouldn't budge.

"Shit, almost forgot," I said to myself.

I reached into my pocket and felt around.

I reached into the other pocket. Nothing.

"Where's the vial?"

I didn't have the vial. I didn't bring it with me.

Ezra? I tried to reach him again. *Ezra, damn it. Answer me.* He wasn't answering. *Think, think, think.*

Examining the book, I ran my hands over every corner, every detail, and couldn't find anything unusual until I focused my attention on the emblem. There was a small hole right above what seemed to be a DNA helix.

That's probably where the blood goes. But I had no blood.

Think, Maeve, think.

Bones said my spirit was strong. Ezra said multiple times that I was special. He also said I was strong enough to go to Hell and that my blood was pure. My blood opened The Gate of the Sun. Maybe it would open the book. I glanced over my shoulder. Shamsiel still had his sword pointed at Sal.

Please let this work.

Placing the side of my hand into my mouth, I bit down hard enough to break the skin. Once I tasted blood, I held my hand over the emblem. Blood dripped into the hole right above the DNA helix. After a few drips, I tried again to grab the book.

It still didn't budge.

I hit my fist on the ground. I wanted to collapse, take a nap, or have a fucking shot of tequila, anything that would help me forget everything I'd gone through in Hell. I felt defeated and hopeless. I knelt forward, laying my head on my lap, and cried. I was acting childish, but what would anyone else do?

The same damn thing. I thought.

Suddenly, a white light shone around me.

I sat up, wiping the tears from my dirty face. The book's emblem was glowing, and the light expanded into a beautiful band of golden sparkles. The snakes on the cover unwound their bodies from the helix before expanding open, with a click, like the sound of a latch being unlocked.

I leaned forward, ready to snatch it up when a thought occurred to me. *What if the moment I touched the book, I died?*

It was right there, ripe for the taking. Hot damn. This wasn't the time to question the what-ifs.

I made it this far and had nearly died too, so I wasn't going to chicken out now. I reached for the book, snatching it from its mossy bed. I held it to my chest and chanted the spell Ezra told me. He'd said the spell would only work if I pressed the book close to my heart and hugged it hard enough to cause discomfort. I don't know how he knew the spell. I'd ask him later. For now, I did what he told me to do.

"*Mans darbs šeit tiek darīts. Mans darbs šeit tiek darīts.*" I repeated the sentence a few more times when I saw blue fire in my peripheral vision.

"No!" I screamed.

If I disappeared with the book, Sal would follow me back home. I had better hurry. I wiped the tears from my eyes and screamed, "*Mans darbs šeit tiek darīts...my work here is done!*"

It happened so suddenly.

My vision went black, and my body felt light. An intense pressure pushed down on me, and seconds later, I was being pulled through a wormhole.

My soul was returning to my body.

A high-pitched ringing hurt my ears. I tried to move, but the pressure was too intense. I felt like my head was placed in a vice, squeezing my brain until it burned.

I wasn't sure how much more I could take when suddenly it stopped.

A hand touched my shoulder. I opened my eyes. Everything was hazy at first. I blinked to clear my vision. Philip stood, staring down at me. He was pale, and his eyes were bloodshot.

"I made it," I croaked.

He smiled gently back at me. "I knew you would."

Chapter Thirty-Two

MAEVE

The room was dim and cold. Philip placed a hand behind my back and helped me sit up. I expected to be greeted by Ezra. "Where's Ezra? I thought he'd be here."

Philip turned his head away from me and sniffled. "It was the only way to save you," he said. A tear fell from his eye.

"What are you talking about?"

"You died, and he saved you."

I shook my head, feeling overwhelmed by everything and now this. "It doesn't make sense…" I remembered seeing him in Hell. I remembered giving up in the cave…I remembered dying, but…. "What happened to him," I muttered to myself. "How did he save me? I thought…I thought he came back here?" Philip shook his head. His mouth was turned down into a somber grin. I gasped, feeling a sudden loss within me. It was a deep-rooted feeling of mourning like a mother losing a child to death, and I wanted to cry. I wanted to scream. I wanted to hit something, but not yet because…how? Why? "WHAT THE FUCK!" I screamed, breathing heavily. I put my shaky fingers to my forehead, rubbing away the tension between my eyes. Then I squeezed my eyes shut, forcing out the tears that had collected in the corners. "I don't understand, Philip," I said in a gentler tone. "I mean…I thought he couldn't even go to Hell."

Philip swallowed before speaking. "Anybody can go to Hell after death."

I stared at Philip as his words slowly sank in. "He's dead?" There was a beat of silence before I laughed and shook my head. "No, he isn't. Quit fucking with me. I'm not in the mood. I just got back from Hell, so tell me where he is."

Bones stepped from the shadows like a damn ghost. I didn't even know he was in the room. He was worse than Philip. His eyes were swollen and red, and there were bruises on his neck. "He died to save you." His voice was a pained whisper, barely audible. "A life for a life. That's the nature of existence."

Bones was straight-faced. "You're saying that he couldn't give me a piece of his life? You bonded our spirits together, basically splitting them in half."

Philip lowered his head and whispered, "God gave us one life that can't be shared, but it can be given as a sacrifice."

I jumped from the bed, letting The Book of Raziel fall to the floor. I looked at Philip. "Where's his body?"

"Your room," Philip answered.

Without another word, I ran from the room. My heartbeat raced as adrenaline pumped through my veins. I thought my heart would explode if I didn't get to Ezra faster. I bounded up the stairs, three steps at a time. When I reached my room, I froze.

Philip and Bones told me he was dead, but I refused to believe them until I saw it for myself.

My hand rested loosely on the doorknob. I held my breath, scared of what I might see behind the door.

Was I prepared to handle the truth?

I guess I would never know standing here.

I slowly turned the knob. My knees trembled, and my hands shook, and little by little, I pushed the door open. The hinges squeaked, and the room inside was eerily quiet. I listened, expecting Ezra to say something smartass. He didn't.

I stood in the doorway.

Falling.

I was falling, spinning faster and faster.

I grabbed the doorframe to keep from hitting the ground.

Philip and Bones were right.

Ezra was dead, lying cold and still on my bed.

I shook my head as disbelief consumed me.

He wasn't dead. I would have felt his death. I was sure of it. I bit my lip as I crept closer.

'A sacrifice is an act of love'.

Ezra's words repeated in my mind like a bad song. I shook all over. I wanted to scream, but nothing came out.

Ezra? Ezra? I tried to reach him telepathically, but nothing came back to me. Tears streamed from my eyes, wetting my cheeks and neck. I threw my head back and screamed, "EZRA."

Still, he didn't answer. I walked over to his body, surprised my wobbly legs didn't give out.

His hands rested on his chest, his eyes were closed, and his lips were pale and sad. I reached for his hands and cringed; they were so cold. I ran the back of my hand down his cheek. His face was cold too.

In the cave, when he came to me, I was weak, barely alive. His energy was bright, a light that wrapped around his body like another skin. Like the heat from the sun, I had absorbed it through my skin.

I could no longer stand, so I collapsed, falling to my knees.

I was dying. Ezra gave me his spiritual energy to save me. Right? My lip trembled.

It was then I knew.

I died in the cave, and it wasn't Ezra's energy I had absorbed. It was...

his life.

I broke down and cried like a child. "I'm sorry," I whispered over and over until my crying turned into uncontrollable sobs. I bent forward and laid my head on my arms, taking deep breaths until the sobs subsided and my body no longer trembled.

Everything was still and quiet until the hinges on the door squeaked.

I sat up. My vision was blurred, so I wiped my hot eyes before looking at the door. I expected to see Philip or Bones, but I saw another man.

My jaw dropped. Did I see clearly? I blinked a few times.

The tall man that stood at the door resembled Ezra, except his hair was long and jet black like his attire: black slacks, black shirt, black shoes, and a long black trench coat. Like a crow, he was all black and menacing.

"Tsk-tsk. Poor chap always had a weakness for beautiful women."

He wasn't Ezra, but he looked familiar. "Who are you?" I asked. I'd seen him before, but where?

He watched me a moment before bringing his attention to Ezra's resting body. I sprang to my feet and made two tight fists. If he tried to go near Ezra, I was going to fight. But something in his expression changed. While looking at Ezra, his eyes softened.

I lifted a questioning brow. "Do you know him?"

"I did," he answered. "He always had a weakness for your kind. Never doubted he'd give you his life." With a click of his tongue, he pushed himself away from the doorframe he was leaning against. "He sacrificed himself for the last time. I thought he learned his lesson from the first miss that broke his heart—ruined him, she did. But you"—he wore a smile that kept growing— "you killed him."

I clenched my fists tighter, making them crack and pop. "Who the fuck are you?"

"You really haven't figured it out, have you? You truly are dim." His manner was like Ezra's, confident and arrogant but meaner. "I'm Levi," he said with a bow.

My mouth fell open as I tried to process what I just heard.

It couldn't be true.

I took a step back, shaking my head in disbelief. He was Levi? I was face-to-face with the jinn that had caused it all.

Levi laughed with a gleam in his eyes. He enjoyed tormenting others. "You, Ezra, and the rest of the dolls fell into my plot perfectly. Perfect little puppets."

I applauded him for his efforts. "Is this what you were hoping for? A pat on the back? Some sort of gratitude for a job well done. Well, I hate to break it to you, buddy, but you can kiss your plans goodbye." I stepped up to him. "You see, *Levi*, I have what you need. You can tell your daddy that you won't be freeing him anytime soon because I have your stupid, fucking Book of Raziel."

He was unbothered by what I said. In fact, he appeared relaxed, slouching against the wall. He started laughing a deep laugh from the pit of his stomach that made me cringe. When he finally stopped to catch his breath, he grinned at me. He changed from hysterical to eerily calm so fast that my mind spun with fear and confusion. He raised his hand and ran the back of it down my check, but I refused to flinch or show fear.

"Are you sure about that, puppet?" he purred.

My thoughts froze.

What did he mean? Of course, I was sure. I had the book.

I scanned the room, hoping I had placed it somewhere. My stomach fluttered when I didn't find it, but then I remembered. *It's with Philip.* Indeed, he would have put it somewhere safe.

I exhaled a breath of relief, but Levi reached into his coat.

"No," I whispered, shaking my head in disbelief. I stepped away, clasping my mouth with a shaky hand. *No. No. No.*

Levi grinned from ear to ear, a damned beautiful smile, as he pulled out the book. After everything I'd gone through, I couldn't let him take it.

I jumped forward, reaching for the book. Levi held up his hand, and I fell on my ass— hard. My teeth hit and rattled painfully.

Levi used the energy around us to knock me back. How? He's a jinn. Do they even have spirits?

I sprang to my feet. "You fucking—"

"Now, now, Maeve. It shouldn't be a crime to take back what belongs to me."

He lovingly stroked the cover. "Ezra, the weakling, handed it over to the Arch Assembly to save my life. Did you know that? I know I should have been thankful, but this book was a gift from Father. He should not have ..."

His words drifted into silence. He ran his hands over the front of his jacket in a calming manner as if to gather himself before he lost control. "I got my revenge," he finished, with no sign of guilt or shame.

"What revenge?"

Chuckling to himself, I watched as he opened the book and flipped to a specific page. He ripped it from its binding and tossed it to me. I did nothing but watch as it fluttered to the floor between my feet. "For your troubles."

I clenched my fists. My nails dug into my hands, hurting me. "Why would Ezra save a fucking jinn?"

He wiggled a finger at me. "Half jinn, puppet. We're nephilim."

"We?"

He watched me for a minute, straight-faced, before turning his attention to Ezra's body. "He's my brother."

A sharp pain settled in my chest. I thought back to what I'd read about the nephilim and their connection to the book and Lucifer. Levi watched me as I connected all the pieces of the puzzle. They came together into one fucked up image, showing me the truth.

"Ezra's a fucking jinn," I muttered to myself.

"What's wrong with being jinn? We're beautiful creatures."

And evil.

I stopped breathing. Levi's eyes were like Ezra's but more reddish, like....

"Fire," I said, covering my mouth with the back of my hand. I remembered where I saw him. He was in Hell. "It's you," I said, pointing my finger at him. "The leader."

He cocked his head, eyeing me. "I'm not sure—"

"You killed my parents."

I remembered him clearly now.

The events unfolded in my mind.

Levi and Ezra are brothers. They are nephilim. Satan's sons. Ezra is half jinn, and I slept with him.

I felt sick to my stomach.

Levi watched me curiously.

My chin quivered as I tried to hold back my tears. I didn't want Levi to see my pain. I needed to stay strong. Plus, I promised myself that I would no longer live with the guilt.

I lifted my chin and rolled my shoulders back. "You killed my Mom and Dad. You wanted me because I'm a threat to you and your plans to end the world." I gritted my teeth. "If I had my knives, I'd slice your heart out."

He smiled. It was an easy smile, relaxed and sure. "Not today, puppet." He lifted his hand. "But I look forward to the challenge." He snapped his fingers and disappeared.

I spun around. Was he gone? Why did he keep disappearing? "Why don't you stay and fight like a fucking man?"

Because he isn't a man. "He's a fucking jinn!"

The nephilim are cursed beings, both human and jinn. That explained how Ezra knew so much and how he fought so well. That was why his spirit was unbreakable and how it could never be weakened. It explained his wealth and beauty. It was why Bones couldn't send him to Hell.

What about now? He's dead, so is he in Hell, trapped in the last two realms like his father?

Bones said he felt something evil connected to Ezra, and Ezra said it was his father.

"He was right about that," I mumbled, my voice hoarse from crying. Ezra's father was evil. He was the Devil.

Ezra's betrayal hurt me the most.

He had lied to all of us. He played us like puppets, just like his brother. He was a jinn hunter. That's what he had said...lied.

He knew how much I hated jinn, half-blood or not, he was evil, and it was his kin, his brother, that killed my Mom and Dad. Did Ezra know that? Did he know it was his brother?

"Why?" I screamed at Ezra's dead body. Anger made the blood rush to my head. I felt ready to explode.

Ezra should have gone to Hell. Nobody would have tried to kill him. "You're a fucking nephilim," I screamed again, wishing he were alive to hear me. The nephilim were fathered by the king of Hell.

I sucked in a breath and held it in until my lungs burned, and upon a slow exhale, I spun around, ready to leave.

But I couldn't.

Ezra betrayed me. My heart felt like it was in a vice, being squeezed until it ached.

Yet, I couldn't leave. Not yet. Not without a proper goodbye.

My arms hung limply at my sides. My eyelids were heavy, my body was tired, my muscles ached. All I wanted to do was go home and get some much-needed rest, yet I couldn't leave.

I stood next to Ezra's body, memorizing every detail: the perfect curve of his lips, the golden waves of his hair, the sharp lines of his jaw and cheekbones. I ran a finger across his forehead, sweeping his hair away from his face and tucking it behind his ear.

That's when I saw it.

I turned his head to get a better look, and hidden just under his hairline behind his right ear was his nevus.

I jerked my hand away and stumbled back, clenching my shirt just over my heart.

Everything, from the lettering to its shape, was exactly like mine, except for two things. Ezra's was smaller and was nearly the color of his flesh.

Memories of what I had read, what Levi said, and the little Ezra had mentioned all came together in my mind. Ezra's nevus connected him to his father— to Lucifer.

If I had the same markings, did that also connect *me* to Lucifer? I reached forward, holding onto the dresser to keep me upright. I bent over halfway to catch my breath.

Holy Fucking Shit.

Would Winston do that? Yes. Yes, he would. I am going to kill him.

I was breathing in-and-out so quickly I thought I would pass out at any moment.

A ringing in my ears, black spots in my vision, my face felt flushed, and my fingers were numb. With my hands on my knees, I leaned over and closed my eyes. In and out, I breathed. Nice and slow.

Finally, my heartbeat stopped racing, and my panic attack went away. I could finally stand up straight without fear of collapsing.

"Don't be angry with him."

With a hand on my heart, I spun around. Phillip walked in and stood by Ezra.

"Don't sneak up on me," I snapped.

Philip stared down at Ezra's body. His shoulders, neck, and back were stiff, yet his face hung low. "He was a good man," he said, his chin quivered as he spoke.

"No! He was a liar. A damn nephilim. A *jinn*." I said the word jinn as if it was poison on my tongue.

Philip stepped away, providing enough space to get a good look at me. "Ezra saved Levi from the bloody hands of the Arch Assembly. Did he ever tell you that?"

"I read about it, and Levi…spoke to me before he left with the book. He mentioned something about it."

"Ezra traded the Book of Raziel for his brother's life. Ezra saved that asshole, yet Levi wasn't thankful. He was angry and hated Ezra for what he did. Because Levi treasured that book and the power it gave him. So, to get revenge, he turned the woman Ezra loved against him. Her name was Sky, and she was his wife. Did Ezra tell you this?" I nodded. "He loved her very much, so Levi slept with her and gave her a child. The firstborn of the Satori race."

"The blood-feeding jinn?" I asked.

Philip nodded. "Levi used the Satori. He turned them into killers, forming an army against the humans. The Satori fed on human blood, killing them by the thousands. That is until The Arch Assembly demanded The Order to stop Levi and the Satori."

"They didn't?"

"Thanks to Ezra, The Order caught Sky. She was banished to Hell, and the Satori was cursed to an eternity in darkness."

"That's why we never see them during the day," I muttered.

Philip nodded. "Eventually, The Order caught Levi and sentenced him to death." Philip shook his head as if disappointed. "But, once again, Ezra saved him." Philip removed his glasses and wiped away his tears. "Ezra promised to work for The Order if they let Levi go."

"That was a mistake."

Philip stared at Ezra. "Maybe, but you see, Ezra was consumed by love and passion, feelings that had blinded him from the truth…that Levi would never be like him—more human."

I choked on a sob. "Why are you telling me this?"

Philip turned his attention to me. Tears left wet streaks on his cheeks. "Don't hate him for what he was but love him for what was in his heart."

I looked away and down at my feet. I wasn't sure I could ever care for a jinn. I knew I could never love one.

Philip lifted my chin with a finger, forcing me to look at him. "But most importantly, you must do what Ezra never could."

"What?"

"Kill Levi."

Chapter Thirty-Three

MAEVE

I looked at Ezra one last time before leaving him forever. I turned my back to his resting body, bent down to grab the page Levi tossed on the floor, and was almost to the door when a sudden thought reached my mind.

Eda.

For a few hours after death, the part of the brain associated with memory can still send signals to the part of the brain associated with consciousness. That's what happened…right? Ezra's brain activity was still creating conscious thoughts, and because of our bond, I heard them.

When I was in Hell, Ezra said that I was the Eda.

Was that why Levi wanted me as a child? Was I going to save the world from his evil plan? I snorted, unable to wrap my mind around the idea.

I scratched my temple. Why didn't Levi kill me? He'd had plenty of chances. I groaned and ran a hand down my face. I was exhausted and mentally drained by the mysteries that surrounded me. I just needed to be me, even if only for a few hours.

Later, I would ask Sal or Winston, but for now…I just wanted to go home.

With my bag and blades in hand, I spotted Sal in the foyer speaking to Bones.

"You look better," I said to Bones. His eyes weren't swollen, and the bruises were gone.

Bones pointed to Sal. "The Watcher cured me."

I smiled at the word *Watcher*. Sal might be an angel, but to me, he will and always will be Sal—my Sal. "What happened to you?" I asked Bones. When I got back from Hell, before Levi came for the book, Bones had bruises on his neck and swollen eyes.

His smile turned into a sad frown. "You were dying, and I couldn't bring you back. Let's just say Ezra lost his control and went a bit crazy."

"So, he beat you up?" I asked.

Bones shook his head, still frowning sadly. "He choked me; nearly killed me."

My mouth fell open. I was speechless.

Bones waved a hand at me dismissively. "Don't worry. I'm not mad at the boy. Philip said Ezra's been known to do stupid things for those he loves," said Bones followed by a wink.

My cheeks felt warm. I was obviously blushing when Sal stepped up behind me. "Who the hell is Ezra?"

I ignored his question with one of my own. "What happened to Shamsiel?" I asked, hoping Sal hadn't killed him.

"The Arch Assembly showed up just in time."

"Really? What did they do?"

Sal took my bag and flung it over his shoulder. "They demanded I return to you and keep you safe."

I tucked my blades into their harness before putting on my vest. "I can protect myself."

"And you're going to have to give the book back to Winston," Sal continued.

My old self would have looked down at my feet, feeling guilty, but not anymore. "I don't have it, but I plan on getting it back."

I was about to shake Bones' hand and thank him, but he jerked me into a hug. "There has never been a soul to return to Earth from Hell," he said. He let me go and reached for my hands, enclosing them in his. "You are a miracle."

"You have no idea," Sal muttered, holding open the front door.

"Thank you for your help," I said to Bones. He nodded and said goodbye.

256

The mid-day air caressed my senses, cleansing my skin. The sweet smell of roses refreshed my thoughts.

I can't believe I made it back.

Sal opened the passenger door for me before placing my bag in the trunk. "Can't you just fly us back?"

He patted his shoulder. "Hop on."

I laughed. "You're funny."

As we drove off, I watched Philip's home until it faded away, leaving behind Ezra and our memories.

Looking at Sal, my smile grew wider. "So, an angel?"

He smiled too. "Yep."

"What did the Arch Assembly do to Shamsiel?"

"They were pretty pissed off about the book, but if he had killed you…."

"What?"

"They would have killed him."

"Because I'm the Eda?" I pulled on the seatbelt, overwhelmed. My body itched to get away, to run and hide.

Sal turned on the signal before immerging onto the highway. "You are the prophesized protector. That's why I am your guardian angel."

I looked out the window in a daze. "How can I protect the world, Sal? I'm only human."

He laughed a condescending chuckle, prompting me to raise a quizzical brow. "Obviously, by now, you should know you're more than that."

Yeah, I knew, but still…. "I don't know, Sal. I don't feel like I have god-like strength."

He glanced at me before looking back at the road ahead of us. "Not yet, but you will."

"When? How?" I already had so many years of training.

"Nobody knows for sure, but Winston said something about being reborn."

I had a sudden sickening feeling in the pit of my stomach. "Like dying and coming back from Hell?"

He looked at me and nodded. "Possibly."

"Is that why you saved me when I was a child?"

"Yes, and that's why Levi, that fucking bastard, couldn't

take you."

I thought back to my conversation with Levi in Hell. "Unless I agreed to go?"

"Exactly."

"Did he know I was the Eda?"

He shook his head. "He made you into the Eda by killing your parents. He heard you were special but didn't know why. Winston heard he's been building an army and desperately wants you on his side."

I laughed to myself, shaking my head at the unforeseen twist of fate. Levi made me into the Eda, creating the very thing meant to stop him from ending the world. Well, isn't that a bitch. "So, Emerich's vision of the apocalypse is true. Levi is a nephilim, and he plans to free the Grigori and end the world."

Sal nodded again. "Yes, and according to the prophecy, you and Levi will fight." Did Sal know more about the prophecy? I assumed so. He was an angel, my guardian angel.

I leaned my forehead against the window, watching the landscape pass by in a blur. I closed my eyes and placed a hand over my heart as I silently vowed to Mom, Dad, and Ezra that their sacrifice wouldn't be wasted.

"And I'll win that fight," I said.

I will destroy the Book of Raziel and kill Levi.

That's a promise.

Chapter Thirty-Four

MAEVE

Emerich poked his head around the corner, looking into my office. "Hey, Mae-bear. We have a meeting in ten."

Glancing up from my computer screen, I took a sip of coffee.

I choked and sputtered, spitting some of it out. Emerich was wearing the large, bright blue glasses he won at the fair last week. "Are you going to wear those to the meeting?" I was now laughing with him.

He threw his head back and laughed. "Of course I am." I smiled so big my face hurt.

He was back to his old self, and I was over the moon happy.

It turned out that the page Levi gave me was a cure for the disease. It took a few stressful days, sleeping at the hospital and waiting hours upon hours, but eventually, Emerich got better. His body fat came back in under a week, and the black circles under his eyes faded away. His cheeks were rosy and full of life.Using my sleeve, I wiped the coffee off my desk. "You're just what I needed," I said, gesturing to my computer screen. "This shit is depressing."

He strolled in like he was cool. "I told you to stop watching the news, but you don't listen." He sat on the edge of my desk and removed his toy glasses.

"I can't help it." I replayed the morning news. "I can't help but feel this is all my fault."

"Numerous attacks and bombings are happening around the world," said the news anchor, "leaving millions of innocent people dead or homeless. Earlier today, the head of

259

state announced that our country will be joining the war against the eastern nations, declaring the third world war is upon us.

Emerich patted my arm. "You can't let this bother you. Let's go. We have a meeting, and Winston's going to be pissed if we're late." He stood up.

I blew out, making a sputtering sound with my lips. "Okay. Give me a minute to collect my paperwork."

He jumped up. "Shit. I have to get my report from last week." With that, he was gone and probably in his office, rummaging through his messy file cabinet.

I stood up into a tall stretch. My joints were stiff and achy. I leaned over and turned off the computer and was headed out when I heard it.

Maeve.

I froze, listening.

"Maeve," Emerich called from the other room.

"I'm coming," I snapped.

I don't know what I expected. It was impossible. Ezra was dead. Sure, I heard him at Philip's, but that was a few hours after his death when his brain was still sending signals to his consciousness.

Ezra had been dead for weeks now.

Yet…

Walking down the hall, scratching my head, a sudden rush of energy flooded my body, creating a specific warmth and static-like energy that pricked my chest.

I stopped, holding a hand over my heart. The last time I felt a rush of warmth in my chest was when Ezra shared his feelings of love for me via our bond. When we were in the cave, and I was dying, Ezra came to me spiritually. He made love to me and gave me his life, but I never felt him again after that time.

Until now.

Ezra is alive.

END

Fantastic Books
Great Authors

darkstroke is
an imprint of
Crooked Cat Books

- Gripping Thrillers
- Cosy Mysteries
- Romantic Chick-Lit
- Fascinating Historicals
- Exciting Fantasy
- Young Adult
- Non-Fiction

Discover us online
www.darkstroke.com

Find us on instagram:
www.instagram.com/darkstrokebooks

Made in the USA
Monee, IL
03 September 2021